M000014843

BROKEN
GLASS

OTHER TITLES BY ALEXANDER HARTUNG

Until the Debt is Paid (Jan Tommen Book 1)

Grave Intent (Jan Tommen Book 2)

BROKEN GLASS

A NIK POHL THRILLER

ALEXANDER HARTUNG

TRANSLATED BY FIONA BEATON

This is a work of fiction. Names, characters, organizations, places, events, and incidents are either products of the author's imagination or are used fictitiously. Any resemblance to actual persons, living or dead, or actual events is purely coincidental.

Text copyright © 2018 by Alexander Hartung
Translation copyright © 2019 by Fiona Beaton
All rights reserved.

No part of this book may be reproduced, or stored in a retrieval system, or transmitted in any form or by any means, electronic, mechanical, photocopying, recording, or otherwise, without express written permission of the publisher.

Previously published as *Auf zerbrochenem Glas* by Edition M, Amazon Media EU S.à r.l. in Luxembourg in 2018. Translated from German by Fiona Beaton. First published in English by Thomas & Mercer in collaboration with Amazon Crossing in 2019.

Published by Thomas & Mercer, in collaboration with Amazon Crossing, Seattle

www.apub.com

Amazon, the Amazon logo, Thomas & Mercer and Amazon Crossing are trademarks of Amazon.com, Inc., or its affiliates.

ISBN-13: 9781542093484
ISBN-10: 1542093481

Cover design by @blacksheep-uk.com

Printed in the United States of America

First edition

For Miriam,
thank you for all your hard work.

Prologue

The sight of the dead girl brought him nothing but sorrow. She had been beautiful once, with kind eyes and long brown hair that fell over slight shoulders. He remembered the way she used to laugh and the excitement in her voice when she would talk about future plans: dreams of a better life, of a family and of getting old. All gone now. Ended by the slash of a knife. Although looking at the many wounds on her body, he couldn't tell which had been the fatal blow.

He gently brushed her long hair out of her face, crossed her hands over her chest and closed her eyes before zipping up the black body bag.

It was a peaceful place to be laid to rest. Away from the city, beside a magnificent spruce, on a hill with views of the Alps. But she deserved better than this. Better than a brutal death and a nameless grave without a cross, where flowers would never be laid. Somewhere, he knew, somebody would miss her. Parents, friends or people from university. But nobody would ever find out how she met her fate. The traces had been too thoroughly wiped and the people behind it were too powerful.

This wasn't the first woman he'd had to bury here, and while he could never get used to it, a long time had passed since he'd had a choice. He needed the job too much and was by now far too involved to be able to leave.

It started to rain. A soft, whispering rain, as if heaven was weeping at the loss of an angel. A cold wind was stirring and it pushed and pulled at the leaves. Shivering, he did up his jacket, rolled the bag into the grave and shovelled the earth on top. He said a prayer, just as he had with the others, hoping that this would be the last. But he knew deep down his pleas would once again go unheard.

Chapter 1

It was the perfect place for an ambush. Down a small side street, hidden from the glow of the streetlight, and outside a derelict block of flats where a homeless man sometimes slept. The windows on the ground floor had all been boarded up, preventing anyone from looking into the building's cold and forgotten rooms. Flurries of snowflakes were waltzing in the cold January wind, savouring their last moments before melting in the brown sludge on the pavements.

Despite the lining in his boots, the cold crept up Nik's legs, making him shiver. A cigarette was anchored in the corner of his mouth and he was rubbing his hands together. The pockets in his leather jacket could no longer keep his fingers warm. He closed his eyes and tried to filter out the noise of passing cars, concentrating on the few people out walking on a cold Monday evening.

He heard heavy boots and the hectic scurrying of paws. The loud click-clack of high heels and the careful steps of a man in loafers, swearing at his smooth leather soles. Nik sucked hard on his cigarette and let the smoke flow through his body, relishing the moment of warmth.

He then heard the tell-tale squeaking of trainers. Each step accompanied by the sound of a neck chain clinking off someone's chest. The man started to laugh loudly, attempting to impress his friends, and Nik's suspicions were confirmed: it was the guy he was waiting for. He opened his eyes, flicked away his cigarette and peered up the alleyway. The group was moving closer.

As luck would have it, Nik's man was walking on the side nearest to him. In one swift move, Nik rammed his elbow into the man's chin, making him fall to the ground. The other three men jumped back in shock and one went to reach inside his jacket. But Nik was already raising his gun.

'What was that for?' screamed one of the men. He was pointing at the man rolling around on the ground.

Nik was cold and had no desire to talk to drug-dealing scum. He pointed the gun at the guy who'd spoken. 'Five seconds.' Nik applied some pressure to the trigger. 'After that, I'll start shooting.'

In less than five seconds the three men were out of Nik's sight. Satisfied, he put away his gun and heaved up the groaning man by his hair. His mohawk was covered in hairspray and snow, making it stick to Nik's hand. At the sides of his head was a tattoo of a spider's web that spread all the way around to his forehead. He had countless piercings, from his eyebrows down to his bottom lip. He tried to get away, but Nik's grip was unrelenting as he slammed him against the wall.

'What the fuck, Pohl?' blared the young man. 'I don't have any coke on me.'

'Inspector Pohl to you, Paddy,' replied Nik. 'And I don't give a fuck where your coke is. I want to know who's selling it for you.'

'Ah, man! Is this about that cripple, Justin, again?'

Nik threw Paddy a heavy punch to the stomach. He gasped loudly and looked at Nik with wide, wet eyes. If Nik hadn't still been holding him up by his hair, he would have been doubled over on the ground again.

'Call him a cripple one more time and I'll smash your head till you forget your own fucking name.'

'What d'you want?' Paddy begged.

'I want you to stop hiring kids.'

'Justin came to *me*,' he cried.

'Stop fucking me about.' Nik pushed him even harder against the wall.

'It's true!' Paddy screamed. 'One of my guys brought him in two weeks ago. Justin said there was loads of cokeheads on his estate, so I gave him a couple of bags.'

'How many?'

'Twenty,' said Paddy. 'Two days later, it was all gone so I gave him his share. And after seeing the money, he wanted to do it again . . . so I gave him another twenty. I didn't *make* him do anything.'

'Do you know what happens to someone if they get caught with that much coke on them?'

'Justin's got a clean record and he's still a minor,' remarked Paddy. 'They can't touch him.'

Nik pushed the man's legs out from underneath him and slammed him into the grimy, wet sludge. 'Get the drugs back from Justin and leave him alone. 'Cause if you don't, Paddy, you'll be begging me to let you crawl away the next time I find you.'

Without another glance in the man's direction, Nik crossed the street and headed towards his local. It wasn't as if he'd be able to sleep, so he may as well grab a couple of beers and catch a bit of the Premier League.

He kicked at a slushy mound of snow in frustration. He'd known it wouldn't be long before Justin was tempted into dealing. His mother barely had enough money to buy him clothes, let alone a mobile phone or a PlayStation. Not even for Christmas. And anyway, living on Munich's Neuperlach estate meant it was only a question of time before he turned to crime.

The snow was getting worse. As a child, Nik had loved this time of year. He'd fetch his sledge from the basement and head over to Olympia Hill with his friends after school. They'd sledge down it until it got dark, over and over again, even after they'd started to shiver. Nowadays, the snow was just a hassle. It caused traffic jams and found its way through even the most waterproof of shoes. Nik zipped up his jacket and lowered his head, swearing under his breath as he made his way along the street.

'Do you sleep in those clothes as well?' a woman's voice called out behind him.

'Not now, Mira,' Nik moaned. 'I just got off a horrible shift. My appearance is the last thing on my mind.'

The woman caught up with him. She was wrapped up warm in a winter jacket, scarf and hat. Her long brown hair sat full and thick under the rim of her hat. She had a small face with a childlike nose and strikingly pale, almost flawless skin. He used to call her Dolly because everything about her reminded him of a porcelain doll.

'There's a hairdresser opposite your flat, you know,' she said, eyeing Nik as he pushed his black hair away from his face yet again.

'No time,' he replied impatiently.

'Yeah, or for a shave either, I see.' She looked disapprovingly at his dark, unkempt beard, scattered with flecks of grey.

'What do you want, Mira?'

'I want you to buy new shoes.' She pointed down at his worn-out boots and the sodden shoelaces trailing along the ground. 'Or at least just do up your laces in this weather.'

'I can take them off more easily this way,' Nik said defensively. 'And I hate laces. So until my favourite boots come with Velcro, I'll just have to walk around like this.' He sighed loudly. 'But I'm sensing shoes aren't the real reason you cornered me.'

'You're a policeman, Nik,' she admonished. 'You can't just go around threatening people with your gun or beating them up.' She made no attempt to mask her accusing tone.

'So how else d'you suppose I get Paddy to leave Justin alone?' asked Nik. 'With a bunch of flowers and a box of chocolates?'

6

'Oh, come on. You must've learned plenty about non-violent methods at police college.'

'Oh, yeah. Loads of theory,' he agreed. 'But the police are treated much worse than the authors of those books like to think.'

She raised her left eyebrow and pressed her lips together, like she always did when she wasn't satisfied with Nik's excuses.

'Let me tell you a little bit about Justin,' he said. 'His father was a notorious criminal who got his girlfriend pregnant when he was out on day parole. Two weeks later, he got shot robbing a bank. Justin's mother only realised she was pregnant five months later. She quit drinking immediately, but it was too late. Her son was already harmed. Not that a deformed hand is the worst of Justin's problems.' He turned to Mira. 'And his mother's always been on benefits. All in all, he's had a pretty awful start in life, if you ask me. So I don't think looking out for him a bit is such a bad thing, do you?'

'And beating up an infamous drug dealer is what you call looking out for someone? If you want to help him, why don't you take him to school so he can finally learn to read properly? Or sort out a job for his mum so she doesn't have to sell her body.'

He turned his back on Mira. 'Jennifer might have messed up her life but she's a good mum. She could have just had an abortion or put him up for adoption like everybody was telling her to do. But she didn't. And ever since, she's been battling with social services so they don't take him off her.'

'And why these two?' asked Mira. 'There are loads of families around here with issues. Why did you specifically seek out the most hopeless one?'

Nik shrugged his shoulders.

'This boy, Justin. He reminds you of you when you were young,' she finally concluded.

Nik frowned. 'I might not be the brightest one in my family, but I don't have attention deficit, and I'm not particularly hyperactive. Plus, my dad didn't rob any banks.'

'But you do know what it's like growing up without a dad. All those things he never did – you're trying to compensate with Justin.'

'I didn't ask for a therapy session, Mira,' said Nik. 'I just don't want Justin to think crime is the only way he can make something of his life. He might have a disability, but he's got opportunities.' He turned towards her. 'Look, don't take this personally, but you just don't get it. It's not like you learn a lot about life on the street by studying art history and working as a gallery assistant.'

'I don't need to know about the streets to see that you're ruining yourself.'

'Ruining myself how?' He was annoyed now. 'Because I wear a tatty old leather jacket? Or because I've got food stains on my jeans?'

'OK. Let's start with your lack of sleep,' continued Mira. 'When was the last time you slept for more than four hours? That's if you sleep at all anymore.'

'I'm on an early tomorrow.' Nik was getting even more frustrated. 'I start at five thirty. No one is properly rested when they have to get up at four after working a twelve-hour shift the day before.'

'So you mean you're working early and instead of getting some rest, you're on your way to the pub to watch football and drink beer?'

'You might not believe it, Mira, but lots of people actually call that relaxing.'

'Yeah, people who want cirrhosis.'

Nik sighed. He hated Mira's constant warnings and clever comments about everything he did. If it was up to her, he'd be working for the road safety department, eating vegetables and drinking green tea.

Thankfully, they'd reached the bar, so he could end this conversation. 'Bye now, Mira,' he said, raising his hand. 'I'm off to get drunk.'

The game had already started when he got inside. He sat down at a small table and gave the barmaid a wave. Had he paid more attention, he would have noticed the man outside the pub, watching him arrive.

◆ ◆ ◆

Nik groaned as the Leicester goalkeeper picked up the ball from the goal for a third time. The easy days from the previous season were gone and the only thing left was the shadow of a surprise title in the Premier League. Downing his beer in one, Nik simultaneously signalled the barmaid to bring him another. As he turned back to watch the game, a man sat down at his table. The first thing Nik noticed was his short, dyed-blonde hair, sticking straight up. The man's winter jacket was undone and Nik could see his large stomach protruding out of a black woollen jumper. The man's lips parted in an unnerving smile, revealing a set of bright white teeth. His nose was small and he had thin lips, more like those of a dainty woman, and his eyebrows were uneven, as if he'd tried to pluck them after a bottle of schnapps.

'Seat's taken.' Nik kept his eyes fixed on the large TV screen as he picked out a small pretzel from a bowl on the table.

'This won't take long,' said the man in a deep voice. 'My name's Jonathan but for as long as I can remember people have called me Jon.'

'Fuck off, Jon.' Nik crunched on his pretzel, eyes still on the TV.

'Oh . . . Inspector Pohl. Did nobody teach you any manners at police college?'

Nik took the man in. He never forgot a face and the one looking back at him wasn't one he'd seen before. He looked at the rest of him: the gaudy hair certainly didn't belong to a CID officer, and his Apple Watch wasn't flashy enough for your typical dealer or pimp. His fingernails had been bitten right back, and his teeth were far too straight and white to be natural. His jumper looked like cashmere and his winter jacket, much like his watch, was more practical than fashionable. His skin was so pale it looked like he hadn't ventured outside in years, and he was sucking on a peppermint as though he was trying to mask his bad breath. Looking back at his eyes, Nik could see no signs of excessive drinking, and the man's non-dilated pupils and steady hands didn't indicate drug use. But there was a waft of garlic and fried chillies, which Nik put down to cheap Asian fast food. That would explain the mints, he supposed.

'Do I know you?'

'Actually, you do,' answered Jon. 'I was down at the police station four weeks ago. But I was wearing a wig and glasses at the time. And I had a full beard.'

Nik tried to remember a man of this description. It finally came to him. 'Oh yeah, you were that fat piece of shit who sat beside my desk for half a day. Lost a fair bit of weight since then, haven't you?'

'Oh, I was padded up in a few places. I've actually put on weight.'

'Only people with something to hide change their appearance.'

'My anonymity is very important to me and there are too many cameras at the station. And vigilant police officers,' said Jon. 'But I wasn't there because of me . . .'

'. . . But because of a missing woman whose case is closed and filed.' Nik remembered the case. He reached for another pretzel and lobbed it in his mouth. 'And if I remember correctly, my colleague, Danilo, told you back then what that means.'

'Yeah, he did. Before I asked him for the case to be reopened.'

'Oh, and why was that?' asked Nik. 'Because of a false statement? Or official misconduct from the judge? Or maybe a violation of the European Convention on Human Rights?'

'No, none of those,' answered Jon. 'It was because if someone would just put the effort in, then they might throw a whole new light on this case.'

Nik sighed. 'Listen, I'm a CID inspector, not a private detective. I'm sorry about your girlfriend, OK, but I'm off duty. So fuck off before I get rude.' His gaze went back to the football again.

'That day I spent down the station, I realised I wasn't going to get anywhere the normal way. So, I've been reading up on you for the last few weeks.' Jon reached for a pretzel. 'The local press was a really helpful place to start. A police officer who beats up a public prosecutor in his office will always get my attention.' He waved the pretzel around. 'And so, I did a bit more research . . . and found out that that particular public prosecutor had actually dismissed a case that had meant a lot to you.'

'All the evidence suggested the husband was the offender, even after he spewed out all that crap about her having a lover,' said Nik. 'A five-year-old could have seen that. Just because the wife's body wasn't found, doesn't mean there wasn't a crime. People don't just disappear.'

Jon nodded. 'The guy deserved the beating. And it made me want to find out more about you. So I hacked your home computer and went into all your private emails. Oh, and I also bribed one of your CID colleagues to get at your personnel file. And lastly, I put a transmitter on your car. Been following you around for quite a while now.' Jon put the pretzel in his mouth. 'The only thing I couldn't crack was your phone,' he said, crunching. 'That thing's so old even the latest computers don't stand a chance.'

Any contentment Nik had felt as he'd drunk his first beer drained away. This nutter had admitted enough crimes to be thrown in jail.

'Nikolaus Jeremiah Pohl.' Jon shook his head. 'I'd like to know how your parents decided on such eccentric names for you all those thirty-two years ago.'

Nik edged his right hand slowly towards his gun holster while his left hand continued to fiddle with the pretzel bowl, distracting Jon's attention.

'So, Jon, if you read my file, then you'll know I'm a bit prone to random acts of violence. And that the other person usually leaves in a bit of a mess. The prosecutor wasn't the only one.'

'Exactly.' Jon nodded. 'I learned a lot from spying on your life. I learned that unlike most people, *you* can't be blackmailed. Your life's turned into such a pile of shit over the last couple of years that you've nothing left to care about. You don't care about money, or your job, or any kind of success or recognition for that matter.' Jon placed an iPad on the table. 'And until about two days ago, I had nothing I could use to force you to work with me. But then I came across an email about a certain Jennifer Keuser and her son, Justin.' He sighed dramatically and shook his head. 'What a terrible situation those two are in. And the mum. Well, she could lose Justin if social services knew she was working illegally as a prostitute, couldn't she?'

Nik tightened his grip on the gun.

'Now, that's not an easy thing to prove. I mean, she'd have to be caught in the act. So, I offered Jennifer a large sum to come and be nice to me in a hotel room.' Jon tapped the screen. A film started. Jennifer was wearing a short skirt and a faux fur coat over a thin blouse. She had a lot of make-up on and her blonde hair fell freely over her shoulders. She was standing at the end of a bed covered with cheap, shiny-looking black sheets and on the wall behind it was a large mirror, equally as tacky.

'Five hundred . . . for the one time?' She was gnawing on a fingernail and having trouble balancing on her high shoes. She didn't seem like a professional prostitute. More like someone just starting out, afraid of what was to come. It broke Nik's heart to see her like that.

Jon came into the shot and handed her five hundred-euro notes, which she accepted with a smile and packed away into a small glittery handbag. But then, any sign of happiness disappeared as she raised her head and realised again why she was there.

Jon turned to the camera and smiled smugly, sending Nik a silent message. The video ended.

Nik had had enough. He pulled out the gun under the table and rammed it against Jon's stomach. 'If you don't delete that video right now, I'll put a hole in your guts.'

'Ah, yes. This was the reaction I expected.' Jon looked at his watch. 'So, in two minutes, an email with this exact video will be sent to the police and to social services, along with Jennifer's address. Now, if you wanted, I could stop the email from being sent. But say, for example, I was shot . . . or you didn't do what I tell you, then Jennifer would be charged with illegal prostitution and her son would be sent off to live in a home.'

'And what if I don't believe you and put a bullet in your stomach anyway?' Nik leaned threateningly over the table.

'Oh, well, then you could wait two minutes and check your own email 'cause I copied you in as well. I suppose then you'll know if I was lying or not.' Ignoring Nik's furious expression, Jon turned to look at the TV screen. 'Never did understand the fascination with football.' He waved over to the bartender. 'Another beer?' he asked Nik.

'What is wrong with you?'

'Oh, I'm just desperate and well prepared.'

Nik closed his hand around the gun so tightly the handle squeaked against his palm. Every inch of his body was telling him to thrash the smug smile from the man's face but there was something so persuasively self-assured about the guy. He was either the perfect poker player or he really was going to send off that email.

Jon's watch beeped. 'One minute, and then you'll know if I'm bluffing. Question is, are you prepared to risk it?'

Nik's breath came hard and fast as his mind whirled with possibilities. Was he telling the truth? And why had he chosen Nik? There were better police officers in Munich. Jon clearly had money, so why not just hire a private detective? What could make somebody so desperate they'd blackmail a CID inspector?

'Thirty seconds.'

Nik's finger was shaking. His rage was boiling. But the risk was too great. He had to restrain himself. Even if there was only the tiniest chance Jon's threat was real.

'OK,' Nik said, putting the gun back in its holster.

Jon picked up the tablet and opened an email program. His fingers flew across the virtual keyboard. 'Good decision,' he said as the watch beeped for a second time.

Almost panting, Nik grabbed the new beer that the barmaid had brought over. 'How can I be sure you've actually deleted the video and that all of this is over?'

'You can't be sure, Nik,' answered Jon. 'I can call you Nik now, can't I? Now that we're business partners.'

Nik groaned with frustration.

'But you should know, I'm not actually interested in ruining random people's lives just for the sake of it. Quite the opposite. I can be quite generous. Help me with the case and I'll leave you alone.'

'It's more a question of whether I'll *let* you go.'

Jon laughed. 'Oh . . . we're gonna work well together.' He turned the tablet to face Nik. 'So, shall we get started?'

Danilo was already sitting at his computer checking emails when Nik got to the office the next morning. He was wearing beige chinos, a white shirt and dark brown leather shoes. He had short, perfectly coiffed, curly black hair and he was wearing a crisp aftershave. His desk was tidy and the few files on it lay in neat piles beside a pencil organiser holding three pens. A cup of coffee stood on a coaster and his phone sat in a holder in the shape of a sun lounger. He briefly glanced over as Nik slumped down into the chair opposite him and shook his head. Nik had barely slept after his encounter with Jon and had only just been able to drag himself out of bed. Showering or brushing his teeth had been out of the question. It was obvious he'd been wearing his jeans for a week and his laces, still undone, were stuffed down the sides of his boots. His shirt was the only clean piece of clothing, albeit unironed.

'You're early,' said Danilo, remarking on Nik's lateness.

'Oh, hi, Danilo. Almost didn't recognise you there,' said Nik, feigning surprise. 'Your head's always so far up our boss's arse these days, I thought your face would be much darker.' Nik picked up a cup from his desk and threw the rest of yesterday's coffee in his mouth. His colleague shivered. Nik pushed the mound of files on his desk around until he finally found his keyboard and started up his computer.

The door from the adjoining office opened. 'Danilo! Nik! In my office,' a man shouted. 'There's work.'

'Up! Up!' Nik said quietly to Danilo. 'There's a good boy.' Nik walked right past his boss's office towards the break room.

'I need a coffee. So how 'bout you warm my seat for me?'

Nik liked his boss even less than his partner, so he took his time getting a coffee and enjoying another toilet visit before eventually knocking on his boss's door, slurping on his coffee. He put his cup on a pile of files on the desk and fell back into a chair, yawning.

'Nice of you to visit, Nik.' Heinrich Naumann was the aged version of Danilo. Proper, always well dressed and fond of talking, but as far as Nik was concerned, he rarely said anything worth paying attention to. He got his hair cut once a week and coloured on a regular basis. He'd sometimes come to work with a swollen forehead, which Nik put down to Botox. Today he was wearing his gold wedding ring. Not a daily guarantee with Naumann. But the light-blonde hairs on his coat told Nik exactly what his boss had been up to the night before. His wife was a brunette. Nik didn't know whether Naumann had a lover or went to a prostitute, but he did know that a young and ambitious female police officer from the other team had hair exactly the same colour and length as the strands currently sticking to his coat. She was the kind of woman who'd be bold enough to start a relationship with a superior thirty years her senior.

There were numerous photos on Naumann's desk: one of him with the Lord Mayor of Munich, one with a Brazilian football player who'd enjoyed the best time of his career at Bayern, and one with a skiing star from Garmisch. Naumann was a master when it came to networking. He courted the right people, willingly accepted orders from above and had no qualms about locking people up just to meet targets. Thankfully, he'd finally given up threatening Nik with sanctions for being disobedient. Instead, he'd managed to sideline him by only giving him cases with very little public exposure. In fact, the cases he got these days barely even made it into the local press.

'Attack on a petrol station.' Naumann let a thin pile of files fall on his desk and Danilo grabbed them instantly. At best, Nik's driving could be described as reckless, so his partner wanted him nowhere near the wheel today. But Danilo's enthusiasm suited Nik perfectly, as it meant he could catch up on some much-needed sleep in the car.

Naumann started summarising the case while Nik examined the contents of his coffee cup. After Danilo had asked all the necessary questions, Nik stood up and shuffled his way towards the toilet. 'I need five minutes,' he said, 'then we can go.' As Danilo started packing his things, Nik slipped past the toilets into an empty office. He closed the door behind him, took out his phone and dialled a number.

A tired voice picked up after the third ring. 'Tilo Hübner.'

'Hi, Tilo. It's Nik.'

'Mate, d'you not know what time it is?'

'Just before six.'

Tilo groaned. 'I'm normally not up before seven.'

'Sorry . . . but we're about to head out to a job and I didn't know when I'd get another chance to call.'

'What is it this time? You been done for assault? Call the chief of police's assistant an impotent son of a bitch again?'

'I'm working on a case and I need to get hold of a file that might help me with it.'

Tilo hesitated. 'You do still work for the CID, don't you?'

'Yes,' Nik said. 'But my permissions got cut – too much poking my nose in where it wasn't wanted, so I'd never get my hands on it.'

'Yeah, I heard about that.' Somewhere in the background Nik could hear the grinding of a coffee machine.

'It's nothing important,' continued Nik. 'The case has actually already been closed. It's about a woman called Viola Rohe.'

Tilo didn't answer. The line crackled.

'You still there?' asked Nik.

'Yeah . . . sorry. Just yawning,' he replied. 'What was the name again?'

'Viola Rohe,' Nik repeated. 'Can you remember the case?'

'No, don't think so,' answered Tilo. 'What about her?'

'Well, she disappeared and her parents reported her missing. At first it was thought she'd been kidnapped or perhaps murdered, but a few days into the investigation, her parents got a letter from her saying she was fine, but never coming home.'

'And what's so strange about that?'

'Nothing,' Nik lied. 'I just want to check something.'

Tilo sighed. 'I'll help you out where I can but your antics almost got you suspended last time. One more offence and you'll be kicked out the service. Then your life really will be screwed. No pension. And the state you're in, you'll be lucky to land a job guarding empty building sites in the winter.' Tilo took a sip of coffee. 'Plus, if this goes to shit, you'll drag me down with you and that would really mess things up for me at Major Crimes.'

'I know,' Nik said, trying to play things down. 'I'll owe you a second round.'

'It'd be a third actually,' interrupted Tilo.

'And this will be the last time I bother you . . . for the time being.'

'Define "for the time being".'

'The next two weeks.'

Tilo laughed. 'At least you're honest.'

'It's a small case that nobody's working on.'

'You know, it's actually *because* I'm your friend that I shouldn't be supporting your solo efforts.'

'You know me, Tilo. I won't give up till I've got those papers.'

'Fine,' said Tilo reluctantly. 'But only on the condition that you keep me up to date with everything. Last time you ruined ten months of drug squad surveillance because you lifted their informant right before a deal.'

'The guy had a suitcase full of money.' Nik tried to justify his actions.

'That was part of the case!'

'OK,' Nik relented. 'I'll give you daily reports.'

'I'll see what I can find and throw copies of anything in your letterbox after work.'

'You're the best.'

'I know,' said Tilo before hanging up.

Nik had only just left the room when Danilo came walking towards him along the corridor. 'You constipated or what?'

Nik raised his middle finger and walked past him. He picked up a camera bag from his desk and headed towards the car park. The petrol station was waiting.

Jon looked at the two photos on his computer screen. On the left, there was Nik as a young police officer at his swearing-in ceremony, and on the right, a picture of him from last week going into the sports bar. They could have been two different people.

Nik Pohl. A quick-tempered, often uncontrollable man who had come off the rails. This was evident from his appearance: his unkempt hair, unshaven face and constantly crumpled clothes. In his worn-out boots and tattered old leather jacket, Nik looked more like a homeless person than a CID investigator. This was a man who had given up; a man who went through life with no fear of death because ultimately, for him, death couldn't be any worse than his current existence.

Any signs of the enthusiastic police officer he used to be had disappeared. Yet, when Jon had threatened to put Jennifer in danger, he'd seen the rage in Nik's eyes. Signs of the alpha male, willing to fight fearlessly for the people he loves. If only Nik would make a bit more effort to dress appropriately or to stop contradicting his seniors, his life would be a lot easier. But despite the blows that fate had thrown his way, Nik still wasn't broken. And this was what made him the perfect man for the job. Jon just needed to evoke the spirit of the younger Nik Pohl, the spirit of the man in the first photo, who would go to any lengths to solve a case and whose belief in justice was unassailable.

It hadn't been easy for Jon to trick Jennifer and treat her like a prostitute. But she was Nik's only weakness. He had seen her desperation. Being forced to earn money that way just so she could keep her child. What he hadn't told Nik was that he hadn't actually had sex with Jennifer and that he'd given Jennifer twice the money they'd agreed upon in the video. Her eyes had shone with happiness when she hugged him goodbye, knowing she wouldn't have to sell herself again for a while.

And Jon still felt cheap when he thought about how he had acted at the sports bar. But it was the only way. He needed Nik to kick things off and then, when he was sure everything was going to plan, he could get on with things on his own. No more threats, no more blackmailing.

Jon needed Nik, otherwise he'd never find out what had happened to Viola.

◆　◆　◆

Morning rush hour was getting underway as Nik and Danilo left the police station. Nik hoped this would make the journey longer and allow him to sleep. But no such luck. As soon as he closed his eyes, he was haunted by the memory of Jon and his obscure request, so the twenty-minute drive proved anything but relaxing.

When they finally arrived, the entrance to the petrol station was blocked by a police car. Danilo parked up beside it and got out. An old man with a bulging beer belly and a terrible haircut was waiting in the sales area, surprisingly composed. He was the manager of the petrol station and immediately began telling his version of events. While Danilo got a detailed description, Nik went to talk to a police constable who was standing at a table going through his notes.

'So, what happened?'

'At 5.31 a.m. a single male threatened the manager with a gun and forced him to open the cash register.' The patrol officer was a young man with shaved hair and a thin goatee beard. He flicked through his small notebook while simultaneously describing the incident. 'Six hundred and forty euros missing,' he concluded.

'Any witnesses?'

The policeman shook his head. 'No, but there's CCTV footage and you can see the offender was carrying a weapon. He looks about one metre eighty tall and around ninety kilograms. He was dressed completely in black and wore a balaclava over his face. He put the money into a blue plastic bag and drove away eastwards.'

'Is a police search already underway?'

The officer nodded. 'The description went out to all patrol cars. We might still find him.'

'Thanks,' said Nik. He went over to his bag, took out an expensive camera and started taking photos.

'Are you going to take DNA samples?' asked the manager.

What a stupid fucking idea, Nik thought to himself. He noticed the man's red eyes. He clearly wasn't used to working the night shift and it was obvious he'd downed something much stronger than coffee to keep himself awake. He kept his shaky hands hidden behind his back.

'Too many people coming and going around here for that, I'm afraid,' explained Nik patiently. 'But I'll be taking fingerprints from the objects that were touched by the offender.'

'We've got a witness,' Danilo called over, pointing towards a middle-aged man whose face was covered in acne scars. 'Tell us what you saw,' he said.

'I was walking past the petrol station on my way home when I saw a man with a plastic bag running out. He had a gun in his left hand, so I pressed myself up close to a big lamppost and tried to keep myself hidden. I saw the guy racing past me in a dark blue Opel not long after.'

'Did you get the registration number?'

'Of course,' said the man, smiling proudly.

Danilo returned the smile and nodded for him to continue. They'd trace the number to the car owner and by lunch, the special task force would have already raided his flat. Case solved.

While Danilo was daydreaming about the praise he would get from his boss, Nik fished out a laptop. He went into a back room and logged on to the free Wi-Fi, which luckily wasn't password protected.

As long as Nik remembered to delete the cache from the browser after he'd finished, Danilo wouldn't be able to see which sites he'd been on. He also ran the CCTV footage from the night before so it at least looked like he was doing some work.

Jon had given him little information on Viola. A photo, her date of birth and her last known address. Despite Nik's repeated questioning, he'd not told him why he wanted him to look into this case, nor what his connection to Viola was. For all Nik knew, Jon could just be bored and fancied himself as a detective. But whatever the case, the missing woman was of secondary importance to Nik right now. First, he needed to find out more about Jon. He'd taken his fingerprints from the beer bottle yesterday so he could enter them into the system along with the ones from today's scene. That might bring up the first clue to his identity.

Jonathan was probably his real name. He was in his early thirties and was good with computers. He didn't come from Munich. He didn't even come from Bayern. To begin with he'd spoken perfect High German, but the more he spoke, the more he slipped back into his old habits. He had a slightly nasal intonation, like people from the Ruhr area. But it was obvious he'd lived in Munich for a good while, as he seemed familiar with local clubs and bars.

Nik considered some possibilities. Jon had probably come from the Ruhr to study IT at the Technical University of Munich, or the TUM as it's known, and after that he must have ended up sticking around in the Bavarian metropolis. He didn't seem to be your typical developer, shut away in a room working for some large corporation, being told what to do. Rather, he seemed more accustomed to giving the orders. It was possible he'd progressed rapidly in his career or he'd founded a start-up.

Nik typed everything he knew about Jon into the search engine. There was a whole array of Jonathans from the Ruhr who'd tried to make it in Munich but none of them seemed to match the blackmailer's description. Nik realised it was highly likely that Jon would have deleted anything compromising about himself from the internet. So a search was probably pointless. But then, fifteen minutes later, Nik came across a TUM article from nine years back about a new lecturer and his group of student assistants, one of whom was a certain Jonathan Kirchhof.

The man was quite young and slim and had barely any facial hair. But then, partly hidden under a dark grey woollen hat, Nik recognised a pair of familiar eyes.

'Hello, dickhead,' Nik said, pleased with himself.

It was easy after that. Although Jon's specialisation had been cryptology, it was his work as one of Germany's first programmers for games apps that had made him famous. With the arrival of the iPhone, these programmers were getting rich, and three years after forming his own company, he sold it to an American firm for a massive seven-figure sum. And after that, he pretty much went off the radar. There were a couple of presentations at symposiums, normally at the Chaos Communication Congress, and then an alumni gathering at the TUM. But year by year, the articles about Jon became more and more scarce. And, as of 2016, there were none. Nik searched for a home address, an email address, a telephone number. But none of the results matched.

He hurriedly finished writing up his notes. At least now he knew more about the man he was up against, and hopefully he'd be able to find a connection to Viola in the files from Tilo. And if Jon's address also happened to turn up, then his new acquaintance would be getting an unexpected visitor.

Chapter 2

Nik had finished his shift and was driving out of the CID car park when his phone rang.

'Listen, I'm going to try and talk you out of this one more time,' said Tilo as soon as Nik picked up.

'Why? What's so bad about it?'

'It's nothing to do with the case. I just don't like the fact you're working on your own.'

'I'll behave this time,' Nik reassured him.

Tilo sighed loudly. 'Mate, you're killing me.'

'Did you put the files in my letterbox?'

'Copies of them.'

'Thank you.'

'Tomorrow you'll tell me exactly what you're gonna do with them and don't you dare start anything without telling me.'

'I won't,' Nik lied.

'Well, good luck.' Tilo hung up.

When Nik got home, he immediately opened his letterbox, took out a brown envelope and headed upstairs to his flat. He cleared away two empty beer bottles from the coffee table in front of his couch, sat himself down and spread out the files.

Viola's disappearance had been recorded by a CID colleague on 26 October and was then passed over to the crime squad. Viola's parents were worried because they hadn't heard from her in a long time and she wasn't in her flat. Her psychology lecturer confirmed she'd not been to the last two lectures. Two days later, a search was launched but then, on 29 October, her parents received a letter from her stating that she'd left Munich and would not be coming back. They had confirmed it was Viola's handwriting and the letter included a reference to Viola's childhood that only she and her parents could have known about. As a result, it was decided the letter was genuine and the case was closed. Nothing strange so far.

Before 26 October 2016, Viola's name had never been registered in the CID system. Her record didn't have any links to criminals or drugs, or to any other offences.

Her life story turned out to be equally uneventful. Born in Munich in 1987, she left school to become a secretary at a car parts supplier. She finished her apprenticeship and worked in the job for three years until 2012, when she started a degree in psychology at Ludwig Maximilian University. At the time of her disappearance she was living in a flat with a friend. It wasn't the best part of Munich, but it certainly wasn't the worst either.

Nik looked at her photo. She had long brown hair that fell below her shoulders, but it was her light green eyes and beautiful smile that really stood out, and both were enhanced perfectly by the blonde streaks in her hair and red lipstick. She wasn't classically pretty: her nose was too pointy and her chin was too strong, but there was a confident maturity about her that was very attractive and made her seem older than her years. There was nothing to suggest she was the type to just up and leave without saying anything to anyone. Obviously, she wouldn't have been the first woman to be tempted away by some rich, handsome man, but her history suggested she was a straightforward woman who valued security and consistency.

Nik put his laptop on the table and started to search for information about Viola. Results came up for a student portal where she'd answered questions in her first semester at university. Her Facebook profile was only visible to friends, but he was able to collect some information from some short posts. Viola took her studies seriously, and in the autumn of 2015 she had completed a work placement at an organisation that provided free school meals to children. There were photos of her at university parties, but none where she was falling down drunk or in embarrassing situations. She was a vegetarian and a member of a cooking group that collected the addresses of regional vegetable suppliers. All in all, her life was hardly exciting, but she had her interests and plans for the future. So why make such a drastic cut?

There seemed to be no link to Jon. He wasn't in a single photo and his name wasn't mentioned once. Viola didn't have any connections to the Ruhr and Jon had never had anything to do with psychology. He was two years older than her. He'd gone to school in North Rhine-Westphalia and there was nothing to suggest Viola had ever been there.

Nik walked over to the wall where he had pinned a large map of Munich. He stuck a red pin on Leopoldpark, near the psychology faculty at Ludwig Maximilian University, and placed another green pin further down at the TUM's Faculty for Information Technology on Theresienstraße. Considering the size of Munich, the distance between the two wasn't that great but it was still too long a trip to make regularly on foot. And anyway, Jon had already finished his degree when Viola started her first semester.

Nik kicked one of the beer bottles he'd placed on the floor. It smashed loudly against the living room wall, but, deep in thought, he ignored it. As long as Jon still had that video of Jennifer, Nik would have to play by his rules. Jon had made it clear that night in the bar that he'd given Nik all the information he needed. Apparently it was none of Nik's business why Jon was looking for Viola and there was no point in trying to get more out of him. So what exactly was Jon's role in all of this?

Was he the jealous lover who wanted his girlfriend back? Very unlikely, otherwise Nik would have found at least one photo of them together. Was it possible that their paths had crossed through Jon's work? He couldn't see why. There was nothing in their interests that seemed to overlap, not even work. But, he supposed, it was possible. Was it likely that a woman like Viola could have been caught up in some sort of industrial espionage? Tech companies were always in competition with each other after all, and maybe Viola led a secret double life, and her good-girl exterior was the perfect cover? Nik shook his head impatiently. He was being ridiculous.

But, that aside, supposing Jon *was* responsible for Viola's disappearance, it was possible that he was using Nik to find and deal with any remaining traces. He sighed. The case had already been closed, so that didn't make any sense. Perhaps Jon was worried that Viola had been killed during a crime. But he'd checked the police database and, since October, there hadn't been any unidentified bodies that matched Viola's description.

Nik grabbed a beer from the fridge and slumped back on to the couch. He switched on the television. He needed a night to mull everything over but then tomorrow, he'd be sure to make good use of his CID badge while he still had it.

After his shift he'd go and visit Viola's parents.

Nik normally couldn't care less what witnesses thought about his appearance but today he needed to make a good impression. When he got home from work, he took a proper shower, washed his hair and dug out a clean shirt from the depths of his wardrobe. Everything could have done with a press and his boots were still untied, but it was his best attempt at the eligible bachelor look.

Oswald and Ines Rohe started to shake when Nik showed them his badge. Their first assumption was that it was bad news.

'It's just a routine visit,' Nik said reassuringly. 'We regularly check in on old cases just to see if anything's happened that we should know about.'

Frau Rohe invited him inside. It was a simple flat that looked like it hadn't been decorated since the 1980s. The living room was carpeted and dominated by dark wooden furniture. In front of an old TV stood a three-piece suite. Nik sat down on one of the chairs while the wife brought him a cup of tea before sitting down on the couch. Her long grey hair was tied up in a bun. She smoothed down her hair and reached over for her husband's hand.

'How can we help you?' Herr Rohe asked.

'Most importantly: have you heard from Viola at all?'

The man shook his head while his wife looked at the floor, trying hard not to cry. Nik felt a flash of sympathy.

'I'm sorry to bring all this up again but I need to know more about the time leading up to your daughter's disappearance. The information in my colleague's report is very vague.' He took a notepad out of his bag. 'Did Viola seem in any way different towards the end of October 2016?'

'Viola might have been a bit stubborn and single-minded but those were really her strengths as well,' said Herr Rohe. 'If she wanted something, she would make sure she got it. She was working at a car parts supplier, but she didn't like it so decided to start a degree in psychology. Not an easy decision. We couldn't be of much support . . . you know . . . with the pensions we're on and she didn't want to move back in with us. So she had to sacrifice a lot for it all. But she did it. And that's why we can't understand why she would just leave it all behind.'

'Was she worried about anything in particular? Had you perhaps had an argument with her?'

'We didn't see her very often because she was either in class or studying or working. But when she did come over, everything was great. She loved my wife's cooking and would normally stay late.'

'Where did Viola spend her time when she wasn't here or studying at the university? Did she have any hobbies?'

'She would go running with friends in the English Garden. And . . . sometimes she went to the theatre. But she didn't really have enough time for a regular hobby.'

'You mentioned she also spent a lot of time working. What was Viola's job during uni?'

'Well, because she had classes during the day, she took on a job in a bar,' explained Frau Rohe.

'In a nightclub called The Palace,' added the husband. 'It's near the main station.'

'I know the one,' said Nik, noting down the name. The Palace was one of Munich's trendier clubs. It had a strict door policy and a varied clientele ranging from B-list celebrities to shady characters on the lookout for new customers, be it for coke or prostitutes. The nightclub was definitely something to look into.

'Did she have a long-term boyfriend?'

Frau Rohe gave a long sigh. 'Not since the whole thing with Volker.'

'I'm sorry?'

'Are you joking?' asked Herr Rohe, irritated. 'You *are* from the Munich CID, aren't you?'

'Yes,' replied Nik, wondering why the atmosphere had suddenly turned so sour.

'And the name Volker Ufer means nothing to you?'

'No.' Nik was perplexed. He had a photographic memory and could always remember names. He'd never heard the name Volker Ufer before and he certainly hadn't read anything about him in Viola's file.

Frau Rohe placed her hand on her husband's arm, trying to console him. He took two deep breaths and managed to compose himself.

'Volker Ufer was a drug dealer. He was arrested in the spring of 2016 and given a three-year prison sentence that he's still serving.'

'And he was friends with your daughter?'

The wife nodded, ashamed.

'Do you know how she got friendly with that kind of man?'

'They met through Viola's old job. He used to work at a garage,' explained Herr Rohe. 'He'd use the job to find rich new customers. Apparently, he dealt cocaine.'

'Did Viola not notice?'

'Volker was a handsome, charming man,' Frau Rohe said sadly. 'He was always very smartly dressed and drove an expensive car. But he was never, you know . . . arrogant. He came across well and had good manners.'

'And was Viola there when he got arrested?'

Herr Rohe nodded. 'Not only that. He told the police that she'd been selling drugs with him.'

'And what happened after that?'

'It was a horrible time for all of us, but in the end, there was no evidence to support Volker's accusations and all the charges against Viola were dropped.'

Nik tapped his pen on the notepad. Having a drug dealer in the picture put a whole new complexion on the case. He would need to rethink everything. But first of all, he needed to find out more about this Volker Ufer. Nik clapped the notebook shut and stood up. 'Thank you for your time.' He nodded to the couple. 'I'll be in touch as soon as I have anything new on Viola's whereabouts.'

Herr Rohe walked him to the door. Although he said goodbye politely, Nik could tell from the man's face that he'd given up any hope of seeing his daughter again.

As soon as he left the Rohes' front door, he took out his phone and dialled Tilo's number. It rang three times before his colleague picked up. 'Are you taking the piss?' Nik began.

'Good evening to you too, Nik,' said Tilo.

'Viola's last boyfriend was a cocaine dealer w
locked up. Why isn't that mentioned in the file?'

'How should I know?' replied Tilo. 'I gave yo
I found.'

'There has to be a cross reference somewhere.'

'There wasn't.'

'Then look harder.'

'Bugger off, Nik. I'm not just sitting around all day in the office waiting for you to call. And it's not my fault if our colleagues don't do their work properly.'

'Then get me everything you can on this guy. His name is Volker Ufer. He was picked up in spring 2016 and is serving a three-year sentence.'

'I'll see what I can find in the morning,' said Tilo, clearly annoyed.

'In the morning?'

'It's 10 p.m., Nik. You might not believe it, but I actually have a private life and I'm not going back to the office just to look for some stupid fucking file. For a case that's already been closed!'

For a moment, Nik was tempted to drive over to the station and look everything up himself. But that would have been pretty much the same as announcing his private investigation on the bulletin board.

'Speak to you tomorrow.' Nik hung up.

He got into his car and closed the door. There had only been a few times in his life when he'd embarrassed himself like he had in front of Viola's parents. He was impatient to see what Volker Ufer's file would hold, but it looked like he'd have to wait. He made his way over to the A9 with his siren on. He needed to blow off some steam before going to bed and a little spin on the motorway would do the trick.

pite having the following day off, Nik was up early. He left Tilo in peace until 9 a.m. and then started calling every thirty minutes until his enraged colleague sent him an email from his private account during his lunch break. The email contained scans of Volker Ufer's file. It was, of course, a gross misconduct of staff regulations but Tilo was high enough up the food chain at Munich's specialist crime division that he'd survive if anyone found out.

The majority of Volker's file focused on his drug dealing, his contacts and his customers. The surveillance report and court transcript were included but they didn't tell him much. The only papers Nik read more closely were those about the arrest.

Viola had unfortunately decided to spend the night at Volker's and was still at his home the next day. After being picked up by the police, the two were separated. She was held in custody and on that same day, she had to stand before the court. Luckily, the surveillance operation had been in place for a long time before the arrest and there was no evidence to show Viola had been involved in the dealing. The fact that Volker had also had two other girlfriends played in her favour and, in the end, she wasn't charged. She was, however, interrogated numerous times and it can't have been easy for her to find out about Volker's cheating.

The dealer was still sitting in jail and Viola hadn't been involved, meaning Nik could rule out revenge from suppliers, two of whom had also been arrested as part of the investigation. Volker Ufer wasn't going to be of any use to the investigation. He would have to follow his second clue and pay The Palace a visit.

Nik sighed and took a beer from the fridge. He hated that kind of club. They were too loud, too expensive and the drinks were never cold enough. Even if he put on his best clothes, he knew he didn't stand a chance of getting past the bouncers, so he'd just have to show up as police on an official investigation. A dangerous game. If a club employee called up the station asking to confirm his identity, Nik would be out on the street by the morning. And he was going to have to behave if he wanted to avoid any complaints. He'd have to be the polite, no-nonsense officer, and that was never the most effective way of getting someone to tell the truth. The travel clock on top of the fridge said 9.52 p.m. He'd wasted the whole day studying the files on Volker's arrest. Nik finished off his beer and slipped into the clothes he'd had on the day before. He pulled his least worn-out leather jacket over his shirt and headed to the U-Bahn. Slipping on the icy street, Nik's temper rose and he screamed at a driver who almost ran him over on a zebra crossing.

The entrance to The Palace was nothing spectacular. Just a metal door and a neon sign with the name of the club on it. Beside the door stood two men and a woman, probably in their forties, each holding a clipboard. The men were about a foot bigger than Nik. They were broad, muscular guys, but they didn't come across as meatheads. They weren't wearing gold chains, their haircuts were pretty standard and their jackets looked like they'd been made to measure. When they turned people away, they did so in a quiet and considerate manner without any threatening gestures. The woman appeared business-like. She sized up every new face meticulously and was friendly towards those she knew, greeting them with a smile and a welcoming gesture. But when she thought nobody was looking, her façade would crack and her expression would turn hollow. It seemed pretty clear she hated her job and was bored out of her mind.

Nik sneaked in from the side while she greeted an older man who was clearly a regular. As she turned to Nik, he was already holding up his badge in front of him.

'Good evening,' he began. 'Munich CID.' He avoided giving her his name. 'Do you have a moment?' The woman nodded, clearly surprised, and moved a couple of steps to the side with Nik.

'Are you the nightclub manager?' he continued.

'His assistant.' She shook his hand. 'Natalja Nowara. What's this about?'

'We're investigating a case in which a former employee of yours might have been involved. Viola Rohe.'

'Viola?' the woman repeated. 'I haven't seen her in months.'

'How long exactly?'

'Can't say. One day she just stopped coming to work. She didn't respond to emails and her mobile just went to voicemail.' She turned towards the entrance as though she was scared somebody might notice her talking. 'Has something happened?'

'I'm not allowed to discuss any details.' Nik avoided the question. 'But perhaps you could take me to the manager? He might be able to help.' The hollow expression had returned. Maybe she felt offended or she didn't like the request but finally she nodded and led Nik around to a door at the back of the building. Using a key to unlock it, she ushered Nik in. The music hit him like a tonne of bricks. He could feel the bass in the pit of his stomach and he resisted the urge to cover his ears. A stairway led from the back door down to the club. A large swarm of people crowded around a wooden bar, all waiting on drinks that were being mixed by three bartenders. Natalja took Nik into an office where the music was considerably quieter. The room had a large glass panel that looked out on to the dance floor. A man of about fifty sat at a large chrome desk. He had a fake tan and the uneven hair growth on his receding hairline indicated he'd had a transplant. Other than that, he was pleasantly free of clichés. He wore a dark brown suit and a white shirt without a tie. His Glashütte watch looked expensive but not showy and his cufflinks were a tasteful white gold. As Natalja walked through the door, he looked up from his paperwork. Nik had perfected the art of reading upside down for moments like this and when he got nearer to the table, he could read last month's figures. The five-digit figure under 'Profits' suggested business was going well.

The man inspected Nik before looking questioningly at Natalja.

'He's from the Munich CID.'

Nik moved closer to the desk and shook the manager's hand. 'Nik Pohl,' he said. Not providing a name at this stage would have been tricky.

'Peer Weise,' responded the man, gesturing towards a leather seat in front of his desk. 'Has something happened in the club?'

'We don't know yet,' replied Nik. He always preferred using 'we' in this kind of situation to give the impression a large group of investigators was on the case. 'What do you know about the whereabouts of Viola Rohe?'

'Viola? She hasn't worked here for a long time. And I haven't seen her here in her spare time either. Is she missing?'

'I need to speak to Frau Rohe and we can't get hold of her at her registered address.' Nik avoided answering another question.

'I could get you her contact details from our computer system if you want?' suggested Weise.

'Like I said,' added Nowara, 'one day she was here, and then the next, she just never came back to work. She didn't say why. She didn't get in touch at all.'

'Did anything out of the ordinary happen on her last day at work?' The woman shook her head.

'We never had any problems with Viola,' Weise explained.

'Do you happen to have CCTV footage from around that time?'

'We don't have any cameras in the club. Just the one at the entrance and we delete the footage every day.'

'What's the point of having it if you delete the footage?'

'To protect our security staff. That way we're able to prove who started any fights.'

'Would you mind if I was to speak to some of your staff or regulars? Perhaps they can give me some more information.'

Weise exhaled loudly. 'You know, we really value our good reputation,' he began. 'A man from the CID might . . . bother a few of our guests.'

'Because of possible drug offences?' Nik was hinting at a raid in 2009 when numerous people had been arrested in the club and the former manager had been found in possession of cocaine. The club had made headlines all over Germany.

'Look, as long as people behave themselves, I don't tell anybody how to live their life.' Weise was trying to defend himself but it was a weak argument. He knew what Nik was referring to. And he knew Nik would need less than five minutes to pick up two underage drinkers, prove three drug offences and uncover various health and safety violations. In a real investigation Nik would have had everything he needed to close the place immediately. It was time to make some demands.

'I'll make a suggestion,' began Nik. 'Frau Nowara introduces me to a few of your employees and a couple of choice customers. And in turn I'll be discreet and leave the detective badge in my pocket. I'll be gone in an hour and I won't mention the visit anywhere apart from my case report.'

Weise bit his bottom lip. He really wanted to turn down Nik's offer. 'All right,' he said finally. 'But please be as discreet as possible.'

'I promise,' said Nik, before turning towards Nowara. 'Shall we?'

Her boss gave her a nod and she led Nik out of the office. The music smacked him again. Nowara had to stand up close and shout loudly for him to hear. Reflections of light sparkled in the disco balls hanging on the ceiling. All the bar stools were taken and a mass of people was pushing to get to the bar. To the side of the bar was a seating area with rigid upholstered seats and black painted tables. On the way to the dance floor there was a pole, around which an attractive dark-skinned woman in underwear was spinning slowly. It was predominantly men who were watching her, their glassy red eyes a clear indication of excessive alcohol consumption. The DJ, a young woman, stood on a raised platform above the dance floor. She bobbed her head in time to the beat, completely engrossed in her mixing decks.

Over the next hour, Nowara introduced Nik to a couple of regular customers and some staff. Most of the people he spoke to knew Viola. Some of them knew her just from the club, while others knew her from outside of work as well. But nobody had heard from her since her last day at work. The deafening noise made it almost impossible to have a conversation and asking people so many questions proved a tedious task. Although nobody could give him any information, one of the bartenders did become very nervous when Nik asked him if he knew where Viola was. The young man was in a great hurry to end the conversation, saying lots of people were waiting to be served. Nowara had introduced him as Finn. He kept watching Nik slyly from the corner of his eye and he suddenly found it very difficult to concentrate on his work. He even dropped a bottle of vodka at one point.

After she'd got through all the bar staff, Nowara introduced Nik to a woman in her late thirties whose name he didn't catch. He thought to himself how attractive she could have been, if she hadn't been wearing so much make-up or a mini skirt that most prostitutes would have considered too short. While they were talking, she kept rubbing her nose. Nik noticed the whites of her eyes were bloodshot and her pupils were dilated. She spoke very quickly and kept laughing. All of a sudden, she grabbed Nik's notebook, tore out a page and wrote down her phone number. She then giggled loudly and stuffed the number in his jacket pocket. Just as Nik was about to talk to someone else, Nowara pressed her earpiece to her ear and listened to something.

'I'll be back in a minute,' she said to Nik before pushing her way hurriedly through the crowd. While she was upstairs, Nik went back to the bar and waited until Finn saw him. Nik nodded quickly towards the toilet entrance area. This was the only place in the club other than Weise's office where the music was a bit quieter.

Making his way over to the toilets, he stood beside the Men's and crossed his arms over his chest. A minute later, the bartender joined him. Finn had blonde hair that fell forward over his face, almost completely covering his eyes. Nik guessed he was in his early twenties. He had barely any facial hair, a scrawny figure and an attractive, childlike face which was surely a hit among the female clubbers.

'Was there something else, Officer?' he asked self-consciously, avoiding all eye contact.

'Ever since I asked you about Viola, you've been very nervous,' Nik commented. 'Is there something else you'd like to tell me?'

Finn looked behind him, as though he was scared to be seen speaking to Nik. A man who was laughing loudly entered the entranceway with two giggling women under his arms. While the women went to the toilet, he waited at the door, straightening his shirt and examining his face in a pane of dark glass.

'Not here,' said Finn, so quietly that only Nik could hear. His gaze went towards the ceiling. 'I finish at two,' he continued. 'There's a kebab place on the street going into town. It's open till three. Let's meet there.'

Finn turned around abruptly and forced his way back to the bar.

Nowara came back shortly after. Nik thanked her politely for all her help and left the nightclub. Outside, the bouncers were holding down a violently struggling man, watched by the crowd around the door, one of whom was enthusiastically filming the scene on his mobile. Nik pushed his way through the mass of people and made his way towards the city centre, taking note of the kebab shop Finn had mentioned. He kept walking until he reached a Mexican restaurant at Karlsplatz and went inside for some food.

Three extra-hot tacos and two weissbier later, he said goodbye to the staff, left a tip on the table and headed to the meeting place. It had started to snow, so he stayed close to the wall and lowered his head to keep the snow off his face. He was walking slowly, shuffling even, but his mind was racing. What was it the boy hadn't wanted to say in front of Nowara? Was it possible Viola actually had been involved in the dealing? The Palace wasn't exactly the worst place to be shifting coke.

It was the middle of the night and it had been a long day. Under other circumstances Nik would have noticed the man closing in on him from behind. But not today. A blow to the head sent him sprawling to the ground. He just had time to glimpse a pair of black leather shoes and some suit trousers before a second blow sent him spiralling into darkness.

◆ ◆ ◆

Nik woke to a thumping headache. He squinted and tried to raise a hand to the wound but both hands had been tied firmly to two wooden armrests. He was sitting on a chair in some building that was clearly under construction. The plasterboard walls were covered in tarpaulin, and the smell of wet paint was in the air. There was a pallet covered in cement bags, and in front of that stood a couple of buckets, a large cement mixer and a drill. A glaring halogen lamp blinded him and forced him to tip his head to the side, blinking rapidly, as he tried to remember what had happened. But other than the fact that someone had hit him when he was on his way to meet Finn, his mind was blank.

The room had no windows and he couldn't tell if it was morning or not. He tried moving his feet but they'd also been tied to the chair. It was old and solid, like the ones found in traditional pubs, and he quickly realised that he wouldn't be able to escape. Someone pushed the light out of Nik's face and he straightened his head. A man stepped forward. He was wearing a dark suit and had short strawberry blonde hair. His lips were exceptionally thin and he had a petite, delicate nose.

'Tilo?' asked Nik. 'What the fuck?'

His colleague came closer, pressing his thin lips together. 'Why do you always insist on getting mixed up in everything?' He hurled the question at Nik.

'Did *you* hit me?'

'I told you to leave the case alone but you just never listen.'

'Have you lost it?' continued Nik. 'Untie me!' He pulled at the cable ties around his wrists.

'I can't untie you,' said Tilo, shaking his head. 'I'm sorry.'

'What the fuck is going on? I thought we were mates!'

'There is no more "we", Nik,' explained Tilo regretfully. 'There's just you or me.'

'What are you talking about?'

'Viola's case should've never been reopened. You can't begin to understand the chaos you've stirred up.'

'What chaos? What's going on?'

'Oh, it's complicated,' answered Tilo. 'You wouldn't get it.'

'You arrogant wanker!' Nik spat on the floor in front of Tilo. 'You've been a right fucking brown nose ever since you got promoted to Major Crimes.'

Tilo smacked him in the face with the back of his hand. 'Nik, not everybody wants a life as shitty as yours, you know.'

'Untie me now or I'll rip your balls off!' Nik screamed. He tugged against the cable ties but it only made the plastic carve deeper into his skin.

'The only thing you're going to do is tell me why you're looking for Viola.' Tilo took out his gun and pressed it to Nik's forehead.

'Could you not have asked me that over a coffee down the station?'

'I did ask you,' responded Tilo. 'And you just fobbed me off with stupid excuses.' He pressed the gun harder. 'I took a look at all the cases you're working at the moment and none of them are linked to Viola. So much for being mates, eh.'

Nik squinted, trying to get a look at the gun. It was a Walther PPQ 9 mm with a silencer. Not Tilo's service weapon. Probably not even registered. 'Fuck you, Tilo.'

Tilo's hand tightened around the gun's grip. He pulled the weapon away and started to laugh. 'I had a feeling you might not be intimidated by me,' he began, 'so I made some preparations.' Tilo put away his gun, walked over to one of the plasterboard sheets and tore it down. There was Finn. Tied up and gagged. His eyes wide with fear. He was sweating profusely and had a cut on his left temple. His trousers were soaked with urine.

Tilo pointed to the young bartender. 'I barely had the gun up to his forehead before he started telling me everything he knew about Viola. When he last saw her. What she was like. Oh, and he also told me about all the secret CCTV down at The Palace.'

'Let the boy go!' said Nik. 'He's got nothing to do with it!'

Tears were streaming down Finn's cheeks and his body was trembling.

'These are the rules,' said Tilo, taking a folding knife from his bag. 'You answer my questions or . . .' – he rammed the knife into Finn's hand, right through to the wood – '. . . the boy gets it.'

Finn's whole body seized up in pain and he braced himself against the ties. He was screaming but the gag covering his mouth reduced the noise to a groan.

Nik squeezed his fists together. He'd always known Tilo wasn't just some coward police officer who sat behind his desk all day eating sandwiches. But this? Taking down the two of them like this threw the case into a whole new dimension. But before he worried about that, he had to get Finn out of there. 'OK,' Nik relented. 'What is it you want to know?'

With one tug, Tilo removed the knife from Finn's hand. 'Why did you dig up this case?' He wiped the bloody blade on Finn's trousers.

'A guy hired me,' Nik explained. 'Offered me lots of money to get the information.'

'Bullshit,' responded Tilo. 'You've never cared about money.'

'I'm in debt with the bank and my landlord's threatened to chuck me out. I'll happily show you my statements.'

'One more lie and I'll poke the boy's eyes out.' Tilo lifted the knife to Finn's face.

'And this guy . . . he's got a voicemail from Viola saying she's afraid someone's going to kidnap her. It was just before she disappeared.' He didn't want to mention Jennifer and Justin, so he thought up a lie.

Tilo lowered the knife and moved one step closer to Nik. 'And why did he tell *you* that and not the police?'

'Apparently he went to the station but nobody cared. Somehow he managed to get his hands on the case file and there wasn't any mention of the voicemail. He thinks one of us is involved and covered everything up.'

Tilo nodded. 'And let me guess: the thought of proving that one of your detested colleagues might be bent got you all excited. Bet he didn't even need to offer you any money.'

Tilo folded the knife together. 'What's your new friend's name?'

'Jonathan Schuster,' Nik lied.

'And where does he live?'

'I don't know. The only thing he gave me was his mobile number.'

'Which number?'

Nik nodded his head down to his jacket. 'In the pocket.'

Carefully, Tilo searched inside Nik's jacket. He took out the piece of paper, went two steps back and looked at the number.

'I'll have the address soon,' said Nik with a hopeful smile. 'And now you tell me what's going on. What is it about this Viola that made you beat me up and torture a boy who's got nothing to do with it?'

Tilo looked at his watch. 'No time. I still have loads to take care of.' He took his gun out of its holster, went over to Finn and shot him point blank in the head. Blood sprayed on to the plasterboard behind.

'No!' Nik screamed, thrusting himself against the ties on his hands. The wood from the chair squeaked but the armrests didn't give. 'Why did you do that?!'

'This thing you're messing with, Nik, it's massive,' explained Tilo calmly. 'I can't afford to have any witnesses.'

'So are you going to shoot me too?'

'Of course.' Tilo's voice had an element of confusion in it, like he couldn't quite believe Nik had asked the question.

He came closer. 'Any last words?'

'You once asked me why I never tie my boot laces.'

'Yeah, and you said so you can slip out of them quicker.' Tilo was now standing in front of Nik. 'Which, to your colleagues' annoyance, you're always doing in the office. What's that got to do with anything?' He shrugged his shoulders questioningly.

'You should have tied my ankles up tighter.'

Nik yanked his feet out of the boots, crouched over like a rugby player before a tackle and rammed his shoulders into Tilo's stomach. Tilo was pushed backwards and a shot went off. The gun dropped out of his hand and he fell back, slamming the back of his head on the floor. He seemed dazed for a moment.

The cable ties around Nik's wrists were still fastened tightly to the chair. Fighting wasn't an option in his crouched position, so he took a deep breath, turned his back to Tilo who was still lying on the floor, and dropped down backwards on top of him. The chair landed on his head. He heard a bone break and knew he'd hit the target.

Nik swung himself up and threw himself down . . . again and again . . . shattering Tilo's skull. The ties dug deeper into Nik's wrists with every plunge. Blood was running down his arms but he couldn't feel the pain. He kept going, slamming on to Tilo until he stopped moving.

Nik lay on the floor, panting. His head pounded, blood was dripping from his hands and his chest burned with anger. He turned to the side. Tilo's face was soaked in blood. His jaw, nose and cheekbones, all crushed. And his eyes stared blankly ahead, void of any life.

'What the hell have I got myself into?' Nik asked himself, shaking his head.

Chapter 3

It took Nik a long time to break the armrests and release himself from the chair. Still in just his socks, he staggered through to the room next door and looked out the window. It was still dark outside but the snow had stopped. As far as he could tell, he wasn't far from the station, but he guessed that because the entire building was undergoing refurbishment, nobody had heard them.

He sank his feet into his shoes, picked up a can of turpentine and washed his blood off the floor and the broken bits of chair. With his job in such a precarious position right now, he didn't want to take any risks. His headache was getting worse and Tilo's beating must have left him with at least a concussion. Every so often he had to prop himself up against the wall and force back the urge to be sick. He kept wondering if he'd imagined everything. How could it be that some closed case had led Tilo to torture and kill an innocent man? Something wasn't right.

After wiping away the traces of blood, Nik looked through Tilo's jacket. No police ID. No work phone. All he found was Finn's mobile, which he put in his pocket. Tilo was still holding the piece of paper with the blonde woman's number on it, so he pulled it out and made his way unsteadily outside.

As Nik reached the door he looked back at Finn. His head was slumped over and his eyes were staring absently at the ceiling. 'I'm sorry,' he said miserably.

The pavements were icy and walking with the head injury proved difficult, but he couldn't risk the cameras on the U-Bahn or being recognised by a taxi driver. He had to go on foot. And anyway, from the way he was walking, the few people who were out and about so early would just think he was drunk. Nik walked until he was a kilometre away from the building site and used Finn's phone to call for an ambulance.

'I've found a body!' he said in a high, hysterical voice. 'Dachauer Straße. Inside that empty block near the station. Hurry up!' He hung up. Another two hundred metres down the street, he took out the battery and SIM from the mobile and threw them down a drain. There was no doubt that when the police found Finn's body, the investigator would ask who had used his mobile to call the police. But that question would now be impossible to answer. Just as impossible as it would be to find out who had battered Finn's murderer to death.

Nik battled his way home step by step. He stumbled up the stairs and with the last bit of strength he could muster, he opened his flat door. Once inside, he fell on to the couch and sank into a long and restless sleep.

Nik stayed in bed all of Friday. He felt dizzy and could only just make it into the kitchen, where he luckily had a hefty supply of painkillers. It was this stash that helped him make it into work the next day for his early shift. Before leaving, he bandaged up the wounds on his wrists and put on a long-sleeved shirt. The bump on his head, however, wasn't as easy to hide, so he put on a woollen hat.

When Nik got to work, he looked through the cases that had come in. He'd expected to find a double murder right at the top of the list but there was no mention of it. There was the body of a homeless man in

Schwabing, an attack on an internet cafe in Neuhausen and a robbery with bodily harm in Moosach. Nothing in Dachauer Straße.

Nik clicked his way through the calls that had come in early on Friday morning and found his own message. He opened up the accompanying document and read the text:

> *On 13 January at 4.36 a.m. an unnamed man called to report the discovery of a dead body at a building site in Dachauer Straße. After he gave this information, the line was disconnected and it was not possible to reconnect with the number. A patrol officer was informed and he proceeded to search a block of flats in Dachauer Straße near the main train station. All flats in the block are currently under renovation. The officer found no evidence of forced entry. Upon being questioned, local residents were unable to provide any additional information.*

Nik pounded his fist down on the desk with rage. 'That's not possible,' he said quietly through gritted teeth. He had even flipped over a piece of plasterboard before he left so that Tilo's body would be easy to spot from the stairway. There was no way his colleagues could have missed the two bodies if they'd been in that building. He'd been sure there was only one block under reconstruction in Dachauer Straße but there was no other explanation: they must have been in another building.

Nik opened up an official website that contained a list of missing people. It was an inconspicuous database which he often used for his work. It was no surprise to him that Tilo's name wasn't there, but Finn's hadn't been registered either. He scrolled down to the unidentified deaths. The last entry was from 1 December 2016: an unidentified male who'd been found in Leinthalerstraße. Other than that, there was a burned body found at the English Garden and a deformed body from the Westend.

'Another rough night?' Danilo interrupted his rumination. His colleague was grinning widely and waving a folder in the air. 'Then this'll make you smile. Residents have complained about a stench coming from a flat in Bogenhausen. Police opened the door to find the rotting body of an elderly woman inside.' He hurled the folder on to Nik's table. 'I'm off to change. Wouldn't want the stench to spoil my clothes.'

While Danilo was in the toilet, Nik got up with a groan and swallowed another painkiller. It was going to be the longest day of his life but that afternoon he'd have to return to Dachauer Straße.

Nik's confusion only increased when he got to the site. This was a crime scene. It should have been cordoned off and investigators should have been searching for clues. But it was as if Nik was the only person who knew anything. Despite it being Saturday, the pavement was blocked by vans from various trade companies. The ground was sticky and the air was thick with the smell of plaster. At the front of the building was a skip full of debris and a rubbish bin overflowing with fast food containers and empty takeaway coffee cups. Men were leaving the building carrying tool bags. Some of them were smoking, while others had already cracked open their first after-work beer. A forklift truck was loading cement bags on to a pallet, which was then lifted up by a pulley. There was nothing to suggest that two people had been killed there two nights before. Nik went up one floor into the room where Tilo had tied him up.

Not a lot had changed. The broken plasterboards had been cleared up, there were now electric cables hanging from the ceiling and the tarpaulin sheets on the windows had been removed and replaced with newly installed frames. No broken chair. No bloodstains. And no bullet casings. Nik leaned against the wall and shook his head. He'd had plenty of crazy dreams in his life but he knew Finn's murder and his fight with Tilo had not been one of them. The wound to the back of his head and his raw, red cheek were proof enough.

Nik went and stood on the spot where Finn had been shot and looked around. He noticed a sharp, chemical smell that was overpowering the general smell of screed. It wasn't the turpentine he'd used to remove his bloodstains. More like bleach.

He went over to the wall, which Tilo's final shot must have hit, and carefully ran his fingers over every centimetre. Finally he found a damp patch of grey filler, the exact colour of the concrete. Pressing his finger into it, he felt a tiny indentation. Nik took a pen out of his pocket and scraped away the filler. The bullet had been removed.

He closed his eyes. According to the police report, his call had come in at 4.36 a.m. By that time, he was already a couple of streets away, so it was likely he'd left the building around 4.20 a.m. The reporting of a dead body is never taken lightly and it typically takes a police officer no longer than five minutes to get to the scene. Searching the ground floor and getting up to the first floor would have taken another five minutes. In total, that would have given somebody twenty-six minutes to move the body and clean up the crime scene. Even if Tilo *had* survived, he would have been in no fit state to remove Finn's body.

This left one other option: somebody else had been in the building. Somebody who didn't want to be seen and who also didn't want Viola's case to be reopened. Somebody who knew how to clean up a crime scene and get rid of a body so that it wouldn't be found. A professional.

Nik exhaled loudly. This case wasn't going away any time soon.

On his way over to Tilo's house, Nik called up a colleague who sat in the office next to Tilo's.

'Friederike Betz,' she said after one ring.

'Hello, Frau Betz, this is Inspector Pohl from Division 91.'

'Hello,' she said, uninterested. Nik wasn't sure if the woman knew of him or if this was just her usual shitty manner.

'I've been trying to get hold of Tilo all day but I'm not getting him on his landline or his mobile. And he hasn't replied to an email I sent him. Perhaps he's still in a meeting? You see, the thing is, I've got some questions about a case and they can't wait. Have you seen him today?'

'No,' she answered curtly.

Nik suppressed a groan. But he had to remain friendly. 'Hmm, that's strange. Tilo's the most reliable police officer I know. Even if he's got the flu, he'll work from home.'

'Very true. Herr Hübner is reliable. But I don't have access to his calendar, so I'm afraid I can't help you.'

'Many thanks,' Nik said before hanging up. Just as he was putting his mobile back in his pocket, he arrived at the expensive housing development on the outskirts of the city where Tilo owned a terraced house. A beautiful beech tree was growing in the middle of his garden and the lawn had been laid with grass. A gas barbecue stood on a paved patio. There was no traffic in the neighbourhood and the cheapest car around was a BMW 3 Series. The streets were clean and well maintained and the nearby Grünwalder Forest looked breathtaking under the setting winter sun.

Nik had been over to Tilo's house twice before. The interior design was modern, with chrome-plated lamps, designer furniture and a luxury kitchen. There was a multi-room audio system, a large flat-screen TV, an outdoor Jacuzzi and a gym in the basement.

Although Tilo had earned good money in his position, it was nowhere near enough to afford this lifestyle or this kind of neighbourhood.

As well as a work computer, Tilo also had his private one. There had to be clues on it about Viola but unfortunately the house was protected by the latest security technology, meaning breaking in would be impossible.

Tilo's BMW was parked in the drive, which was no surprise – driving it to the building site would obviously have been a bad idea. There were no lights on in the house, so Nik could be sure nobody was home, but he rang the doorbell anyway. There were no footsteps and nobody opened the door. Today's post was still in the letterbox along with the morning paper.

A woman with a blonde ponytail appeared from the house next door. She was wearing pink jogging bottoms, a shabby sweatshirt and had a bag full of rubbish in her left hand. Nik had seen her at Tilo's birthday party once. They hadn't been introduced to one another, but Nik could read 'A&G Ebbers' on her front door.

'Good evening, Frau Ebbers.' Nik walked over to her. 'Nik Pohl,' he said. 'I'm a colleague of Tilo's. We met at his birthday party?'

'Oh! Hello, Herr Pohl,' she said politely, although her facial expression said she had no idea who he was.

'I'm supposed to be meeting with Tilo to discuss a case. But he doesn't appear to be home and isn't picking up his phone either. Do you have any idea where he might be?'

'I haven't seen him since Thursday evening,' said Frau Ebbers. 'He came home and cleared away some snow from the drive.'

'Ah, OK. It's just a bit strange because his car is still in the drive, you see.'

'You're right, yes. He normally leaves for work early on a Saturday but when I left this morning to take the children to the park his car was still there. I just assumed he'd taken the weekend off.' She came a little closer. 'Do you think something's happened to him?'

'No.' Nik brushed off the suggestion. The last thing he needed now was an investigation into Tilo's disappearance. 'He's probably just at work. I'll drive to the station and see if I can find him there.' He raised his hand. 'Thanks for your time.'

Nik arrived at his car and called Jon. It went straight to voicemail.

'Listen, Jon,' Nik said angrily. 'I have no idea what happened to Viola but I've been beaten up, tied up and very nearly shot by a colleague. Plus, a guy who'd done nothing wrong was murdered in front of me just because he knew Viola. So I'm not making one more move until you tell me what you've got to do with all this.'

Nik hung up, started his car and drove home.

◆　◆　◆

Nik's phone rang in the middle of the night. It was an unknown number. Only a few people had his number, and he'd killed one of them the day before. So chances were it was Jon.

'Good evening, arsehole,' Nik answered, taking some pleasure in his bad-tempered greeting.

'Good evening, Nik,' Jon replied in a friendly manner.

'Before I tell you anything about what happened, I want to know everything,' Nik said angrily. 'Who is this Viola and how do you know her?'

'Sounds like your relationship with Jennifer isn't as solid as it once was. I can't imagine any other reason why you'd want to give her up to social services. Did she throw you out of bed or something?'

'Oh, much better than that,' answered Nik. 'There's actually a case in the system where an unidentified man blackmailed a woman with a raunchy video. The woman works for the city council. The case is only slightly similar to yours but I'll make the connection somehow. Together with your photo, your name and a statement from myself that Jennifer just needs to sign, I'll put you on the wanted list. And then you can make your game apps in jail, where I'll spread the word you're a kiddy-fiddler. Your stay there will just be one massive party.'

'Not bad, Nik,' said Jon, laughing. 'Shame you're such a prick. With your skills, you would've had a long career ahead of you at the Munich CID.'

'Tell me, or this is over!'

'You're forgetting I hacked your computer, Nik.'

'And what's on it that could force me to work for you? You'd need to make something up.'

'Oh, that won't be necessary,' responded Jon. 'You know, my father always used to say it's important to have a good plan. But what's even more important is a good back-up plan.'

'How fascinating.'

'Do you remember copying some case notes and taking them home with you to work without authorisation?'

'You mean that? That's already on my record.'

'Yes, but what I find interesting is that initial period of all your lone-wolf antics. Your downfall, you could say,' Jon went on. 'Christmas 2013. The case of Rachel Preuss?'

Nik held his breath. The name still made him shudder.

'Until then, your record was spotless. You were given a promotion, two commendations. And your supervisor predicted you'd have a successful career as an investigator. But then it all changed. You became disobedient, there were breaches of internal security regulations, not to mention the bodily harm to other public officials.'

'You wouldn't get it,' said Nik softly.

'I think I would, Nik. You see, that case was just like ours: a search that had been underway for weeks was called off after the husband received an email from his wife saying she'd left to start a new life in Thailand and was never coming home. Your colleagues ignored the police reports on domestic abuse and the passport that was found during the house search.'

Nik closed his eyes. The details of the case started to haunt him all over again. The car full of shopping at the supermarket. The conversations at the station. His boss's stubborn attitude. And of course, his consequent demotion because he leaked information to the press. The image of Rachel's husband, grinning triumphantly, hounded him to this day.

'Here's my second offer,' continued Jon. 'I'll get you Rachel's case files just like I got hold of your personnel folder.'

'What would I need them for?'

'The files have been securely locked away since 2014 but since then, there have been three additional entries.'

'How d'you know that?'

'Ah, money . . .' Jon mused. 'You wouldn't believe what you can achieve with money and bribes.'

An image of Rachel came into Nik's mind. Her friendly smile, and that gentle face.

'You'd never get hold of that file in your position,' Jon said, interrupting Nik's thoughts.

'I'm done with that case.'

'No, you're not,' Jon argued. 'I looked through your server history. In just the last couple of weeks, you've been looking at photos of Thailand. Lots of them from travel companies but also lots of holiday snaps people had posted on social media. And when I looked to see what time you were looking at these photos, I saw it was mostly in the middle of the night. You couldn't sleep, so you kept checking to see if Rachel maybe *was* in Thailand. Leading a happy life. And not buried somewhere in the woods.'

'Bastard,' mumbled Nik.

'You won't be able to lead any kind of normal life until you know what happened to Rachel.'

'You don't know that.'

'Not only am I giving you the chance to get your hands on all the paperwork, I'm also offering you my help. I'm not just a good hacker,

I've got a lot of money,' Jon went on. 'That opens doors which, until now, were firmly shut for you.'

'You have no idea what you're getting yourself into,' said Nik. 'These people are everywhere and all your money and IT skills can't hurt them. They won't be blackmailed by videos and you wouldn't believe how powerful the people on their payroll are.'

'So what do you have to lose, Nik? What do you have left that's worth fighting for?'

Nik laughed ironically. Good question. Right now, he actually wouldn't care if he disappeared down a dark hole and was never seen again. On the contrary, he might enjoy it.

Nik went over to the fridge, grabbed a beer and sat down on the sofa. After the third gulp he began to tell Jon everything, starting with the visit to the club and Finn's death, right up to the cleaned-up crime scene and lack of any bodies.

'Shit. I hadn't expected it to be as bad as that,' said Jon sincerely. 'So, what d'you want to do now?'

'No idea,' Nik admitted. 'Finn was the only link to Viola we had.'

'And what about your colleague, Tilo?'

'Too risky,' said Nik. 'Somebody cleaned up the crime scene and whoever it was must have been in the building when I killed Tilo, otherwise they wouldn't have had enough time between my emergency call and when the police officer arrived.'

'And where would this unidentified person get stuff to clean away all the traces at that time of night?' asked Jon. 'It's unlikely they popped into a DIY store.'

'The clean-up had been planned in advance,' explained Nik. 'Tilo wanted to kill me and the young barman. The fact that the tables turned to a certain extent didn't seem to change anything in the cleaner's mind. It just meant there was a different second body to dispose of.'

'And how did Tilo find out about Finn?'

'He must have had this unnamed cleaner follow me. Must have come in behind me when I went into the club and saw me speaking to Finn . . . twice. And then finally, whoever it was picked up Finn on his way to our meeting point.'

'Who are we dealing with here? Organised crime, sex traffickers . . . ?'

'No idea. But other than Tilo, at least one more police officer is involved.'

'What makes you say that?' asked Jon.

'Tilo was never officially assigned to Viola's case. The connection to her boyfriend was probably one of many details removed from her file. And somebody else was responsible for that.'

'OK, so you need to write up a list of everyone involved in the case. And then one of them is the rogue.'

'Yeah, but I can't prove which one without any evidence,' Nik pointed out. 'Up to now, neither Tilo's nor Finn's body has been found. At some point, both will be declared missing but even then, nothing will link their disappearances to Viola's case or give me anything to use against the former investigator.'

'Viola must have had something really big on Tilo. Why else would he try to murder two people?'

Nik took a swig of beer. 'No idea, but he didn't give the impression he was involved. He barely even asked about Viola, just what I knew about her disappearance. He was probably just doing someone's dirty work.'

'Who on earth could be controlling a CID officer who's that high up?'

'Somebody even higher up,' answered Nik.

'We need to find out more about Tilo.'

'Well, going down the normal routes won't work,' said Nik. 'Whoever he was working with won't let me out of their sight for two seconds. And we can forget doing any research at the station.'

'So then what?'

'I need another way to get into the police server. I can barely order a pizza on my account.'

'Hmm,' said Jon pensively. 'Maybe there's another way.'

'You want to hack the CID?'

'No, but maybe our dead friend Tilo will be of some use to us yet.'

Chapter 4

Munich was pleasantly crime free on Sunday morning. Danilo was engrossed in writing up a report, leaving Nik in peace to work on Viola's case. A cup of coffee stood on his desk and salt crystals from the pretzel he'd just eaten were strewn across his files.

Jon hadn't been exaggerating when he'd said he was good with computers. Thanks to his skills and his knowledge of Tilo's preferred passwords, which Tilo had once given to Nik over a beer, Jon was able to get on to the police server. Tilo had had loads of access privileges, so now Jon and Nik could access the entire system to read reports and look for cross references. Thankfully, Tilo's disappearance had still gone unnoticed, so his account hadn't been locked.

Nik started with the numerous folders his ex-colleague had saved on the server. He found photos from work outings, CID events and newspaper reports, all of which had been neatly arranged by date. He opened every single document and found drafts of employee appraisals, summaries of internal correspondence, but no mention of Viola. He then searched through Tilo's address book. Most of the numbers were of other public officials, friends and tradespeople but nothing seemed suspicious. He clicked through the calendar, checking who he'd had meetings with, but nothing connected back to Viola.

Nik closed his eyes and tried to remember every gesture and every word from the other night. Tilo had been so calm and composed, not at all like someone who was being blackmailed or whose life depended on covering up the case. But he'd played a big part in the whole thing. Voluntarily. Tilo had been a smart guy, too smart to have ever saved anything incriminating on the CID server. Maybe on his private computer, but Nik was never going to get his hands on that. The people Tilo had worked with weren't going to let his house out of their sight and any evidence had probably been disposed of by now.

Up to now, Nik had thought of two ways Viola could have been involved. Firstly, she could have been right at the centre of something big. For example, she was heading up a drug cartel, or knew a secret or was a principal witness. But other than the incident with her boyfriend, there was nothing leading Nik to believe any of these could be possible. The second possibility was that she'd been the unintended victim of a crime. Maybe she'd seen something she shouldn't have, or got in the way of a crazy, violent criminal who then decided to live out his sick fantasies on her. If this was the case, then there might be other victims. Once was rarely enough for a psychopath.

Nik opened up an internal database and started a new search. He limited the search to women between twenty and thirty-five who'd been registered as missing and who shared Viola's general physical appearance.

Thirty results came up. So as not to miss anything, he didn't restrict the search any further and read through each report, one by one. Most of the women were adult runaways who'd left home for various reasons, be it domestic abuse, drug addiction or family problems. Sometimes, the reason for leaving was unknown but those women had only gone missing for a short period of time, so the cases were useless to Nik.

The nineteenth entry was a case about a woman from Schwabing who looked a lot like Viola. Twenty-six-year-old Kathrin Glosemeier had gone missing on 11 July 2016 after going to the gym. Her parents informed the police the next morning and a missing persons announcement was released. Kathrin had left the house with just a sports bag and her gym clothes. She'd left her phone at the house, hadn't packed a suitcase and hadn't told anyone she was planning a trip.

Three days later, one of her friends received a letter from her, much like the one Viola had supposedly written, and as a result the search was called off. But then, only a month later, on 15 August, Kathrin's body was found at a climbing rock near to Flintsbach. There hadn't been any sightings of her since she'd been reported missing.

Nik clicked on the report from the local police who'd been at the scene. The rock face where her body had been found was a popular climbing area. There were easier routes for beginners and there was also an adjoining car park. Nik looked at photos of the crag online and read some descriptions from climbers about the difficulty of the routes. 'The Quarry', as it was called, was a steep limestone rock face, overgrown in some areas and not very high. But it was very challenging in many spots. One mistake up there without the right gear would have been fatal.

Nik looked at the climbing area on Google Earth. Flintsbach lay around seventy kilometres south-east of Munich. A nice place, but far too close if Kathrin had been aiming to leave her old life behind. Plus, it was a popular destination for day trips from Munich and not the best choice for somebody who intended to stay hidden.

Nik closed the browser and read the next part about the state of the body when it was found. Kathrin's body was discovered by someone out walking in the area. There was little doubt from the photographs that she'd died from a fall. Her head lay in a pool of blood and her leg was twisted out unnaturally to the side. The left side of her face was crushed and her jaw was broken. Her tongue hung out of her open mouth and her eyes stared ahead rigidly.

Nik opened the attachment with the death certificate. There was a non-confidential page with Kathrin's personal data. Her identity had been confirmed with her German ID card. The climbing area in Flintsbach had been entered as the place of death and 'Unnatural' had been marked as the cause of death.

Nik found more detailed information on the yellow pages that followed. There were observations on the certain signs of death and on the signs that the death had been unnatural. Overall, Kathrin's demise had been declared an accident. Case closed.

Nik stood up, grabbed his coffee and shuffled into an adjoining office to make a call. Thankfully there was barely anyone around. He dialled Jon's number.

'We've got a problem,' Nik said as soon as Jon picked up. 'I've found a case that's similar to Viola's and so full of contradictions a drunk, coked-up colleague would have noticed.'

'Go on,' said Jon.

'Kathrin Glosemeier went missing in July 2016. A search began, and not long after it was called off because a friend received a letter. What's not similar to Viola's case though is that Viola is still missing. Kathrin's body was found a month later on 15 August at the bottom of a popular climbing crag near Flintsbach.'

'She fell while climbing?'

'That's what it says in the final report but there are so many inconsistencies I reckon it's a cover-up.' Nik drank some coffee. 'Kathrin's body was found at dawn by somebody out walking. By the time the ambulance got there, rigor mortis had set in but only in the eyelids, jaw and neck. It takes at least two hours for rigor mortis to kick in, so it's very likely she died during the night. And another thing, the ground where she was found was wet, so it must have rained at some point.'

'Can't say I've ever heard of a climber who likes to go out alone, at night and in the rain.'

'Exactly. No car was found in the car park and there isn't any public transport that goes out there. So you could assume someone brought her there but then nobody got in touch when the announcement went out. Whoever took her there was never identified, or more to the point, nobody ever made any effort to find out who they could have been.'

Nik sat down on a chair in the meeting room. 'On top of that, Kathrin had nothing on her when she was found. No ID, no climbing gear and no jacket. It was hours before someone got in touch to say he'd found a rucksack hidden in a bush. All the typical climbing things were inside. A harness, a rope and a chalk bag, and also her purse. Going by the photos, all the gear was brand new, which is pretty strange, especially for a climbing harness. Plus, Kathrin wasn't wearing any climbing shoes. Just a pair of dirty trainers.'

'Was there an autopsy?'

'Cause of death was determined as a skull fracture with a brain haemorrhage, which would support the theory that she died from falling.'

Nik heard Jon typing in the background. 'Kathrin Glosemeier . . . She came from a well-off family,' began Jon. 'Her father's big in the brewing industry and she founded a start-up which created marketing campaigns for small companies with a focus on social media. She studied abroad and came back to Munich three years ago. That's all there is about her on the company website. Have you found any link to Viola?' asked Jon.

'Can't see anything in the file,' replied Nik. 'The similarities stop at their physical appearance. Long brown hair, light eyes and an attractive smile. Kathrin would have had admirers, just like Viola.' Nik took another sip of coffee. 'The whole case is fishy. But once again, no leads. The man who found the rucksack can't be reached at the registered address and the man who found the body was a tourist from Thuringia.'

'And what about the investigators who worked on the case?' asked Jon. 'Any of them also work on Viola's case?'

'No correlation,' said Nik. 'And Tilo's name is nowhere to be seen either.'

'So yet again we've got nothing.'

'Very little.'

'You got any ideas?'

'Wouldn't call it an idea, more like an act of desperation.' Nik took a deep breath. 'We could look at Kathrin's body.'

'You want to exhume her?' asked Jon. 'What's that gonna achieve?'

'The photos of the body are useless and the coroner's report could be described as shoddy at best. They stuck to all their due diligence obligations, but it looks like they put it down to an accident from the word go. It's pretty obvious that wasn't the case but I need proof that something was covered up. A couple of discrepancies aren't enough. There might have been injuries that weren't caused by a fall. And her death is still recent enough that we'd be able to detect traces of drugs in her hair.'

'And how d'you plan on getting permission for an exhumation?'

'I don't,' explained Nik. 'But I'll deal with the body. I need *you* to find somebody corrupt enough to do an autopsy on an illegally dug-up corpse.'

Jon was silent for a moment. 'There is one guy.'

◆ ◆ ◆

At 10.47 p.m. Nik noticed his fridge was empty and that his favourite kebab shop was about to close.

He sprang into his boots, pulled on a winter jacket and left the flat. He cursed briefly as the cold air hit him, but then, as he mulled over the fates of the two women, all other considerations retreated. Viola and Kathrin were three years apart in age; they didn't know one another from school. Kathrin did her undergrad in England and never studied at any Munich university. Viola had never been climbing and didn't know anybody from Flintsbach. Other than the way they looked, the only thing similar about the two was the way they disappeared.

All of a sudden, a woman called his name. 'Hi, Nik.' Nik stopped abruptly and turned around, perplexed. A woman with long black hair was standing in a side street. She was wearing a hooded winter jacket with a faux fur collar, a short skirt and black knee-high boots. Her eyebrows, which were extremely thin, looked like they'd been tattooed on. 'You haven't forgotten me, have you?'

Nik was exceptionally good with faces and he was certain he'd never seen the woman before but the way she was acting and the fact she knew his name was annoying him. He looked at her more closely. She had brown eyes, a small nose and strong cheek bones. He imagined her with blonde hair – first of all short and then with a ponytail, but neither image brought any names to mind.

'Have we met?' He edged over to her.

'Elvira,' she said, with a fake tone of indignation. 'Your memory must be fading.'

'I've met three Elviras in my lifetime. The first was an aunty on my mother's side who died in 1992, the second my German teacher, and the third a clerk at work with an arse like an Asian water buffalo.' As Nik spoke, he took in the woman's desirable figure. It clearly wasn't the clerk.

The woman crossed her arms over her chest and tapped her foot. Nik was so focused on her, he failed to notice a young man approaching him from behind. And then it was too late. In a flash, the man managed to get his hand inside Nik's jacket pocket and grab his wallet, then he jumped back, holding two notes in his hand.

'Oh, Pohl . . . you're getting old,' Nik sighed as he turned to look at the thief. He was small and wiry with dark messy curls and a cut above his right eye.

'I just need a little spare change, mate,' he said, giving Nik an arrogant, toothless grin. Then he tossed the wallet back to him, stuffed the two notes in the back pocket of his scruffy jeans and turned to make his way back to the main street.

'Give me my money back, you worthless piece of shit.'

The boy raised his hands, turned around to look at Nik again and walked backwards away from him. 'Please don't hurt me. I can't pay you tonight.' The disdainful grin was gone and fear had spread across his face.

'What the fuck!' said Nik, confused by the boy's sudden surrender. 'Give me my money!'

'Please! No!' he begged, his hands still in the air.

Nik walked over to the boy and threw a punch to his stomach, making him stumble to the ground. Quickly twisting the guy's arm around his back, he pushed his face to the ground. With his knee pressed firmly on his back, Nik took the money out of the guy's back pocket and stood up. The boy started to cry, making no attempt to get up. Nik looked quickly around; the woman was nowhere to be seen.

Nik shook his head and moved on. For a flash it occurred to him that he might have just fallen for an extravagant trap, but by the time he made it to the kebab shop, his thoughts had returned once again to Viola and Kathrin. While he was waiting for his food, he drank a black tea – there'd be no sleep for him tonight, so the caffeine would do him good. He did have a dead body to steal after all.

Winter still had an icy, uncomfortable grip on Munich, but for tonight, the snow drifts and slippery ground were a welcome aid for Nik's plans. Nobody would leave their house unless they really had to. All the night owls would be home by now and it was still five hours before the rush-hour traffic would begin. Nik parked his car in Regerstraße, put on the rucksack he'd filled with tools and walked alongside the S-Bahn tracks until he reached the rear end of the Ostfriedhof, Munich's eastern cemetery. It was surrounded by a high fence, overgrown with weeds, and high trees stopped anyone from seeing into the grounds. But Nik wasn't worried about getting in. It was the exhumation that would be the tricky part.

Even if the ground hadn't been frozen, using a shovel to dig up Kathrin's coffin would have taken forever, but not far from the crematorium was a garage which stored everything he would need. He went over to the garage door and examined the padlock. Taking out a large pair of bolt cutters from his bag, he cut the shackle. He made no attempt to cover his tracks – the first cemetery employee to get to work in the morning was going to notice a gaping hole in the ground and a missing coffin, so an investigation was pretty much guaranteed. Nik pulled the chain away from the lock, opened the door and shone his torch around the room.

There were two broken cemetery benches at the entrance, and next to them some artificial grass mats, a device for lowering coffins, a ring-beam formwork, and even a chiller cabinet for coffin trolleys. There were also some tools and gardening equipment hanging on a wall. But it was the small orange digger that Nik was interested in. All that work he'd done during college holidays would come in handy now. The digger was a Kubota KX. It weighed two tonnes and had a high-performance engine. He'd driven its predecessor and would quickly find his way around this one. Thanks to the track pads, it wouldn't get stuck in the snow, and since it wasn't a wide model, he'd be able to drive it down the narrow paths of the graveyard. Luckily for him, Bavarian burial law stipulated that a grave for an adult must be 1.8 metres deep. The digger's bucket could reach down 2.3 metres, so he was confident he wouldn't have any issues reaching Kathrin's coffin. The law also said that the distance between graves had to be at least 60 cm. So although the digger was powerful, he wouldn't damage any neighbouring graves.

Nik took a copy of the cemetery map out of his bag and followed the way from the garage to Kathrin's grave with his finger. Once he'd memorised the shortest route, he took the digger key from the cabinet, started the engine and set off. The noise from the digger was deafening but hopefully the snow and thirty hectares of cemetery would be enough to absorb it.

When Nik got to Kathrin's grave, he hesitated. A beautiful bunch of red flowers had been placed on top of it and was glowing against the sparkling snow. Beneath a crying marble angel stood a large, gold grave lamp. It was the only light for miles around, shining calmly like a reminder to the dead that they wouldn't be forgotten. Nik closed his eyes and apologised to Kathrin, wherever she might be. But although he was sorry, he was sure she'd accept his actions if her death turned out not to have been an accident.

The first layer was the most difficult, as the icy winter frost had made the earth almost impenetrable. But with each rise and fall of the digger, the mound of earth beside the grave slowly grew taller. Nik paused twice to measure the depth of the hole before carrying on carefully. As the bucket started to scrape over wood, Nik turned off the engine and went back to the garage.

He took a shovel and two strong chains, which he then laboriously pulled under the coffin. It was a peculiar feeling to be so near a corpse but Nik kept working relentlessly. Finally, he attached the chain to the arm of the digger. Climbing out of the grave, his boots caked in mud, he could feel his heart pounding from the exertion, and underneath his winter jacket his clothes were soaked with sweat. He desperately needed a rest but he couldn't risk it. Had he been alone, he probably could have evaded a police officer but not while pushing a coffin with a human corpse inside.

Nik ran back to the garage to fetch a coffin roller, a simple device made up of metal poles and rubber wheels, which he placed next to the grave. After that he started the engine and lifted the digger arm upwards. The wood creaked but the coffin was solid enough not to fall apart. Nik placed it carefully on to the metal poles and released the chains.

Getting back to the garage with the trolley would have been difficult enough, but Nik needed to get across the cemetery to St Martin's Square. The snow had become heavier and the rubber wheels on the roller were not designed for snow. Terrified that it would get stuck in a hole, Nik kept his eyes to the ground. Finally, he came to a point where all the paths in the cemetery met. From here, across the expanse of lawn, he had a good view of the gabled main building, with its large cross and round copper roof. He paused, stamping his icy feet and stretching his aching muscles. Suddenly he noticed the flashing blue light of an emergency vehicle through a window in the main building. Hurriedly, he pushed the coffin further westwards before cutting down a small path, and parking it up against a large oak tree. He'd only just got back on to the main pathway without the coffin when he saw two figures walking towards him with torches. Nik took out his CID badge, and got ready to show it to the officers.

'Inspector Walter,' Nik said. Giving a false name was a risky move but thanks to the hat, scarf and snow in his beard, the officers wouldn't be able to recognise him. Plus, he looked a lot like Walter from the 14th Division. 'Did you get a call about the digger noise?'

'No,' answered the officer. 'Because of a silent alarm in the garage.'

'Ah, OK. I was just passing by and heard a digger. Probably somebody trying to steal it. The garage is over at the back there.' Nik pointed north-east. 'I'll stay at the gate and make sure any thieves don't leave this way.'

The two men nodded and headed off in the direction Nik had indicated. He waited until they had disappeared before running back to collect the coffin and continuing towards the entrance. Between pushes, he texted '2.45 a.m.' to the number Jon had given him. He had five minutes to get out of the cemetery. The officers would soon get into the garage and find a visible trace back to Kathrin's grave. That would keep them busy for a while.

Cursing himself and his stupid ideas with every step, he pushed the coffin through the snow towards the copper-roofed house. Large white mounds were collecting at the end of the trolley, making pushing almost impossible. Finally, he reached the house, where a side gate led him to the street. It was 2.46 a.m. A dark-grey hearse was waiting nearby, and slightly up the street, a police car was parked on the pavement, its blue lights still blinking. With its headlights off, the hearse cruised silently towards him and stopped. A man in dark jeans and a thick winter jacket got out. He was wearing a woollen hat and glasses with extra thick lenses.

'Let's get this over with as quickly as possible,' he said nervously, gesturing to the police car with his thumb. Briefly, he made the sign of the cross when he laid eyes on the coffin, then quickly opened up the car boot. Nik had no idea whether Jon had blackmailed this man as well or if he'd just offered him money, but in that moment he didn't care. He was sweating and freezing at the same time and they had to get away from that cemetery there and then. Once the coffin was in the car, Nik pushed the roller back inside the grounds, closed the gate and got into the passenger seat beside the stranger.

'Where to?'

'Pathology Institute at LMU. Thalkirchner Straße,' replied Nik. The man nodded, saying nothing, and drove off. The LMU, or Ludwig Maximilian University, was one of Munich's oldest and most prestigious universities.

Nik closed his eyes, grateful for the warmth of the car heater, and prayed that he was right – that the real cause of death had been covered up and it wasn't simply down to his colleagues' sloppy work.

Because if he didn't get another clue tonight, the investigation would be over.

As the hearse was driving into the courtyard at the Pathology Institute, Nik looked across the street towards Munich's southern cemetery, or Südfriedhof. He wondered whether it was merely a coincidence that the institute sat directly opposite a cemetery or if it had been planned that way. The driver seemed to be familiar with the route and had no trouble finding the shortest way from the Ostfriedhof to Thalkirchner Straße without any GPS. The hearse's engine had barely cut out before the man sprang out and ran over to a chrome-coloured rack on wheels. The rack's upper surface was covered in snow, as though it had been standing outside for a while. Nik got out of the car as the man pulled the coffin on to the rack in two swift moves. He then pushed the rack underneath a small awning at the back entrance to the building and, with a curt goodbye, rushed behind the wheel of the hearse.

Nik waited until the car was out of sight before going inside. The door to the institute was open and the light was on in the hall. Someone was expecting him.

Nik's memories of his visits to the Forensics Institute weren't good ones, so he didn't imagine a visit to pathology would be much better. The smell that hit him as soon as he got inside the building overwhelmed him. It was a repulsive, nauseating stench, as though someone had relieved themselves in the hallway. Entering the dissection room, he saw the corpse of an elderly man lying on the first table, staring up at the ceiling. Dressed in only his underwear, he was desperately thin and his mouth sat open, as if frozen during his last desperate inhalation. On the second table was another body that had already been cut open, and over it stood a man in wellington boots, a face mask, green overalls and a blood-splattered plastic apron. A chrome trolley and tray stood to the side of the table. It reminded Nik of a large breakfast platter, but instead of rolls and jam, this platter was spread with pieces of intestine, most likely the source of the stench.

The man in the mask didn't seem perturbed by the work in the slightest and hummed a tune as he inspected the intestines with gloved fingers. The pathologist was the same height as Nik but apparently had more stamina in the eating department. His belly was astonishing. He had a clean-shaven head and a round, deathly pale face. He repeatedly lifted pieces of intestine up to the light and observed each one attentively.

'Aha!' he said at last. 'I knew it.' He turned to look at Nik. 'Cause of death: a small ulcer in the stomach which led to internal bleeding.'

'Oh.' Nik didn't really know what to say.

The man pulled down his mask, peeled off a bloody glove and went over to a wooden table in the corner of the room. Picking up a lavishly painted porcelain cup from a coaster, he took a delicate sip, holding his cup with one manicured pinky extended, as if he were at a reception in Buckingham Palace. Closing his eyes, he drew in the scent of the tea through a nose that looked as if it had been flattened in a boxing ring. The contrast between his manicured hands and his flattened nose was disconcerting. Let alone the fact that he was drinking tea in front of a dead body and its extracted intestines.

'You must be Inspector Pohl,' said the man. 'Jon's friend.'

'Oh, we're definitely not friends,' responded Nik, taking in the rest of the room.

'You seem disappointed.'

'Look, don't take it personally but I would have preferred a forensic scientist over a pathologist.'

'I find it impressive you know the difference,' said the man. 'But we pathologists do have an advantage. You see, we have to be far more specific during our clinical autopsies than forensic scientists do during their legally requested post-mortems. Forensic scientists only clarify whether the death was natural or not. The actual cause of death is of secondary importance to them. Pathologists, on the other hand – we can't rest until we've found the actual reason.' He took another sip of tea. 'Perhaps you'll be reassured to hear that I worked for a year in a forensics department.'

'Are pathologists allowed to do that?'

'No, but I sort of . . . tweaked . . . my CV.' He gave a throaty chortle that made his chins jiggle up and down.

'How did Jon convince you to work with him?' asked Nik, changing the subject.

'My pathologist's salary isn't sufficient to meet all my needs.' He set down the cup and walked over to Nik with an outstretched hand. 'Balthasar von den Auenfelden, at your service.'

Nik took a step back. 'Under the circumstances, I think I'll pass on the handshake.'

'As you wish.' He reached for a chocolate biscuit from a plate and slung it into his mouth. 'Well, now that we're going to be working together whether we like it or not, you can call me Balthasar, but please, not Balthi, or Sasar or Smart Arse.'

'Who calls you Smart Arse?'

'Most of my incestuous relatives, who can't stand the fact I'm intellectually superior to them. And my greengrocer, when I explained to him that sweet potatoes are from the morning glory family and *not* the nightshade family. Then there was my apparently well-read neighbour when I explained that the word "uniquest" doesn't exist because unique is an absolute adjective. And lastly, my colleagues, who can't stand the fact that I possess more expertise than the whole department put together. The colleagues, however, tend to add on a "blue-blooded" before Smart Arse.' And with that he concluded his speech. 'Is Nik your real name or is it short for something?'

'My parents couldn't afford any more,' replied Nik tersely, fed up with the small talk. 'Could we maybe leave the fraternising to another time and concentrate on the reason I'm here?'

Balthasar shrugged his shoulders. 'Where's the body?'

'Coffin's at the back entrance,' said Nik.

'Push it round into the common room, please.' He signalled towards a small room with chairs, a table and a coffee machine. 'I'll go ahead and forge the paperwork,' he said with a wide grin.

'You do that often?'

'What, forging paperwork?' Balthasar chortled again, as if Nik had asked him if the earth revolved around the sun. 'Best you don't know the details,' he said, settling down at his computer.

On his way to the entrance Nik asked himself what on earth he was doing there. First of all, he'd killed a colleague. Then he'd used that dead colleague's computer account to search the CID network illegally. Then he'd broken into Munich's Ostfriedhof garage, exhumed a corpse and lied to two colleagues while stealing that corpse. With the help of a dubious hearse driver, he'd then brought the dead body to a corrupt pathologist, who openly admitted forging documents, despite the fact Nik worked for the CID. All things considered, he thought grimly, his misdemeanours of recent years were child's play compared to all of this.

Nik pushed the coffin into the common room and set off home. It was six o'clock in the morning and there was nothing else he could do at the institute. His work was done.

Now it was down to oddball Balthasar to find some clues.

Nik didn't manage to sleep more than four hours. The exhumation had shaken him and he kept dreaming of Kathrin's grave. In one dream, her coffin wasn't in the ground, and in another, Tilo's corpse was down there. He couldn't remember his last dream but when he woke up, he still had the sickening smell of the pathology lab in his nose. His body was yearning for rest but his mind could not stop replaying the events of the last few days. There was no point staying in bed.

Nik's back was sore from all the midnight coffin-pushing, so he allowed himself two aspirins with his morning coffee. Yawning, he shuffled into the bathroom, where he trimmed his beard and the hair that was falling over his eyes. After a short shower he went into the living room and observed the mountain of files that he'd gathered over the last few days. So much paperwork and he still had more questions than answers. But before he could work any further on the case, he'd have to wait for the autopsy results. He stuffed his hat, scarf and winter jacket into a large bin bag, slipped on his shoes, pulled on his leather jacket and left the house.

It had stopped snowing and the pavements had been cleared. The cold in his face was invigorating. He lit a cigarette and relished the warm smoke in his lungs. He had moved barely five metres when a woman in a thick coat joined him, looking him up and down accusingly.

Nik sighed.

'Why d'you look more knackered on your days off than when you've got work?'

'I had to exhume a body and bring it to the pathologist.' Nik conveniently omitted the fact he'd done this outside his function as a CID inspector. 'And since I can't shift the stench of dead body from my jacket, I'm getting rid of it.' He went over to the used-clothes container, threw everything in and headed towards the supermarket.

Mistrust crept across her face. How did she always know when he wasn't telling the truth?

'Why are you still wearing that?' she asked, pointing to the heart-shaped locket hanging on a silver chain around Nik's neck.

'It was Mum's. Isn't that reason enough?'

'I don't have a problem with its emotional value. I have a problem with the stuff inside it.'

He shook his head. It was apparently impossible to hide anything from his sister. Nik tugged on the locket and opened it up. 'It's just a little tablet,' he said.

'Nik, that's horrible.' She took a step backwards. 'Why do you do it?'

'Freedom of choice.'

'Freedom of choice?' Mira repeated. 'So poison lets you choose freely, does it?'

'This isn't just any old poison,' explained Nik. 'This is cyanide. Two seconds and it's all over.'

He looked at the pill. It was barely bigger than the nail on his little finger but it was deadly. 'I've lost control of my life. At least with this I get to have some control over my death.'

She stared at him in utter disbelief.

'It's comforting to know that when it all gets too much, I can just swallow the cyanide and it'll be over. No more worries. No more problems. Just an eternal sleep. Wonderful, isn't it?' He closed the locket.

'How did you even get your hands on that stuff?'

'In a drugs raid,' answered Nik. 'And it wasn't just coke and heroin in the hideout. There were weapons, ammunition and a small bag of cyanide tablets. I was in charge of the inventory, so I pocketed one.' He shrugged his shoulders.

'What the hell is wrong with you?'

'Mira, I'm tired,' he said with a sigh. 'I just want to go shopping. Then, I'm going to bed so I can get some rest before work tomorrow.'

She raised her eyebrows, which Nik took as an act of approval. She stood still and watched him go into the supermarket. And by the time he came out again with his shopping, his sister had disappeared.

His phone rang. He put down his carrier bag and answered. 'Nik Pohl.'

'This case will go down as having the sloppiest post-mortem examination in the history of forensic medicine.' It was Balthasar.

Nik could hear the agitation in the pathologist's voice. It was a mixture of indignation and hysteria.

'Formally, everything is perfect,' he continued. 'Even the smallest of details was recorded in the report. Livor mortis, rigor mortis, even abnormalities on the facial skin. The problem isn't how the examination was conducted. It's that any inconsistencies were deliberately ignored.'

'OK, what else?' Nik leaned against a wall and pulled a cigarette out of his pocket with his free hand.

'Kathrin had two injuries which could have arisen from a fall. One on the face and one on the back of the head.'

'OK. And how could that have happened?'

'Either she was hit on the back of the head with a rock and then fell, landing on her face, or, she hit the back of her head on a rock while falling, turned over and fell face first.'

'Unlikely, but not impossible,' said Nik. 'But that rock face is really steep. If she fell, she'd probably have scratched herself, but not suffered severe injuries to the back of her head. There aren't any overhanging rocks to hit on the way down.'

'Well, that's definitely one good indication she didn't hit her head during the fall,' began Balthasar, 'but I also found tiny wooden splinters in the back of the head, and that's after her body was washed and prepared for the funeral.'

'But maybe she hit her head on a branch when she fell?'

'Well, I'm not an expert on the trees in Flintsbach, but I very much doubt there are any that contain adhesives, dissolving agents and colour pigments.'

'The wood was coated in varnish?'

'Just a small amount but enough for the mass spectrometer.'

'So Kathrin was hit on the head with a piece of wood?'

'Yes, a hundred per cent.'

'OK. Sounds like a climbing accident just turned into a murder case.'

Chapter 5

Nik read through all of Kathrin's paperwork again. Officially, there wasn't anything wrong with it. As the death had been classified as unnatural, a medico-legal autopsy had to be performed on the body. This took place one day after Kathrin's death. The German Criminal Code stipulated that two doctors had to be present at such an autopsy, and at least one of them had to be a registered pathologist. The registered pathologist at Kathrin's autopsy was Dr Beate Cüpper, who worked at the LMU's Institute for Forensic Medicine. Originally from Ulm in the south of Germany, Dr Cüpper got her doctorate in Medicine from Freiburg University. Her first position as a doctor was at the Forensics Institute at Würzburg University, and in 2011 she moved to Munich, where she still worked today. She received an award for her PhD and was a member of the German Society for Forensic Sciences.

Nik found very little information about Cüpper online: three entries about events at LMU, some photos on Facebook and some handouts from a presentation she'd given at the University of Bern. Not nearly enough to build up an accurate profile and nothing to suggest she was having difficulties in her private life or at work. Nik found a couple of minor driving offences in the Flensburg traffic register. But other than that, her record was squeaky clean. Going by her publications, Cüpper was a very proficient doctor, and this only made Kathrin's mediocre autopsy seem even more dubious.

Nik wasn't a fan of conspiracy theories but everything he'd come across over the last few days had just added to his suspicions. The enquiries he'd made into Viola's case had pushed his colleague Tilo to kill an innocent stranger and to very nearly kill Nik as well. And then there was Kathrin Glosemeier's case – similar to Viola's in so many ways – where a competent and renowned pathologist apparently forgot everything she'd ever learned during her highly successful career.

There was nothing questionable about the death certificate and if it weren't for the exhumation, Nik wouldn't have had any reason to criticise the pathologist. And that meant any aggressive enquiries were out of the question. The desecration of Kathrin's grave still hadn't made the news. Officially, she was still buried in the Ostfriedhof.

Speaking to police and investigators would be something Cüpper had to do on a regular basis. A couple of questions weren't going to spook her. Nik would just need to make sure he used his best CID-guy-next-door tactics when questioning her. And stage one of that involved a shower, a clean shirt and some mouthwash.

The doctor lived in a beautiful detached house in Munich's Pasing district, not far from the city park, with views of the Würm river. Two steps led up from a small garden to the front door. The windows were made of safety glass and fitted with burglar-resistant fixtures and lockable handles. The halogen motion sensors would make any creeping around very difficult. There was a reinforced door panel and a high-grade lock. Burglars would think twice before trying to get into this house.

There was a light on in the kitchen. According to Nik's research, Cüpper was single, so it had to be her in the house. He rang the doorbell and a woman of about forty, with full lips and a delicate snub nose, opened the door. She was wearing very little make-up and her black hair was tied up in a ponytail; she looked older than the photograph on the LMU homepage, and noticing the wrinkles on her forehead and around her eyes, it was clear to Nik that the picture had been Photoshopped. Nik could tell from the way her blue eyes squinted at him that she was probably short-sighted, but as there were no tell-tale dents on the sides of her nose, it was likely she normally wore contacts.

Apparently he'd interrupted her while cooking, as she was wearing a black apron over her white blouse and was holding half an aubergine. On her wrist was an Oyster Perpetual Rolex adorned with diamonds. While LMU pathologists were certainly paid more than CID officers, their salary still wouldn't be enough to afford a 35,000-euro watch.

'Yes?' Her voice was deep and powerful. She was standing up tall with a straight back, looking Nik directly in the eyes. He held up his CID badge.

'Inspector Pohl, Munich CID. Would you happen to have a moment for me?'

'Do we have an appointment?' asked the woman.

'No,' Nik replied. 'And of course, I would have normally just gone to the institute but there've been some developments with a case, you see, and you were in charge of the autopsy.' He forced a smile. 'I need to hand in the preliminary report by early tomorrow morning and need your opinion. It'll only take five minutes.'

She stood silently, regarding him with raised eyebrows, making it clear she was not impressed with the interruption. But finally, she stepped to the side and let him in.

'As long as you don't mind if I cook while we speak.'

Things didn't start to look any cheaper after stepping inside Cüpper's house. The ground floor consisted of one large open-plan living space that stretched from the front door back to the garden patio. There wasn't a single wall, just one large supporting column in the centre of the room. The floor had been laid with light tiles that matched the furniture and the designer kitchen glistened with expensive chrome.

There was a replica of Neo Rauch's *Vater* hanging on the left wall. Or at least it was probably a replica.

All the ingredients for a vegetable bake were set out on a cooking island with a polished marble countertop. Deep-purple aubergine sat on a chopping board already sliced and waiting to be used. And beside that was a baking dish with tomato sauce topped with mozzarella and boiled eggs. Everything looked top quality. Probably not just your regular packaged, supermarket range. Whatever the case, Nik couldn't spot a single plastic bag or container lying around anywhere.

Nik was relieved the pathologist showed no intention of asking him to eat with her. The only thing he hated more than a vegetable bake was a vegetable bake with aubergines.

'So, which case are you talking about?' asked Cüpper, slicing another aubergine. The oven was preheating and its light formed a warm glow behind her.

'The case goes back to 15 August 2016,' Nik began, sitting himself down at the kitchen table. 'That morning the body of a young woman was found near Flintsbach. Her name was Kathrin.'

'Doesn't ring any bells. Can you tell me anything else?'

'The body was found at a climbing crag called The Quarry.'

'Ah, yes, the climbing accident,' she went on casually. 'What about it?'

'How certain were you it was an accident?'

She stopped slicing. 'Listen, I take my job very seriously. If I determine a death as accidental, it means I've ruled out all other possibilities. Did you read the report?'

'Yes,' replied Nik. 'But I still wondered why she had severe injuries on her face *and* the back of her head.'

'Can happen in that kind of situation. One injury is caused during the fall and the other on impact.'

'But the right side of The Quarry is really steep. If you fall there, the only thing you're going to hit is the ground. Not any rocks.'

'Aren't there any small trees there?'

Nik nodded.

'Well, they could have caused the injury.'

'But no bark or leaves were found in the back of the head.'

Cüpper salted the rest of the aubergine and placed it in the baking dish. 'Inspector Pohl,' she said, sighing, 'I'm a pathologist, not an investigator. I can barely even remember the case. If I concluded that Kathrin Glosemeier died falling, it means I found nothing to suggest third-party involvement.'

She sprinkled parmesan over the aubergines and put the dish in the oven. 'We deal with numerous unexplained deaths every day. You can't expect me to have every single detail from each case in my head. That's what the report's for.'

'Of course,' Nik responded. 'But if you can barely remember the case, why did you remember Kathrin's surname?'

Cüpper pursed her lips. 'What are you suggesting, Pohl? Are you trying to blame me for this woman's death?'

'I just want to know how you and the scene investigator managed to miss some very obvious discrepancies. Things an amateur would have seen.'

'Then you should ask the investigator.'

'He's up next.'

'Why are you opening up this case again?'

'As long as you keep lying to me, that'll have to stay my secret.'

'And how d'you know I'm lying? Because of the two wounds? I could show you ten falling accidents where the person had injuries all over their body. Front and back. So many injuries I couldn't tell which one had killed them.'

'I've read other reports from you and they are all far more detailed and precise than Kathrin Glosemeier's. And if you'd taken a closer look at the head wound, you'd've found little bits of varnished wood.

Not really something you'd expect to see after a fall. After a fight perhaps.'

'How do you know about the varnished wood? I never wrote about it in my report.'

'Magic.' Nik cast an imaginary wand with his hand.

Cüpper glared at Nik and let out one long, loud breath. 'You need to leave.'

'That won't help you, you know. I'll just ask you to come into the station. Whatever the case, this conversation isn't over.'

'I think you overestimate your power a bit, don't you?' she asked with a snicker.

'I know Kathrin Glosemeier's half-arsed autopsy wasn't just coincidence. Somebody made you do it that way. Somebody very powerful. More powerful than I'll ever be. And I know the case will probably be closed again before I can write the word "varnish". But d'you know what?' Now he snickered. 'I'm going to play really dirty here. I'll take the files home with me, beef them up and send them on to a couple of bloodhounds in the press. You know, the kind of journalists who've always had it in for the police and who'd sell their own grandmother for this kind of story. And I couldn't give a flying fuck if I go to jail for it. And you . . .' – he pointed a finger at Cüpper – '. . . you'll go down with me. Because no matter how powerful this second employer of yours might be, I'm sure they really wouldn't like this kind of publicity. And at some point, they're going to need a scapegoat. And it's not going to be me.'

Cüpper took two steps to the side, opened a drawer and pulled out a gun.

'Out! Now!' she screamed.

'Jesus! Calm down!' said Nik, raising his hands. She was holding a .22 Arminius HW 3. Easy to handle and small but each of its eight bullets could easily kill him. 'Shooting a CID officer would be a really silly thing to do.'

'I'm not going to shoot "a CID officer". I'm going to shoot a man who managed to get into my house under false pretences and tried to rape me.'

Cüpper didn't have a firearms licence, which meant she'd sourced the gun illegally. She probably hadn't ever shot it. The table he was sitting at was made from simple safety glass. It wouldn't offer any protection. And the couch and door were both too far away. The marble cooking island was his only chance. If he squeezed himself up tight against its drawers, Cüpper wouldn't be able to shoot him. She was too small.

'Please.' Nik stood with his hands in the air. 'Can we just calm down?'

'No!' she screamed, her face contorted with hatred.

'The rape idea wouldn't work. I never even shook your hand.' Nik attempted to coax her into a conversation. He was still too far away to throw himself on to the floor and roll towards the cooking island. Cüpper would have ample time to shoot and it could be deadly. He needed to get closer.

'So I wouldn't be able to prove you raped me, but still, a brutal attack?' And with that, she slammed her forehead against a wall cabinet. When she lifted her head, blood streamed down her eyebrows. But rather than grimacing in pain, Cüpper started to smile.

'Last chance, Inspector Pohl. Leave!'

Realising what Nik was planning, Cüpper edged over to the cooking island. Now she had a clear line of fire.

'OK.' He walked to the door with his hands still in the air. He'd only ever been threatened with a gun three times in his life and each time had felt just as shit.

He made no sudden movements, opened the front door and went outside. He didn't look back once. As he stood on the street he heard the door slam and blinds being rolled down.

There was no point pushing Cüpper any further, so he got in his car and drove home. He'd evaded death by the skin of his teeth for the second time in a week and he still had no idea why.

He'd reached yet another dead end. The more information he came across, the more bizarre the situation became. He needed help from the man who'd got him into this trouble in the first place.

◆　◆　◆

The small loft space would have made an ideal little flat. All it needed was flooring to cover the concrete, some new windows and a lick of paint. But this place wasn't meant for relaxing, it was Jon's office. The plaster on the walls was cracking and electric cables had been clamped to the ceiling. Some underfloor heating would have warmed the room perfectly, but instead there were just two electric heaters, both attached to some kind of metal cage. Inside the cage were Jon's four PCs and a Cray supercomputer. The Cray was one of the smaller models, but it was still exceedingly fast and perfect for hacking.

Since Tilo had tried to murder Nik, Jon had moved into this hideout and stepped up security. To this end he had installed two extra screens above the PCs, which he used to keep an eye on the area surrounding the loft and the front door. At the side hung a large red cord attached to two canisters full of an aluminium-based fire accelerant that sat on top of the Cray. If the canisters were ever to be ignited, the aluminium mixture would burn through the computer like acid, irretrievably destroying any data.

Some might call him paranoid, but the fact that a high-ranking CID agent was involved, and, it seemed, had no qualms about committing murder, meant there was every reason to be careful. Gaining unauthorised access into strangers' computer systems was nothing compared to that. So until this case was solved, Jon had decided to hole up in his office, venturing out only to buy the bare essentials.

There would be no pizza delivery and no meeting friends, not even Nik. His post would be delivered to a PO Box which he'd registered under a false name and he'd manage with the belongings he'd packed into a bag before he left. Money, a couple of sets of clean clothes and a fake ID were all he'd brought.

Jon's phone beeped. He read the SMS. '**Need a connection between Viola and Kathrin. Call me at 10 p.m.**' Jon set down his phone and laughed a little to himself. Never any unnecessary niceties with Nik. He always got right to the point.

Jon turned on his computer and started searching.

◆ ◆ ◆

At 10 p.m. Nik's phone rang.

'So, I looked for connections between the two victims,' Jon began. 'The bad news is I couldn't find a single link. Not even a Facebook like.'

'And the good news?'

'That I still had hope *you'd* find something.'

'Nope. Everywhere I look I hit a brick wall. All these discrepancies, I've almost got myself believing it's a conspiracy.' Nik sat down on the couch and took a swig of beer. 'The fact Viola's file doesn't mention a single thing about her boyfriend being a drug dealer could just be down to sheer laziness. But not the fact my ex-colleague tried to kill me because I was looking into the case. In all my days here I've never seen anything like that before. And Kathrin Glosemeier's death is turning out to be just as messed up.'

'Balthasar wrote to say she'd been murdered.'

'Yeah, and he found serious shortcomings with the autopsy. I just went to see the pathologist who carried it out.'

'Did she try to shoot you too?'

'Yes,' replied Nik.

'Are you serious?' Jon asked. 'That was a joke!'

'It was all pretty harmonious to start with but then as soon as I upped the pressure a bit, she whipped out a gun and said she'd tell the police I attempted to rape her if I didn't leave immediately.'

'This is insane!' Jon blared. 'What the hell would push a CID agent and a pathologist to do all this?'

'If it wasn't for the involvement of Tilo and Dr Cüpper, I'd be tempted to think we were looking at a serial murderer. But that would be the worst-case scenario from our point of view.'

'Why?'

'A serial killer has a plan and similar motives for all their murders, but their victims tend to be random and have nothing to do with the killer before they die. So, until you know the pattern or motive, there's no point looking for a connection between the victims' lives or their surroundings either.'

'What do you mean?'

'So, for example, the Woodward Corridor Killer raped and strangled at least eleven prostitutes in the 90s, apparently because he hated hookers. But it wasn't until his pattern became clear that undercover officers were put out on the streets. It took them months before they finally caught the bastard.'

'OK, so you try to find out what a serial killer's motive is and when you know that, you can predict their next victim.'

'Yes. But our first problem is the lack of connection between Viola and Kathrin. Both are women, they're around the same age, and they look pretty similar. And that's all we have. We also don't know enough about how they were killed,' added Nik. 'Kathrin was hit and fell off a rock. Although the fall was probably just a cover-up. And we don't even have a body for Viola. She might still be alive.' Nik drank his beer. 'The Son of Sam shot his victims or attacked them with a knife. The Freeway Killer strangled or stabbed his victims to death. It was committing a violent act that was important to them. They never went for poison or built a bomb or ran over their victims with a car. So in our case, we don't have enough information to be able to recognise any patterns. And if we include Tilo and Dr Cüpper in the picture, then the whole thing completely blows up in our faces.'

'Why?'

'Serial killers are crazy loners. OK, so sometimes they work in twos, like the Lonely Hearts Killers, who looked for well-off single women in lonely hearts columns. But I've never come across any case where a CID agent and a pathologist have assisted a cover-up.'

'Before you ask, I've not found any link between Tilo and Dr Cüpper, or between them and the victims,' said Jon. 'All we have left is the conspiracy theory.'

'On what?' asked Nik. 'Neither Viola nor Kathrin were hiding secrets from people. Neither had particularly remarkable jobs and neither was friends with any important people. Even if they were murdered, why is there so much effort being made to cover it up? Why would Tilo and Dr Cüpper risk their careers and be willing to murder to make me leave the investigation alone?'

'I don't know and the longer I think about it the more frustrated I get.' Jon was silent for a moment.

'Now would be a good time to tell me the truth about Viola,' said Nik. 'How did you know her?'

Jon sighed loudly. For a second, Nik thought he was going to fob him off with another excuse but then he started to speak.

'I met Viola at a university event. I was fascinated by her from the moment I saw her. By her intelligence, her enthusiasm and her will of steel. When she talked, everybody listened to her and when she didn't, her presence just seemed to fill the room. You couldn't escape her. She was literally radiant.'

'Was there something between you?'

'We were just friends. Good friends. Not the kind of friends who saw each other every evening. But when we did see each other we'd completely lose track of time and I was always sad when we said goodbye.' He was silent for a moment. 'I remember the last time we met. Down at the Chinese Tower. We sat on a bench, drinking beer and watching the kids on the carousel. And then suddenly it started raining. We'd been chatting so much we hadn't seen the dark clouds. The other guests ran under the wooden roof of the tower or under the trees, but Viola put down her bottle, closed her eyes and raised up her hands to the sky like a shaman. Removed from the world. Just completely captivated by the rain.' He sighed. 'So, now you know. What next?'

'I need to see Cüpper again. She's the only thing that can help us crack this secret about Kathrin's death. But this time I need to meet her in a safe place. Getting done for attempted rape now would be the end of me. The only way I'll get to speak to her next time is by going to her work. I'm CID, so I can turn up without an appointment. Hopefully, there's far less chance she has a gun in her desk and she won't be able to accuse me of attempted rape.'

'Be careful, Nik,' warned Jon. 'With Tilo's death and the visit to Cüpper, you're on their radar now. Whoever "they" are. And if they can get a top CID officer and a pathologist on their side, then they've obviously got what it takes to keep you silent. And they won't stop there.'

◆　◆　◆

Nik was pleased he was on the late shift. It meant he didn't have to get up early and could work on the case during the day. He was in an infuriating position. The only evidence he had that the case needed to be reopened had been uncovered via an illegal exhumation. An anonymous tip-off would make no difference and the discrepancies in the files wouldn't be enough to get a second investigation started.

The traffic wasn't on Nik's side, but he finally made it to the Institute for Forensic Medicine, not far from Nussbaumpark. He checked the time. It was already past ten. Even if the pathologist was a late riser, she should definitely be at work by now. Deciding against driving into the LMU grounds, he parked his car on a side street and walked the last couple of hundred metres. To Nik, the outside of the forensics building looked more like an office block. It was painted completely in white, had large windows and was surrounded by a grass verge with four concrete benches. A set of steps led up to a nondescript glass entrance area.

Nik had only been able to find Dr Cüpper's telephone number and department online. The rooms at the Forensics Institute stored highly confidential files, and security had to be accordingly tight. Even with his CID badge, getting into the building would prove a challenge. But he had to try. He walked past the public waiting area and rang a doorbell. A female employee answered and asked to see his ID.

Two locked doors and a brisk walk down a corridor later, he arrived at Cüpper's door and, without stopping to knock, he walked in.

Inside the room, two desks stood opposite each other. One of them was clean and tidy with just a small cactus and a trophy on it. The other was covered with books, files and notes. A young man lifted his head from behind the pile and blinked, as if Nik had interrupted him mid-thought.

'Yes?' he said, visibly confused. He inspected Nik over the top of his glasses, scrunching up his nose and munching at something like a little rabbit. He had a coffee stain on his white lab coat and short, shiny fingernails. It was clear from the state of his nails and the bitter smell of Stop 'n' Grow in the room that biting his nails was an issue. A pennant with a white D on a red background hung on the wall. Nik recognised it as the Dynamo Dresden football team's flag, which confirmed his suspicion that the man had spoken with a light Saxon accent.

'Inspector Pohl.' Nik showed his badge. 'I urgently need to speak to Dr Cüpper.'

'Beate isn't here today,' answered the man.

'I see. And you are?'

'Dr Uwe Ettel.' The doctor stood and shook Nik's hand. 'I've been Beate's colleague for two years now.'

'And where is Dr Cüpper?'

'I got an email from her this morning saying she's got a terrible cold and wouldn't be coming to work.'

Nik analysed the man's gestures and facial expressions. The handshake suggested he was right handed. If he'd been lying about Cüpper, he would have looked up to the right. But he didn't. He just kept looking at Nik without blinking any quicker or rubbing his eyes. He seemed calm and spoke at a normal pace.

'Maybe I can help you?' asked Ettel.

'It's about an autopsy performed by Dr Cüpper. Do you ever assist her?'

Ettel shook his head. 'We're very low on staff, so we usually use hospital physicians or the LMU emergency doctors.'

No delays in his answer. No evasive phrases and a direct manner. There was nothing to suggest he was lying, so he probably wasn't involved.

'I only have a death certificate and an LMU pathology report for the case. Do you usually take other notes?'

'We record any ideas or facts as we work,' explained Ettel. 'We wear a microphone on our lapels so we can use our hands for the examination.'

'Are these recordings saved?'

Ettel nodded. 'On the forensics server.'

'And the information on these recordings . . . Is all of it transferred to the death certificate and report?'

'Well . . . the recordings are of course more detailed and include assumptions that are often rejected further down the line,' explained the pathologist. 'We see our work as the last service to our patients, so we go about it very carefully and write down any deciding factors.'

'Thank you,' said Nik. Ettel had said all he could and the fewer people who knew of his investigation, the better. 'I'll be in touch again at the end of the week. Maybe Dr Cüpper will be better by then.'

Nik fought off his urge to swear out loud. He'd hoped he could avoid visiting Cüpper again at her home. But at least this time he'd be prepared for the gun in the drawer. He hoped Ettel wasn't also involved, because if he was, he'd be able to warn Cüpper before Nik arrived at her house.

The traffic going out of the city wasn't nearly as heavy, so thanks to this and Nik's complete disregard for the speed limit, he was at the pathologist's house in fifteen minutes.

Nothing much had changed since yesterday. The garage was still closed and the only difference was that the roller blinds at the front of the house had been rolled back up. Nik went to the front door and rang the bell, knocking loudly at the same time.

'Frau Cüpper!' he called. 'Munich CID. Please open the door.' He knocked again, even louder, and left his finger on the bell but nobody came to the door.

Nik went to the nearest window and looked into the kitchen. The vegetable peelings and crockery had been cleared away but other than that, the room was in the same state as it had been yesterday. But no sign of Beate Cüpper. Nik went around the house, past a herb bed and into a grassy garden. Thankfully the garden was surrounded by high hedges, so Nik was able to creep about without being seen by any nosy neighbours.

It was just as neat and orderly as the inside of the house. The herbs in the bed had been meticulously planted and exceptionally well looked after. The little fountain in the middle hadn't sprouted any moss and the perfectly positioned stone slabs on the patio were clinically clean. Not a single blade of grass would pop up between those slabs in the summer. Next to the patio was a small spiral staircase which led to a balcony on the first floor.

He went up the stairs and peered through a full-length bedroom window. To his surprise, the bedroom was nowhere near the pathologist's pedantic standards. All the cupboard doors were wide open and clothes had been flung across the floor. The bed was unmade and the light in the bathroom was still on.

Dr Cüpper was gone. She'd probably guessed Nik would come back looking for her. Nik was wondering how he could organise an official search for her car when his phone rang. It was Danilo.

'What is it?' asked Nik impatiently.

'I'm used to you fucking things up at work but I never knew you were such an arsehole in your free time as well.'

'What are you talking about?'

'Come to the station, Nik. You're in deep shit,' said Danilo. He sounded exasperated. 'And come in the back door.'

Nik was used to colleagues talking about him and it was normal for conversations to stop and for heads to look away when he walked past. But when he walked into the station today something was different. Everybody was staring at him like he was Charles Manson, not Nik Pohl, the fucked-up Munich CID officer. The entire team from the early shift was clustered around the coffee machine but before anybody had time to make a comment, Naumann had already dragged Nik into his office.

'Congratulations, Nik,' his boss said. 'You've really done it this time.' Cynicism oozed from each word.

'What's going on?'

'Do you not listen to the news? Watch TV? Go on fucking line?'

'I had a lot to do,' explained Nik. 'I only watch the TV for sport. The radio just plays shit and I only use my mobile for making calls.'

'Then let me show you the 9 a.m. local news, shall I.' Naumann reached for the remote from his desk. A blurry recording of a pavement came up on the screen. Cars were parked along the street. It was night time but you could see a few details thanks to the street lamps.

'*In recent years, the crime rate in Munich has gone down consistently and the number of successful prosecutions has increased,*' explained a female news reporter. '*Various events have recently proved challenging for the authorities. For example, the numerous football games with potentially violent fans from across Europe, or the mass demonstrations surrounding the G7 Summit. But Munich, with over a million inhabitants, still managed to keep its place as Germany's safest city. And there is no doubt that's all down to our police force. But unfortunately, not even this public service is immune to corrupt employees.*'

Nik moved closer to the TV. He recognised the street corner. It wasn't far from his flat. '*The following shocking images were sent to us this morning. According to experts, the recording is authentic. The video has not been manipulated and everything happened exactly as you are about to see.*'

The film started. A short young man appeared, walking backwards out of a small side street. He held his hands above his head. His face was only visible from the side. He looked scared and appeared to be saying something.

'Oh, shit.' Nik knew what happened next. A second later, Nik came into the picture.

The film made it very clear how angry Nik had been about his stolen wallet. He watched with a sinking stomach as the film showed him go over to the man, punch him and twist his arm behind him, before pushing his face into the ground and pressing his knee into his back. Finally, Nik stuck his hand into the man's trouser pocket and pulled out some money. The video ended with the man lying on the ground, crying.

'*Muggings are an everyday occurrence in the city*,' continued the reporter, '*but we have never heard of one that was executed by a CID officer.*' A photo of Nik appeared on the screen. He was scrunching his eyes together in an unflattering manner and was clenching his fists. There was no doubt the man in the photo was angry and violent. '*The attacker in the video is an agent from the Munich CID. Inspector Nik P. has already attracted attention for violence and disobedience and was subsequently disciplined. He lives near the street where the crime was committed and a number of sources from the neighbourhood have revealed that Nik P. has often demanded protection money from numerous individuals.*'

'That's a lie!' Nik shouted.

'*None of the people affected were willing to speak in front of the camera out of fear of reprisal.*' The video played again from the beginning. '*And this was also the reason nobody reported the attack to the police. Were it not for the neighbour who managed to record the incident, nobody would have known about it. The video has been sent to the relevant CID department in Munich along with a request that a statement be made.*'

The video stopped just as Nik had pushed the man to the ground.

'*We promise to cover this story until Nik P. no longer poses a threat to the citizens of Munich. And we request that the chief of police remove the man from the police force.*'

Naumann turned off the television and threw the remote on the floor. 'Do you have any idea what's been going on here for the last hour?' he asked. 'We've only just finished dealing with the mass shooting in the shopping centre and now you come along with this? You thick piece of shit! Always dragging us down into the dirt with you. So now the chief of police, the mayor and even the Minister of the fucking Interior have got my number on speed dial. And not because they want me at the VIP tent at the Oktoberfest!'

'It didn't happen like that,' Nik attempted to explain.

'Oh, so that isn't you?' Naumann pointed to the black TV screen.

'Yes, but . . .'

'Then why did you hit a defenceless guy and steal his money?'

'Because a minute earlier, he'd trapped *me* in the alley and mugged *me*! It's *my* money I'm taking back.'

'And is there a video of this mugging?'

'All this was deliberate.'

'What do you mean by that?'

'I mean, I was framed!' screamed Nik. 'Am I seriously the only person here who can see that?'

'And why would someone want to frame you, Pohl?' asked Naumann. 'You're not famous. You're not particularly powerful and you're not even working any big cases.'

Nik bit his tongue. He desperately wanted to tell Naumann everything but he knew that he'd probably be chucked in jail if he told him any of the details. Plus, he had no idea who he could trust at the CID anyway.

'Maybe it's not just about me. Maybe they're just using me to discredit the entire police force.'

'Oh! Well, they've found the perfect scapegoat then, haven't they?' remarked Naumann. 'And not only is that video on every channel possible, we've also probably got an internal breach of data on our hands because details of your caution were given out.'

'There was another person there. A woman. She was about twenty-five. Had long dark hair and wore a short skirt and black boots. Give me a day and I'll find her.'

Naumann waved Nik over to the window. A mass of people had congregated around the main entrance. There were two camera teams, numerous photographers and a bunch of reporters waving their phones around in the air expectantly.

'There's an equally large mob waiting outside your flat as well,' said Naumann. 'And we've already had three enquiries from political groups who want to hold a demo against police brutality tomorrow.'

'And what about the fact the journalist could identify me from a blurry video in just a couple of hours? Does nobody find that a bit odd?'

'It happened right in your neighbourhood, Nik,' explained Naumann. 'Somebody would have recognised you and known that you work for the CID. Someone published your address on some Facebook page and it was already out before the deletion centre could get rid of it.'

'I'll testify today and say that the supposed victim attacked me first and that I was taking back the money he'd stolen from me.'

'It wouldn't make any difference,' responded Naumann. 'Look at it from a neutral perspective. On this video, you grab a defenceless man, you throw him to the ground and then you take money from his pocket. Along with the warning and the witness statement claiming you're involved in blackmail, there's a pretty damning case against you that no testimony on earth could help. The public are expecting a verdict.'

'All that stuff about protection money is bullshit. And supposed witnesses . . . who aren't willing to go on camera? You surely can't believe that?'

'It doesn't matter what I believe. I need to put out this fire and keep the damage to a minimum.'

'And here was me thinking your colleagues' well-being was so important to you,' said Nik. 'At least that's what you so touchingly said at the last Christmas party.'

'And how am I supposed to protect you?' He pointed to the TV again. 'The evidence against you is indisputable and you don't have a single thing to prove otherwise.'

Nik shook his head. It was pointless trying to discuss this with Naumann. His only interest was in saving himself. His boss sighed loudly and straightened himself up. Nik knew what was coming.

'Inspector Pohl, in light of compelling evidence, you are hereby suspended from any work-related duties until further notice. I advise you to urgently seek legal assistance for the forthcoming disciplinary proceedings.' Naumann stretched out his hand. 'Please give me your service weapon and service ID.'

Chapter 6

The open bottle of vodka on the table was tempting. It promised Nik a warm, comforting escape. Maybe also a long, dreamless sleep. With that amount of alcohol in his blood, he wouldn't be able to walk in a straight line . . . and that would mean he couldn't walk to Ettstraße and destroy the chief of police's office. So many benefits. But Nik knew, despite the raging anger coursing through his entire body, he would never come back from a low like that, and neither Viola's disappearance nor Kathrin's murder would be explained. He shook his head and thought back to the night with Cüpper. How she'd aimed her gun at him and hit her own head against the cupboard.

'Fucking crazy,' he mumbled. He finally stood up and kicked the bottle violently. Vodka ran down the wall and under the couch. There were shards of glass everywhere. But Nik didn't care. He left everything as it was and made his way to his bedroom. A boxing bag hung down from the ceiling beside his bed. The ceilings in his flat hadn't been fitted with plasterboard, so although the soundproofing was awful, they could hold a good deal of weight. He hit the tough leather with his bare hands, imagining himself punching Naumann, then Danilo, and then finally Jon, who'd got him into this nightmare to begin with. His punches became more precise. He began to sweat and his knuckles ripped. But he kept hitting the bag, imagining it was the little shit who'd tricked him in the alley, and then Tilo, his supposed friend. And last of all, Dr Cüpper. The one who got away. The chain squeaked under the strain and the bag jolted back and forth. Blood sprang off the leather and splattered on to his bed. He cried out in rage, throwing hit after hit until finally he fell panting to his knees. He didn't move. He just focused on the pain from the raw, wet wounds on the backs of his hands. It felt good.

He waited until his heart had stopped racing and stood up. He took off his sodden clothes and got into the shower, letting the cold water stream over him, washing away any last doubts.

Ten minutes later, he was on his way to Forstenried to visit Laura Kabus. Laura had been a friend of Kathrin's and her name was mentioned in Kathrin's file. While Viola's letter had been addressed to her parents, Kathrin's had been sent to Laura. Maybe visiting her would throw some new light on the case, just like Nik's visit to Viola's parents had done.

But Nik was suspended. He'd be limited in what he could do. He only had a fake badge, no ID, and his only service weapon had been confiscated. And even if he had had a second gun, he wouldn't have been able to take it out with him anyway.

Despite the snow, Nik managed to reach Munich's south-western borough of Forstenried without hitting any traffic. When he arrived, he noticed the red roof of the Heilig Kreuz Church lying hidden under a blanket of snow. He wasn't a religious man but a large part of him wished the church's crucifix really could perform miracles; God knew, he needed one if he was to solve this case.

Laura lived one street over from the church in an old block of flats which looked on to a sports field surrounded by large trees. It was nothing like Nik's neighbourhood. Rather than the booming bass from tuned-up BMWs, the air was filled with children's voices as they sledged under the glow of street lights. They didn't seem in the slightest bit bothered by the cold or the onset of darkness.

Nik rang a backlit buzzer with the name L. Kabus on it. He hoped Kathrin's friend hadn't seen the local news today or it was going to be a very short conversation.

'Yes?' answered a clear and bright female voice.

'Good evening, Frau Kabus,' Nik began. 'My name's Inspector Pohl. I'd like to speak to you about Kathrin Glosemeier.' His suspension would be made public at the press conference at 6 p.m., so he still had some time before every Munich resident would know he was no longer a police officer. For a moment, nothing happened. The intercom crackled and the door remained closed. Nik was about to ring once more, when the door buzzed. Somewhat relieved, he pushed the door and went upstairs. A woman with long dark hair was waiting for him at the door to her flat. She was wearing black jogging bottoms, a baggy jumper and thick woollen socks. Looking at the thin scarf around her neck and cup of tea in her hand, Nik wondered if the heating had broken down. She asked him to come inside.

Laura's flat was really more of a nest. There was carpet on the floor and countless cushions and blankets on the couch. Dreamcatchers and crystals hung from the ceiling. The heating was turned up full and her wallpaper was covered in nature images. A waterfall, a forest and a small stream. All of this, together with numerous plants, made the room feel more like a tropical rainforest, and it was worlds away from the dark, crisp winter Nik had left at the front door.

Laura said nothing and gestured to a chair. Nik sank into it while she sat down and crossed her legs on the couch opposite him. She was staring at the steam escaping softly from her tea cup before dissolving in the air. There was sadness behind the stare, like she was still suffering from the loss. There were no signs of guilt.

'As you probably know, your friend's case has been closed but we still need to make some enquiries to find out if there have been any changes,' Nik said confidently. 'New investigators have been put on the case to try to gain some new perspective and that's why I'm here.'

'OK. How can I help?' she asked.

'You and Frau Glosemeier were good friends, right?' asked Nik.

'Best friends.'

'Why did Frau Glosemeier send her farewell letter to you?'

'She had a difficult relationship with her parents,' Laura began. 'Her father wanted her to go into the family business but she wasn't interested in beer. New media, apps, start-ups. Those were her life.'

'I see. Now, let's go back to the day you last saw Frau Glosemeier. Did anything appear strange at all?'

'No.' She put down her cup. 'I've asked myself that question hundreds of times, but I can't think of anything. We saw a film at the cinema, then we went for Italian food and then, around eleven o'clock, we both went home. It was a nice evening. Like loads before. I sent Kathrin a couple of texts over the next few days but she never read them. I was worried that she might have relapsed, but she seemed so well and happy that night that I didn't believe she would have. I know the signs. Then just when I thought I should go and see her, I got the letter.' She stood up and went over to a small box made of polished wood and took out a piece of paper in a clear poly pocket. Nik had seen a copy of the letter in Kathrin's files.

'Relapsed?' Nik's eyebrows rose. He hadn't expected that.

'Yes, Kathrin had had some problems with drink and drugs, but she'd got treatment and it really seemed to have helped and she was back on track.'

He nodded. Balthasar hadn't mentioned any drugs in Kathrin's body, but maybe any traces would have disappeared. He'd need to ask him later. 'Did it seem like an unusual way for Frau Glosemeier to say goodbye?'

'Unusual?' she laughed. It was a cold, mocking laugh without a streak of humour. 'It was absurd. Kathrin would never do something like that. And even if she *had* planned on taking her own life, she would have said goodbye to me personally. I told the police that already.

But they didn't care. For them the case was closed.' She threw Nik an accusing look.

'Do you know the name "Viola Rohe"?'

'No, who's that?'

'Just another case,' said Nik dismissively. 'Were you and Frau Glosemeier ever in The Palace nightclub?'

'I've heard of it, but we were too old for that kind of place,' explained Laura. 'We were never really into clubbing. We hung around in bars where the volume was a bit more bearable.'

'Did Frau Glosemeier get in touch at all after the letter?'

Laura shook her head. 'It was the last sign of life I had from her.'

'Kathrin was found at a popular climbing area,' Nik continued.

Laura closed her eyes. 'Kathrin was a keen mountain biker. But climbing? With no gear? On that kind of crag? Not in a million years. She'd never been climbing in her life.' She picked up her tea again and took a sip. 'I told the police that too,' she added, quietly dismayed.

Nik took out his notebook. Laura had just confirmed exactly what he'd been thinking. A heap of discrepancies that even a constable just out of training would have noticed. But apparently in this case they'd been completely overlooked by an entire team of investigators. It was the confirmation he needed that none of this had anything to do with incompetence. The motive for the cover-up might still be unclear but Nik had thought of a way he could get a bit closer to explaining it.

'Would you mind if I took the letter with me?' he asked the woman. Laura nodded and handed him the poly pocket. 'Do you have any other letters from Frau Glosemeier?'

'Just postcards.'

'Could I borrow one? I promise to return it fully intact.'

She shrugged and went back to the wooden box. She took out a postcard and handed it to Nik. It was from the Maldives. 'It's from 2015,' she said.

'Thank you very much,' said Nik, putting everything in his pocket. He said goodbye to Frau Kabus and went back out into the cold. He'd barely got around the corner when he took out his phone to call Jon. It went straight to his voicemail. 'I hope you've got a bit more dosh in the bank 'cause we're gonna need another expert. I've got a new theory and it needs checking.'

◆ ◆ ◆

Kornelius Oberlander was being so quiet it made Nik nervous. The man sat reading the letter, neck bent right over with his face as close to it as possible. It was as if he had trouble reading the words, despite the glasses on the tip of his nose. A second pair also sat on his forehead. He'd follow each sentence with a gloved finger and when he got to the end, he'd shoot his head and hand back to the left to start the next line.

Other than Oberlander's desk, which was illuminated by a bright lamp, the rest of the room was submerged in darkness. Each wall was hidden by a fully stacked bookshelf and there was only one small window, right beside the door. Although it was almost the middle of the day, its roller blinds were firmly down, as if Oberlander was afraid of seeing the sun. His sallow face, scrawny figure and bald head made him look like Count Orlok from the silent horror film, *Nosferatu*.

Nik had expected a high-tech lab, with computers, halogen lights and large magnifying glasses that would be able to identify each and every dash and flick. But instead, there was a bony man huddled over his desk in a chamber that hadn't been aired since the turn of the millennium. Minute specks of dust danced around the lamp like a swarm of tiny moths and beside the lamp was a membership certificate from the Association for German Graphologists. Oberlander stood up, interrupting Nik's quiet thoughts of drinking a cold weissbier in Munich's English Garden. Already accustomed to the darkness, Nik had to blink hard to get his eyes to focus on the man.

'I'm sorry, I've forgotten your name,' said the man in a scratchy voice that completely matched his appearance. 'You are Herr . . . ?'

'Pohl,' answered Nik. 'My um . . . acquaintance, Herr Kirchhof, told me to come and see you so you could help me with the two letters.' Jon had reassured Nik that he'd not blackmailed Oberlander into helping, but had simply offered him good money.

'Do you need a graphological analysis or a writer identification?'

'Um, both?' stuttered Nik, who had no idea what the difference was.

'OK. Let's start at the personality aspects.' The man cleared his throat. 'Frau Glosemeier is a very ambitious person.'

'How can you tell?'

'Mostly from the consistent leaning to the right. She is intelligent. Determined. The kind of woman who listens to her head more than her emotions.'

'OK,' said Nik, hardly convinced.

'Frau Rohe is different. A soft hand that's adorned with round swirls which indicates a calm but persevering nature.'

Nik frowned. 'Swirls?'

Oberlander pointed to the letter. 'Here, you see the "n" looks like a "u",' he explained. 'A lot of thought is put into this writing and there is a big focus on its shape.'

'Ah.'

'Graphology is more my hobby really,' continued the man. 'I'm actually a handwriting expert and write forensic assessments for the Munich Court.' He cleared his throat again, as if trying to emphasise the importance of what he'd said. 'When comparing handwriting, the composition of the strokes, the pressure applied and the level of saturation all play a role. The vertical extension, the size of the letters, as well as the contrast between the long and short elements are all important for the forensic report.' He pointed to a microscope beside the table. 'By analysing the writing with a stereoscopic microscope under reflected, transmitted and diffused light, you can recognise where pauses were taken as well as other nuances. A handwriting comparison can help determine whether or not the letters were written by the same person.' He picked up the letters. 'You gave me two letters and two handwritten documents for comparison. I can tell you for certain that the letters were not written by the same people who wrote the other documents.'

'They do look very similar though,' said Nik, thinking back to how even the CID officer in charge of the case had believed them.

'Oh, yes. It's fantastic work,' said Oberlander. Nik sensed the admiration in his voice. 'A handwriting expert less gifted than myself would have missed it. But the analysis under the microscope showed up significant differences.'

'Were any pauses taken?'

Oberlander shook his head. 'I couldn't find any signs of pauses but the forger invested a lot of time and energy into the letter. If only it wasn't part of a crime, I would have written to the person to express my praise.'

'Is it possible that the writing is different because the women were under high levels of stress?'

'No, not this type of difference,' the man explained. 'Obviously, someone's handwriting changes when they are under strain but the differences we have here came about because it was a different person who wrote it.'

'You're sure?'

'Entirely,' confirmed Oberlander. 'Both farewell letters are fakes.'

◆ ◆ ◆

'We've got our link,' Nik said as soon as Jon picked up the phone.

'I didn't even say hello, Nik.'

'Yeah, but you were going to.'

'You know, it's hard to get away from you these days if you watch local news or read the newspaper.'

'That little shit stole my money first. I was framed perfectly.'

'I did warn you,' said Jon. 'Whoever's got a CID agent and a pathologist on their payroll knows how to get rid of some annoying little investigator.'

'Wish they'd just shot me in the head.'

'Far too obvious,' remarked Jon. 'Then there would have been questions and an investigation all of its own. This way, they get you out the way and screw up your reputation at the same time. Even if your private investigation did uncover something that could be used to get the case reopened, nobody would trust it now, thanks to your little show.'

'I've lost my badge, my gun and my limited computer access. They did a good job.'

'We'll still get on to the server with Tilo's details. And if they close his account, we can just use a new profile I was able to set up thanks to all those permissions your ex-colleague had. It runs under admin's radar, so no one can find out about it.'

'Somebody must have noticed he's missing,' said Nik. 'It's been six days.'

'Doesn't take much. A forged doctor's note to the employer and a message to the neighbours. Tilo didn't have any family in Munich, so nobody'll get suspicious before the end of the month. Then the letters will start piling up . . . and people will wonder why he hasn't replied to their voicemails. But then nobody will find his body. An investigation will run for a while but they won't find anything.'

'It's obvious from the fake letters that we're dealing with professionals.' Nik changed the subject. 'The only fingerprints on the letters are from the victims and the recipients. I checked. The paper is normal printing paper without any special marks. And the pens are no help either. Just your typical ballpoint you can get at the supermarket.'

'So, we've got more signs that point to a large-scale cover-up, but we still don't know who's behind it or why they're even doing it.'

'And the two people we know who *are* involved can't help us because one is dead and the other's missing.'

'No matter how hard I look, I just can't find any link between the victims. I've set up a web search that runs constantly and notifies me if anything new appears. But until now, there's been nothing on their connection.'

'We need a new suspect,' decided Nik.

'You're not allowed in the station and forensics is out of bounds for you too. But you could try hanging out with some of the women's friends.'

'I'll go back to The Palace.'

'To Viola's old work?' asked Jon. 'I thought you'd asked everyone.'

'Yeah, the owner was very helpful but I remember something Tilo said before he tried to put a bullet in my head. He mentioned something about secret cameras.'

'And what d'you hope to achieve?'

'Everything suggests Viola's last day at work was the day she disappeared. She wasn't kidnapped from the bar but somebody was there that night and they've got something to do with the whole thing. Maybe I'll find something on the videos.'

'That kind of recording is illegal and you don't work for the CID anymore. That owner's never going to just give it to you.'

Nik smiled. 'Then I'll just have to use my charm.'

◆ ◆ ◆

Normally Nik didn't mind the winter. Except when he was on a stakeout. It had stopped snowing but the thermometer was showing minus twelve. He'd been waiting in the freezing car for two hours but Peer Weise still hadn't left the club apart from for a few minutes when he'd come out for a cigarette, which meant he still had to be inside. Nik hadn't noticed a sofa bed anywhere when he was last there, so it was unlikely he was going to stay the night. The clock read 3.30 a.m. The Palace had been closed for half an hour and there wasn't much to see, thanks to the night's lack of clientele. Nik had taken three caffeine tablets to stay awake and he'd already started to feel the effects. First there was the headache and then came the uneasy restlessness that affected every part of his body. At one point he'd got out of the car and done push-ups on the frozen ground just to try and release some energy. And the three cigarettes he'd smoked had only eased things for a minute. His heartbeat had become irregular and his breaths were short.

He was playing with the new phone Jon had given him when Weise finally came out of the back door. His clothes were just as smart as the last time, but instead of his assistant, Nowara, he was unfortunately with one of the bull-necked bouncers. Nik sighed. He was slowly starting to appreciate the meaning of bad karma. But compared with everything he'd been through recently, this was merely a ripple in his turbulent and unpredictable life. Nik waited until the two men were walking past the car and got out. The bouncer was wearing a thick winter jacket, big enough to use as a child's tent, and a bulletproof vest was sticking out of his sports bag. While waiting in the car, Nik had noticed some old floorboards that had been dumped on the pavement. He went over to the pile and grabbed one, about the length of his arm, and smashed it into the bouncer's kidneys. His jacket provided little protection and he fell to the ground, groaning in pain. Nik was going to need silence for the next couple of minutes so he rammed the plank into the man's chin as he tried to get off the ground.

Weise put his hands in the air and looked at Nik, terrified. 'I saw you on the TV.' His voice was trembling. 'D'you want money?' He took out a wad of notes and threw them in front of Nik.

'Take it. Just, please, don't hit me.'

'Wow. For a man from the club scene, you're pretty easy to scare.' Nik put down the piece of wood and stepped over the unconscious bouncer. 'But I don't want money. I just want the video footage from the nightclub.'

'We only record the entrance.'

'Herr Weise,' Nik said with a smile, 'I know there are cameras inside the club.' The man looked about slyly, trying to locate an escape route. 'The good news is that the CID won't hear about any of it because I'm suspended. But the bad news is I've got absolutely nothing to lose and still have access to all the CID material I'm banned from using.' He took a step towards Weise. 'And don't bother trying to run away,' Nik warned him. 'I've always been an excellent sprinter.'

'I'll give you whatever you want if you just leave me alone,' said Weise desperately. 'I've got nothing to do with all that stuff.'

Nik punched the man on the chin, sending him staggering to the ground. 'Now, that was the first lie. I'll forgive you, this time.' Nik pulled the man back up on his feet. 'But I really wouldn't recommend doing it a second time.'

'What have I done?' Weise asked, wincing in pain.

'Let me summarise the night we first met.' Nik started pushing the man towards the club's back door. 'I came into your office, introduced myself as a CID officer and asked about Viola Rohe. Apart from one shit-scared barman, not a single person could tell me anything about her. And then, just a few hours later, that very barman is attacked by a high-ranking CID officer and tied up right beside me, all because he wanted to tell me something about Viola.' He gave Weise a push. 'What a coincidence, eh?'

'I didn't have a choice,' the man tried to defend himself. 'Your colleague Hübner had been to see me. He'd left his number and told me to call him if anybody came and asked about Viola, otherwise he'd give orders for the biggest drugs raid I'd ever seen.'

'When was that?'

'About a week after Viola went missing.'

'And you didn't find it a bit odd?'

'I just thought Viola had got herself involved in something and she was being investigated.'

'And when did you tell Hübner I'd been to see you?'

'As soon as you left my office.'

'And then what happened?'

'He told me to get my people to watch you and let him know if anything looked suspicious.'

'Like my second chat with Finn the barman?'

'Yes,' said Weise.

Nik pushed him to the ground for a second time. 'You know, two hours later Hübner put a bullet in Finn's head.'

'I didn't know that.' Weise seemed surprised. 'When Finn didn't show up for work the next day, I just thought he'd been arrested.'

Tilo had probably made everything sound like an official investigation that nobody was allowed to know about.

'I really liked that guy,' said Weise, brushing the slush off his suit. He seemed genuine enough.

'Well, if you want Finn's murderer to be punished, you need to tell me everything you know about Viola.'

'I already have,' explained Weise. 'Viola was a reliable employee and I never had a single problem with her. I never asked Hübner what he wanted with her and I never noticed anything strange about her. I also asked my assistant why Viola wasn't at work but she couldn't tell me anything.'

'OK, enough of the obvious bullshit,' said Nik. 'Were there any rumours going around about Viola? Did she ever hang about with shady people from the club? And when I say shady, I don't mean pickpockets. I mean people involved in drug dealing or money laundering. Serious stuff.'

Weise shook his head. 'It was just a bar job for Viola. She never chatted to anyone and always ignored any flirting. I don't think she spoke to a single punter for more than five minutes.' Weise unlocked the back door and took Nik into his office. He started the computer. 'Which time frame do you want?'

'The missing persons announcement went out on 26 October. Viola had already been missing for three days by that point. Her last day at work was the 22nd into the 23rd. So I need that whole week and one week later.'

Weise nodded.

'Why d'you make the recordings?'

The club owner took a USB stick from his desk drawer and started copying over all the footage.

'There've been more pickpockets recently. And vodka's been going at double the pace even though sales have stayed the same. I reckon one of the staff's stealing it.'

Nik sat on a chair and kept his eyes on the entrance. Ten minutes later, he was going back to his car. It was time to find out what had happened on Viola's last day at work. But before anything else, Nik needed to go home and sleep.

Chapter 7

The reporters had thankfully got fed up of the cold and gone home the night before, so Nik could get into his flat unseen and watch the videos of the nightclub.

There were three cameras in The Palace. The first one recorded the entrance, just as Weise had said. The footage, however, wasn't deleted the next day. The second camera was near the toilets. That's why Finn had been so nervous. It mostly recorded the dance floor and then a bit of the toilet entrance. The third camera was above the bar and focused mostly on the staff side. The customers could only be seen at the edge of the shot.

Nik let all the videos play simultaneously and at eight times their original speed. He tried to remember the faces and sometimes stopped the videos to take stills of the regulars he'd spoken to. Viola worked Fridays and Saturdays in the club and only appeared on a couple of Sundays. The young woman who normally did the shift wasn't there, so Viola had apparently covered for her.

The club was always busy at the weekend. The dance floor would fill up and people would push at the bar. It took a lot of effort from staff to collect empty glasses and working behind the bar was stressful. From the looks of things, they barely had time to breathe. Viola was constantly making drinks, handing out drinks or washing out Finn's blender. Her long hair was tied back in two plaits. She always wore a short skirt and a tight top, both of which accentuated her figure perfectly. She was attractive in a refined way. Not at all cheap. And men were continually trying to start a conversation with her. She mostly just smiled, thanked the men for the generous tips and politely accepted a business card which she'd then subtly toss in the bin at the next possible opportunity. For her, it was just a job and definitely not something she planned on doing for the rest of her life.

After midnight, the strain would start taking its toll. She'd slow down and sometimes pause for a moment. But other than a toilet trip, there were no breaks and the crowds didn't start to dwindle until around 2.30 a.m. Soon after that the staff would stop serving and begin preparing the bar for the next day. The lights would go up, the glasses would all be put through the machine and the fridges would be stocked. The last customer would normally leave the club around 3.30 a.m. Finally, the lights were switched off and it would stay dark until the cleaning team came in the next day at lunch time.

Once Nik had an idea of what a typical day looked like at The Palace, he started looking for things that seemed out of the ordinary. First of all, he focused on Viola. He noticed two pushy admirers who tried their luck more than once. The first was a hipster with a long shapely beard and muscular, tattooed arms. He showed off his well-trained body with a tight-fitting vest. The videos didn't have any sound, so Nik couldn't catch any names. Not that sound would have made any difference with all the pounding music in the background. The hipster reminded Nik of a friend from school, so he decided to call him Christoph. He watched Christoph, imagining he might be the perpetrator, but despite his intimidating appearance, he was harmless. He just liked to play the big, generous guy, letting champagne flow all around him while slithering his way into conversations with women. He was at The Palace for three nights and on each of those nights he went home with a different girl. And each girl was more attractive than Viola. If you're judging attractiveness by cup size, that is.

And then there was Ivan. The man had slightly Mongolian features and looked like he could have come from Russia, which was why Nik had decided to call him Ivan. He was always at The Palace with an older man who sat in the separate VIP lounge talking to numerous people. Going by the older man's body language, some of them were friends, some fleeting acquaintances and others were strictly business associates. Ivan stayed near him almost all the time, apart from when he was occasionally sent away by the older man. Ivan was the classic bodyguard. He was clearly interested in Viola but he also acted in a pushy, almost vulgar, manner with lots of other women in the club as well. Viola was just one of many.

Nik focused on the night of Viola's disappearance. Nothing seemed strange. The club was full as per usual and it was mostly the regular crowd. Viola was going about her work as normal. And then Nik saw something. It was just before 1.00 a.m. on 23 October. Viola had dried a chrome cocktail shaker and handed it to Finn when she stopped dead in her tracks. Her mouth was open slightly and she stared straight ahead with a mixture of fear and astonishment. The dishcloth she was using fell to the floor and she started walking backwards away from the bar, her eyes still fixed on whoever it was that had given her such a fright. She was moving towards the stairs that led to Weise's office and the back door. Nik tried to see what she was looking at but there was nothing inside the shot. Seconds later, she raced up the stairs and vanished. Nik wished he'd seen someone follow her, but nobody used that door again until the club closed. The person who'd scared her hadn't run after her.

'It had to be a weekend, didn't it!' mumbled Nik. If Viola had gone missing on a Wednesday, he would have had half as many customers to look through. He was going to be there all night, taking stills of each and every customer in the hope of finding somebody suspicious.

Six hours later he'd collected over four hundred photos and still hadn't got through everybody entering the club. The ringing of his phone jolted him out of his state of concentration and he looked around for a moment, bewildered, before remembering where he was. He noticed his extreme hunger pangs and realised he desperately needed to go to the toilet. He looked at his phone. There was only one person who'd be calling from a private number.

'It's not looking good,' said Nik.

'What d'you mean?' Jon replied.

'The footage is useless.'

'I thought you had the footage of the day Viola went missing? There has to be something.'

'Viola saw something from behind the bar, got really scared and ran. She was a confident woman and not easily shaken but whoever she saw made her nervous.'

'Can you see who it was?'

'Nope, wrong camera angle. The only thing to do is take a still of every person entering the club.'

'Jeez, how many is that?'

'Over four hundred.'

'Any familiar faces turned up yet?'

'Nobody,' replied Nik. 'No Beate Cüpper, no Tilo and no friends of hers that I'm aware of.'

'So what good are the recordings then?'

'Pretty much no good right now. And lots of people are keeping their heads down, so I can't even get a decent shot. The footage will only be useful after we've got a suspect we can compare with the stills.'

'But we don't have any suspects.'

'We have to go back to the serial killer theory,' explained Nik. 'We still don't have any link between the victims. We've got the fake farewell letters that were really well written. We've got nothing on the similarity of the deaths because we don't even know what happened to

Viola. Viola and Kathrin are similar in age and appearance, which fits the serial killer theory. But they are not so incredibly similar that other women wouldn't also fit the bill.'

'But the fake letters *are* a common thread, maybe not with the women but with the perpetrator. What is it that's still bothering you?'

'How powerful the perpetrator is,' explained Nik. 'He had a high-up CID agent on his side. And a well-known pathologist . . . and a professional handwriting forger. Not the kinds of things you can just pick up down the high street. And he managed to set the perfect trap to get me suspended. What kind of serial killer has that sort of power?'

'Look at it as an advantage,' suggested Jon. 'We're looking for a very influential person, which means we can rule out regular citizens.'

Nik took a moment to think about the comment. 'True,' he said at last.

'So, d'you know what you want to do next?'

'Can you still get on the CID network?'

'Of course.'

'Then go through all the cases from the last twelve months involving women who look like our victims. I'd set the age group to between eighteen and thirty-five. Slim, dark hair. Concentrate on violent crimes like armed robberies, rape, bodily harm and murder. Oh, and kidnap and attempted kidnap. We can rule out domestic abuse, theft, break-ins, fraud and traffic offences.' Nik could hear Jon typing. 'Use a less specific filter for the appearance. We don't want anyone to slip through the net.'

'OK,' said Jon.

'I'm gonna order something to eat and go through all the people at The Palace, even if it is unlikely to give us a new lead. Give me a call when you're done. The perpetrator's bound to hear about my visit to the club owner at some point. And I'm sure he'll try something else when he does. Very much doubt I'm gonna get away with just a suspension.'

◆ ◆ ◆

Nik was enjoying an hour of rest when he was woken by his phone ringing. Falling asleep at the desk had been a bad idea for his neck and it cracked as he straightened up to answer.

'You got something?' Nik asked, yawning.

'Uh, maybe,' Jon answered hesitantly.

'Why maybe?'

'I searched the CID database like you said and came across a woman who fits the appearance but other than that has little in common with Viola and Kathrin.'

Nik could hear Jon typing again. 'Her name's Olga Rasic. A prostitute who went missing. It was a social worker, Corinna Drung, who reported it. I've sent the files to your private email address.'

Nik opened up Jon's email and the attachment. He looked at the photo. Aside from the fact that Olga looked Eastern European, her age, face shape and hair were very similar to Viola and Kathrin's. She wore a lot of make-up and a tight leather top which clung to her chest. She looked blankly into the camera, as if she didn't care that she was about to be chucked in jail. It was probably better than going back to work on the streets.

'She was picked up a number of times for illegal prostitution at the main station and down on Schillerstraße. According to her file, she wasn't registered to work in Germany, so chances are she came over here after being promised the world and then never got away.'

'OK, so she moved in different circles to Viola and Kathrin.'

'Olga's disappearance was reported on 25 February 2016,' Jon went on. 'According to the social worker, her flatmates hadn't seen her for two days. She just never came back to the flat after work one morning. So Drung went to the police.'

'OK, so she went missing at night between the 22nd and 23rd of February.'

'Nobody noticed anything, which is pretty normal for that scene. There's no description of possible customers, no registration number or any other kind of clue.'

'I've already looked through the missing persons database,' said Nik. 'There have been no unidentified bodies in the last twelve months who match her. Olga's either still alive or her body hasn't been found yet.'

'Well, she couldn't have met our perpetrator at The Palace, because at that time it was closed for refurbishment.'

'OK. And I can't imagine she'd have gone to the same gym as Kathrin, so that's unlikely to be the common thread between them either.'

'And . . . nobody ever got a farewell letter from her. She's still registered missing. So maybe her disappearance has nothing to do with our perpetrator.'

'What've you got on this social worker?'

'Corinna Drung used to be a prostitute herself. She now supports prostitutes who are working illegally and have no health insurance. I found over twenty entries for her where she'd reported men for either bodily harm or people trafficking. Olga's disappearance was an exception. D'you want to speak to her?' asked Jon.

'No use,' replied Nik. 'Drung probably looks out for hundreds of women and wouldn't have anything on Olga's customers. I need to speak to the other prostitutes. Have you got Olga's address?'

'A flat in Schillerstraße, not far from the main station. Looks horrible.'

'It is,' agreed Nik. 'There's this dilapidated block where the girls are shacked up four or five to a room that's not even big enough for one person. I'll head over tomorrow around noon.'

'The pimps aren't gonna be happy to see you, you know?'

'Let me worry about that,' said Nik. 'A little bit of physical activity always helps clear my mind.'

The courtyard was just as dingy as the last time Nik had been there. The few bits of wall that weren't crumbling had been covered in graffiti and there were random metal rods lying around on the ground. Water was leaking out of a broken gutter from above and a thick mixture of mould and moss had started to grow where it hit the ground. The building was five storeys high and let barely any light into the narrow courtyard, and the small balconies hanging off the flats made it feel even more claustrophobic. There was a disgusting, heavy smell in the air which clung to every corner like a sticky fog. It was a mixture of rotting rubbish from the overflowing bins and cooking fat that had been used far too often.

The only improvement since last time was the lack of a dead body lying on the ground. When Nik had been there two years ago, a young prostitute with a shattered skull was lying in the middle of the courtyard, clearly too far away from the building for it to have been an accident. She had also had a swollen eye and burst lip from being beaten up not that long before. The other prostitutes in the building had been far too scared to say anything and her pimp gave some blabbering speech about suicide. So the case was declared as just that.

Nik had never managed to get Kevin Otte's contemptuous grin out of his head. It was a mixture of contempt for the police and smugness because he knew he was going to get away with everything. As if his thoughts had conjured him from thin air, the very man appeared from a small door and walked straight over to Nik. He looked exactly the same. The tattoos of the devil on his shaved head and the word 'hate' on his knuckles only riled Nik even more. The man was scum. Otte's strong, muscular body was clearly outlined beneath his black jacket and he obviously had metal caps on the tips of his combat boots. Just like the last time, he stank of sweat: a musty, filthy smell, which perfectly matched his torn, stained jeans.

'Hey, dickhead!' the pimp said, chewing on something. It looked like Nik had interrupted his dinner. 'You're on private property, so fuck off!'

'Kevin!' said Nik, like he'd just seen an old friend. He showed him his fake badge. 'You've got even less teeth than the last time we met. Get smacked in the face again or just bad dental hygiene?'

The thug looked confused for a second as he tried to work out how he knew Nik. Then it finally clicked.

'What d'you want, you prick?' Otte asked.

'Your mother never teach you any manners? Swearing at a police officer, I don't know.'

'Fuck you! Tell me why you're here or I'll smash your face in.'

'I want to talk to some prostitutes. Prostitutes who knew Olga Rasic.'

'Aren't any prostitutes here,' Otte continued. 'Just decent women who hired me to protect them from dickheads like you.' He pointed to the courtyard entrance. 'Go!'

'How about I make a suggestion? We fight on it.' Nik pointed to his clenched right fist. 'If I win, I'll walk around and speak to the decent women. And if you win, I'll disappear and never come back.'

'You really think I'm stupid enough to fight a copper?'

'Oh no. I think you're much more stupid than that. But how about I make it easy for you?' Nik threw his badge over his head behind him and took off his jacket. 'See, now I'm not a copper.'

Otte grinned and threw a left-handed cross as hard as he could. Nik managed to bend back a bit, but he still got hit hard in the face.

'Not bad,' said Nik, spitting out the blood that had run down from his nose into his mouth. Otte didn't stop – he cracked Nik on the chin and rammed his fist into his stomach twice. He pushed Nik backwards, then piled in with a second round. Nik protected his head with his arms and doubled his body over, trying to dodge to one side. But Otte followed and threw a punch so hard, it emptied Nik's lungs. He fell to his knees, gasping for breath.

'What the fuck?' Otte cried. 'Is this a fight or d'you want the shit kicked out of you?'

Nik hummed a tune.

'What the hell is this?'

'It's no wonder a dipshit like you likes the Nine Inch Nails.' Nik sprang to his feet, threw a tidy punch to Otte's face, dodged quickly out of the way and hooked him hard in the ribs.

'I just needed a bit of a thrashing so I could see things clearly again,' Nik said as Otte winced back at him. 'I prefer it to yoga, even if it does have a few painful side effects.' Now it was time for Nik's second round. He used exactly the same sequence. 'Plus, I used the opportunity to study you.' Otte bawled from the double blows and stumbled backwards. 'You almost always hit with the left and you kept your right arm locked in tight . . . like you were trying to protect something. In your case, a broken rib.'

'Wanker!' Otte screamed. For a moment, his rage erased any pain and he started to swing his arm. But Nik ducked down quickly and on his way back up, kneed Otte powerfully between the legs.

'And the way you pull your arm back before you punch. Looks like you're on the phone, mate.' Nik shook his head as Otte fell to the ground, groaning. 'Thanks for that. Always good to know where the punch is coming from. Gives me time to get out of the way. And that hook! The way your hip always buckles so I know which punch is coming before you even raise a fist.' Nik stood directly in front of Otte. 'Now, if you did any training, you'd admit defeat and give me a tour, but unfortunately you're just a piece-of-shit pimp, so I'll need to meet the women myself.' He rammed his knee into Otte's chin and watched his bald head bouncing unconscious on the floor.

Nik pulled a knife and a knuckleduster from Otte's jacket and tied him up with his leather jacket. It turned out they'd attracted quite an audience. Nik lifted his head to see a group of young women moving away from the window and curtains falling back into place. He rubbed his knuckles, trying to soothe the pain and went in the door Otte had come out of. He entered a small, rotten kitchen where the smell of old cooking oil almost choked him. He washed the blood from his face at a filthy metal sink that had turned brown. He was going to look pretty broken for the next couple of days but that would actually be an advantage for what he was planning. Fear was an ally if you knew how to use it. His show in the courtyard had fulfilled its purpose.

He went up the creaking staircase, taking his time. He heard women whispering in another language. They sounded scared, almost panicked, but as he got to the first floor they went silent. Nik opened the door on the right-hand side of the corridor. The room was just as dirty and decaying as the outside of the building. The wallpaper was torn and stained. Cables were exposed on the walls and the only light came from a grimy light bulb in the centre of the ceiling. There were three girls to the one old and worn-out sofa bed, and other than a mirror on the wall, the room was bare: no furniture, no pictures, no ornaments. Not even an old TV.

The air was damp and warm. Condensation dripped heavily down the window in the corner and a layer of mould grew around the frame. The three women were standing against the wall on the right side of the room, none of them showing an inch of fear. They just stood there looking down at the ground. You could tell from their body language that they'd all been hurt so badly they were immune to the threat of violence. Any hope they might once have had of getting out of the hell they'd landed in was well and truly gone. Nik would have loved to get the women out of there: find them a decent flat, get them out of the sex trade, but that wasn't going to save anybody. In fact, it would do exactly the opposite. Nik knew the way Otte would take his rage out on these girls after being beaten up. But this was his only option.

'I'm looking for someone who used to know Olga Rasic,' Nik said immediately. He didn't try to console the girls and didn't show his badge. It felt horrible but it would be better for everybody if he just got out of there as quickly as possible. A woman with dyed pink hair and smelling of cheap perfume stepped forward. She had tried to make herself look older by wearing blusher and eyeliner but Nik could still make out the smooth, teenage facial features. She was a pretty girl but any sense of youth was gone. No sparkle in her eye, no smile. And she'd applied much more concealer to her right eye. Probably to cover up a bruise. She wore a baggy, stretched jumper that fell over her hips, as if she was trying to conceal anything alluring about her body.

'I knew Olga,' she said with a Russian accent.

'What's your name?'

'Roswitha.'

Nik waved her over to the hallway and closed the door behind them. 'What happened to Olga?' He spoke quietly. He didn't want the others to hear what she said.

'One day, she just never came home,' said Roswitha without any emotion. 'Like lots of us.'

Nik closed his eyes and suppressed a sigh. He might not work in vice but he knew all too well how these women lived. They were a commodity. And when they couldn't work anymore, they'd be shifted out. Some would be sold, with the lucky ones ending up in a brothel, while the not so lucky ones might find themselves with some sick punter who'd live out his sadistic fantasies before getting rid of the dead body.

'Did you notice anything strange about that day?'

Roswitha shook her head. 'We were near the main station. I had a customer who'd paid me for the whole night, so I never saw who Olga drove away with. And then she wasn't there when I got back. The pimps looked for her the next day but never found her.'

'Did any of the other girls see anything?'

'No. It was too long ago,' she replied. 'All the ones who knew Olga are gone.' Roswitha lowered her gaze. Nik recognised the dark place the girl was in and paused for a moment.

'Did she maybe run off or hide somewhere?'

'Olga didn't have the nerve for something like that. She wouldn't have done it even if she'd had the chance. She would've preferred to die in this prison than go it alone out there,' explained the girl. 'And the pimps had her passport anyway. They told her if she ever got in any trouble, they'd go to her family in her home country.'

'What can you tell me about Olga?'

'She came from a small village where it was impossible to live a decent life. She dreamed of becoming a model and made her way to Prague, but then the agency turned out to be a sham. A day later she woke up in a freight container on the way to Munich. She'd been pumped full of drugs, abused and robbed of everything. Her money, her passport and her phone. She tried to defend herself to begin with but it didn't last long and the next day, she had her first punter.'

'Where did she work?'

'We were mostly at the main station or here in Schillerstraße. Sometimes we got special jobs.'

'Special how?'

'As escorts for businessmen or hostesses at parties.'

'Did Olga get more special work than other girls? Did she have a sugar daddy?'

'No, nothing like that.'

'So which jobs did Olga get?'

'Two nights at the opening of a strip club in Schillerstraße. Then a New Year's party at some sports agent's house. Luckily enough there were so many drugs at that party that most of the guests were out of it.' She closed her eyes. 'And the last one was an expensive rehab clinic for addicts. The patients were allowed visits from women every two weeks.'

'What was the sports agent called?' asked Nik. 'And do you know the name of the clinic?'

'We never got any names or knew where we were being taken,' said Roswitha. 'We were packed in the back of a van with no windows. I know the sports agent didn't live far from here but the clinic was out of town. We were on the road for about half an hour. Absolute agony in a van with no seats or cushions. It was out in some wood with no other houses nearby.' She shrugged her shoulders. 'It was all so long ago. I can only *just* remember Olga.'

Nik sighed. None of this was very informative. A sports agent might show up in the photos from The Palace but even then it would still be difficult to link him to Viola and Kathrin.

'Thank you,' said Nik with a smile, and without another word, he turned around and went downstairs. He knew he couldn't change the world or save the women but he still felt guilty as he left the courtyard.

◆　◆　◆

Sara looked down at the pool of blood on the filthy courtyard ground, her arms crossed. She had a pretty good idea of how the fight had gone. Her blonde ponytail fell past her right shoulder and over her large breasts, which pressed against her black jacket. Her glowing skin and blue eyes would have been more fitting on a Swedish runner but then her big nose and sickly yellow teeth, stained from all the cigarettes and coffee, ruined that image. A large man in a black jacket was waiting beside her. He stood in a military position with his hands crossed behind his back. His figure was impressive. Two feet taller than the woman, with wide shoulders and enormous arms. His black hair was short and he had a well-groomed goatee which hid his small lips. The only thing ruining his stylish businessman look was the scar that ran from his left eyebrow over to his ear. He was looking at Kevin Otte, who was holding an ice-pack to his chin and shifting nervously from side to side. He kept his gaze on the woman, not daring to speak or move from the spot.

Finally, Sara lifted her head.

'I'll keep this short,' she began with a direct voice. 'Was this the man who beat you up?' She held up a photo and showed it to Otte.

'That's the wanker,' he confirmed.

'Nik Pohl. CID officer until not that long ago.' She put the picture back in her pocket.

'Give me that fucker's address and I'll put his lights out.'

'We'll deal with him.'

'Then I'm coming with you. Nobody beats me up and . . .'

In one fast move Sara grabbed an extendable baton from her jacket and before it was fully extended, hit Otte in the face with it. He hadn't been expecting the blow. His nose broke and blood streamed on to his shirt. He groaned loudly and fell to the ground.

'I don't like saying things twice.' Her voice was quiet as she pushed the baton together and slipped it back in her pocket. 'You had your chance and you obviously blew it.' She pointed to the bloodstains on the ground. The large man stepped behind him. Otte screamed as his arm was twisted sharply behind his back. But his screams were cut off abruptly as the man's foot stamped on his head and stayed there, pinning him to the ground.

'So . . . you'll forget the name Nik Pohl,' she ordered. 'You won't look for him, you won't ask anyone for him, and if you run into him on the street, you'll turn around and run away.'

'OK, OK,' moaned Otte.

The man with the scar tightened his grip around Otte's arm further just to make sure he got the message. When he was satisfied, he let go and moved to stand beside the woman again.

'And now fetch the whore Pohl was speaking to.'

It wasn't easy getting up. Blood dripped from his nose and he was holding his injured arm. Finally back on his legs, he staggered inside the building. A minute later, he was coming out again, pulling a girl behind him by the hair. He walked so fast the girl could barely keep up. Her cheek was swollen and her jumper was badly torn. Her eyeliner had run down her face and her eyes were bloodshot. When Otte was two metres in front of Sara, he gave a last tug on the girl's hair, throwing her to the ground.

Sara shook her head at Otte as if to show her disapproval of such violent behaviour. She looked at him and quickly signalled towards the door with her head. It was time for him to leave. He clenched his fists and looked at her for a moment in disbelief. Maybe he didn't like being sent away or maybe he had something to say, but in the end he turned around silently and went back inside.

The large man lifted the girl to her feet and straightened out her jumper.

'What's your name?' Sara asked.

'Roswitha,' the girl replied quietly.

'Did you speak to this man?' She pulled out the photo again and showed it to her.

Roswitha nodded. 'Who is he?' she asked.

'What did he want to know?' asked Sara, ignoring her question.

'He asked about Olga.'

'Olga Rasic?'

'Yes.'

Sara pressed her lips together and looked at the man. He looked worried for a second.

'What's happened to Olga?' asked Roswitha. 'Is she OK? Do you know . . .'

Sara shot her hand forward and grabbed Roswitha by the throat.

'You're here to *answer* questions. Not ask them. You've already caused enough trouble by speaking to Nik fucking Pohl.'

'But you should've seen him,' she replied, wheezing through the grip. 'How he beat up Kevin and threw him on the ground. What was I supposed to do?'

'Not say anything! You fuck him or you jump out the fucking window . . . but you don't say a fucking thing. Not about Olga, not about anything,' answered Sara, letting her go.

'She's been gone so long, I hardly know anything about her anyway,' she said, trying to defend herself.

'Well, we'll soon find out if that's the case.' Sara watched a snowflake as it fluttered to the ground and started to melt. 'But we can discuss this inside that shithole you call home.' She nodded towards the kitchen. 'Air the room and make some coffee. We'll be there in a minute.'

While Roswitha walked inside, her head hung low, Sara turned to the man beside her. 'I underestimated Pohl, Zeljko. I thought he'd be out of the picture once he was suspended.'

'Why's he doing this?' Zeljko asked. 'No one in the CID told him to look at the case and it's not like he's got a personal connection.'

'If Tilo hadn't messed up, then we wouldn't have to ask that question.'

'We should sort this out ourselves.'

'No. As long as I don't know the background, it's too risky,' explained Sara. 'Pohl is a disaster. Most people in his situation would have drunk themselves to death. He's working with someone, and we need to find out who it is.'

'OK. Then let's send them both a clear message.'

Sara nodded. 'But first of all, coffee.' She signalled with her head towards the kitchen.

'I've never been part of an investigation before,' said Balthasar. You could hear his agitation over the phone. 'At least not on the investigator side,' he added. The pathologist had annoyed Jon with so many messages that in the end, Jon had just asked him to join the conversation. Nik didn't care. Balthasar was already so involved, he could've already blabbered to someone by now.

'How'd it go with the prostitutes?' Jon asked.

'Um . . . refreshing.' Nik rubbed his swollen nose tenderly. 'But not very enlightening.' He went to the fridge and grabbed a beer. 'I only found one woman who knew Olga. But she never saw who Olga got into a car with that night or who might have abducted her.' Nik squeezed the telephone between his shoulder and ear and opened up the bottle. 'She wasn't sold on, because after she disappeared her pimps went crazy and tried to find her.'

'Maybe the men finally found Olga and shot her,' suggested Balthasar.

'People traffickers like this work with the women's fears,' explained Nik. 'They do kill, but in this case they would've beaten her half to death and then shot her in front of the other prostitutes just to show them what happens to someone who doesn't obey the rules.'

'What could the woman tell you about Olga?' asked Jon.

'She didn't have a sugar daddy or a regular customer who wanted to save her. She was just a normal prostitute who one day went out to work at the main station and never came home. Her colleague also told me about some special jobs for a sports agent and in a rehab clinic, but she couldn't tell me any names.'

'Rehab clinic?' asked Balthasar.

'Apparently there are these parties with prostitutes for the patients.'

'Hmm,' said Balthasar.

'Why a rehab clinic?' asked Jon.

'Disulfiram,' replied Balthasar.

'What?' asked Nik.

'Disulfiram. It's a drug that can be used to treat alcohol addiction. It inhibits the enzyme acetaldehyde dehydrogenase, which is used by the body to convert alcohol into acetaldehyde. As a result, there's a build-up of acetaldehyde which causes the acetaldehyde syndrome.'

'Didn't understand a word,' said Nik.

'It's basically a drug that makes you feel bad when you drink alcohol. The resulting acetaldehyde syndrome is actually just poisoning. It starts off with sweating and flushing of the skin which leads to intense itching, all of which is still harmless. What *is* dangerous, however, is the increased heart rate and strong fluctuations in blood pressure. After that, there is normally sickness, stomach cramps and breathlessness.'

'Sounds like a good remedy for alcohol addiction,' Nik remarked.

'And that's exactly what it is. But disulfiram can only be used if the patient plays along. If you drink one too many with the substance in your system, it's over. The doctor can't take any risks.'

'And how is this useful to us?'

'I found traces of disulfiram in Kathrin's blood,' said Balthasar. 'I didn't think twice because her liver showed no signs of cirrhosis but together with the addiction clinic it's certainly noteworthy.'

'So could Kathrin have been in the rehab clinic when Olga was working there?' Nik wondered aloud. 'Yes, that makes sense. I meant to ask whether you found any traces of drugs in Kathrin's body because her friend told me she'd had problems with drink and drugs in the past but had got treatment. Said when Kathrin disappeared, she was worried she'd relapsed.'

'Well, that would certainly explain the disulfiram.'

'Could Kathrin have taken it for some other reason or by mistake?'

'Unlikely.'

'I didn't find anything related to any health treatment,' said Jon. 'There was nothing mentioned on social media and no payments from her bank account.'

'Well, it isn't the kind of drug that's pushed on the street, is it. Anyway, don't expect she'd want to broadcast her problems to the world. But where would she have got it?'

'There are quite a few rehab clinics in the Munich region,' said Balthasar. 'Do you have any idea which one it could be?'

'The woman said it was about a half hour journey from the flat and situated near a forest, far away from any houses.'

'Well, Munich doesn't have any remote clinics near to any woods,' Jon remarked.

'Half an hour from Schillerstraße and you are outside Munich. Depending on the traffic and time of day you could get to Fürstenfeldbruck, Anzing or maybe even Starnberg. The last two places in particular have a lot of wooded areas.' Jon was typing enthusiastically in the background. 'But there aren't any rehab clinics out there.'

'You mentioned Starnberg,' said Balthasar. 'There's a very exclusive country beauty resort near there. There's a well-known rumour that it's actually a rehab clinic.'

'What's the place called?'

'Meadows Beauty Resort.'

'There's a website with very little information,' said Jon after searching for a moment. 'A photo of the main building, an email address and a phone number. Then some text about micro-needling, HydraFacial and laser treatments. Nothing about withdrawal.'

'Could be a cover,' said Nik. 'Having absolutely nothing online would be suspicious, so it's better to have a website saying nothing.'

'How can we get in?' asked Jon. 'It's not like we can call up and ask about Kathrin Glosemeier or ask when the next prostitute party is.'

'If the resort really is that exclusive, I won't get near the entrance before security picks me up.'

'Then we should have Nik referred,' suggested Balthasar.

'I don't drink that much beer these days.'

'Money wouldn't be an issue,' said Jon.

'But money on its own isn't enough,' Balthasar explained. 'With this kind of place, you need to have a pretty good contact, or something of the sort.'

'Do you know anyone?'

'I'll need to ask around,' said Balthasar. 'But I think there's one person who could help.'

'The quicker the better.' Nik suddenly heard a strange noise, like a rope being pulled tight and squeaking over wood. It was coming from the staircase. 'Wait a minute.' He stood up, turned on the hall light and opened the flat door. The noise got louder. One metre above the staircase on the next floor up he saw Roswitha hanging with a rope around her neck, jerking frantically as she struggled to breathe. Her tongue was hanging out of her mouth and her face had turned blue. She had a cut on her forehead, her eyes were swollen and her lips were burst. Her fingers were cramping up around the noose and her legs were flapping as she tried to reach the bannister to stabilise herself. Nik shot forward, untied her lower legs and lifted her up. 'Help!' His voice echoed up the staircase. 'Somebody help!' he called out. But there was no answer. He looked up. Roswitha's head hung lifelessly to the side. She'd stopped breathing. 'Jon! Balthasar! Call an ambulance!' Someone on the floor below opened a door. 'A knife!' Nik screamed. 'Bring me a fucking knife!'

It seemed an eternity before he was able to cut the rope and lay Roswitha on the floor. He tried to resuscitate her but she wouldn't breathe. At some point, a paramedic pushed him out of the way and put an oxygen mask on her. Soon after, she was on her way to hospital, still unconscious.

Chapter 8

The crime scene investigators packed away the rope and looked for fingerprints on the rails. The blue light from the police car blinked through the window in the staircase, its usual glare softened somewhat by the falling snow. It was particularly heavy tonight, as if it was trying to erase the evil act with a layer of purity. Nik sat on the floor outside his flat, watching the group of investigators and playing subconsciously with the locket around his neck. All of a sudden, Danilo and his boss were amongst the group. He hadn't even noticed them come into the building.

'Everything OK, Nik?' asked Naumann.

'No, it's not,' Nik answered, irritated. 'A young woman was just murdered outside my front door, and when I noticed, it was too late.'

'She's still alive, Nik. But she's in a coma,' said Danilo.

'Yeah, well, it'd be better for her if she was dead. Whatever's waiting for her on the other side can't be worse than this.' He turned to his ex-colleague. 'Did you see the mess she was in? Bleeding from her head, her face swollen from being hit?'

'Did you know her?'

'No,' Nik answered. There was no use in telling the truth. They wouldn't be any help. And anyway, he couldn't trust anyone as long as Tilo's partner was still out there.

'The girl's name is Roswitha Sowa,' said Danilo. 'We've already got her fingerprints in the system. She's been picked up numerous times for illegal prostitution. Does the name mean anything?'

Nik shook his head. 'Maybe you should ask her pimp.'

'We will,' said Naumann. 'Do you know why she was here?'

Because somebody wasn't happy I'd asked her questions and they wanted to send me a message, Nik thought to himself while shaking his head slowly.

'Does someone in the building get regular visits from prostitutes?'

'I barely know who lives here and I couldn't care less what they get up to. But I know none of them would've tied a rope around that girl's neck and hanged her for the sake of it.'

'We can't rule out suicide.'

'Bullshit, Danilo,' said Nik. 'You obviously didn't see the look in her eyes when she cramped up. Pulling hopelessly at the rope and trying to catch a breath. She was scared to die and tried as hard as she could to save herself.' He turned to Naumann. 'Let the investigators inspect Roswitha. They'll find signs of that. Then lose the bullshit suicide theory and find the evil bastards who did it.'

'We'll do everything in our power to—'

'Yeah, yeah,' interrupted Nik, standing up and going into his flat. 'I'll come into the station tomorrow and give a statement. Don't bother me again tonight.' He pushed the door shut and called Jon.

'How's it looking?' asked Jon.

'Not good. Roswitha's in a coma. Five seconds earlier and I could've saved her.'

'How did this happen? You were at the prostitutes' place just a couple of hours ago.'

'I was careful,' said Nik. 'Their pimp was the only man there and I spoke to Roswitha quietly in the hall. The other women couldn't have heard a thing, even if they'd put their ears up to the door. I'd hoped the girls were tight . . . that nobody would say anything. Apparently that was a fucking stupid idea.'

'It's not your fault.'

'Yes, it is, Jon,' Nik responded. 'If I hadn't gone to that flat and spoken to Roswitha, she wouldn't have ended up battered and fighting for her life in hospital.' He sat back down on the couch. 'Whoever's behind the disappearances and Kathrin's death wanted to warn me and show me who's in charge. They wanted me to know they're watching me and that they'll sabotage every attempt I make to find out who they are. And they definitely can't risk Roswitha waking up again.' Nik sighed. 'Look, Jon, I've no idea what you're capable of with your money and computer skills but that girl has to be admitted into another hospital under another name. You'll get whatever you want from me.'

'I'll deal with that,' Jon promised. 'Nothing'll happen to her. But first of all we need to get you out of your flat.'

'Don't worry about me. Nobody's going to put a rope around my neck and chuck me over a bannister.'

'That's not what I mean, Nik,' said Jon. 'As long as they know where to find you, we can't get on with the investigation. The pimp you beat up won't have been given the same instructions as the owner of The Palace. Someone followed you.'

'I would've noticed.'

'No, you wouldn't. Not with today's technology,' said Jon. 'The transmitters these days are minuscule and can be easily stuck to clothes. Your follower can be three streets behind you and they still won't lose you. Your flat might not be bugged but your car's got a tracker on it that you just can't see.'

'So what d'you suggest?'

'I've got a flat you can go to. You'll be safe there. I'll send the address to your new phone. Check your clothes for transmitters and don't take anything that isn't essential. Don't take the car, and slip out during the night. Go by taxi or public transport so no one can follow you. And lastly, you'll need a new look. We were going to do that to get you into the rehab clinic anyway, so we'll just do it a bit sooner.'

Nik let out a crabby groan. Jon's suggestions all made sense. He just really didn't want to go to the hairdresser.

'I can't be seen in public,' Jon continued, 'so I'll ask Balthasar to drive you around. I need to deal with Roswitha. Her attacker won't take long to find out where she is. And they won't mess up a second time.'

'All right,' said Nik. 'Hope you've got a big fridge in this flat.'

'Oh, don't worry. I'm sure you'll be satisfied.'

It was strange waking up in someone else's bedroom, but Nik was sure he could get used to his new luxury accommodation. There was a deluxe box-spring bed, the water from the showerhead didn't spurt in every possible direction and he could follow the latest news on a small screen in the bathroom while he brushed his teeth. The living room was equally as lavish. There was a projector instead of a television. The surround sound was exceptional, and Jon had signed up for every streaming service money could buy. And most importantly, the freezer would fit enough food for a month and you could slide a whole crate of beer directly into the bottom of the fridge. But the material joy didn't last for long. As soon as he woke up, pictures of Roswitha came flooding back to him. He thought about her blue, bloodless face and the cut on her head. About all the punches she must have endured because she'd spoken to him. Jon had at least managed to get her on a different ward and changed her name in the hospital database. That gave Nik a slight sense of peace but he still felt guilty.

It was eight in the morning. Balthasar would be there in a minute to pick him up. He was in charge of getting Nik ready for his visit to the exclusive addiction clinic, whatever that might entail. Nik got dressed and finished off another coffee from the automatic machine before shuffling his way outside. The pathologist was standing beside a yellow Z4 Cabrio with white leather seats and a wooden dashboard. As if that wasn't eccentric enough, he was wearing black and white striped trousers and a white blazer with one blue arm. Underneath that, he wore a dark blue shirt, which clung to his belly, and on his feet he wore light beige loafers. He had blusher on his cheeks and his bald head looked like it had been oiled.

'Hello, Nik,' Balthasar said, hugging him.

Nik was so flabbergasted by the pathologist's appearance he went along with the hug. 'Please tell me this wasn't what you meant when you talked about pimping me up,' Nik said, looking Balthasar up and down.

'Oh, Nik, you don't have the figure for Jean-Paul Gaultier.'

'What a pity,' mumbled Nik as he got in the car. The smell inside was so strong he almost choked. 'What is that stench?'

'It's called "Wow!". It's one of my favourite scents,' answered Balthasar with pride. 'Very aromatic, with a hint of vanilla.'

'Did you spill it on the floor or something?' Nik scrunched up his nose and let down the window despite it being freezing outside.

'No, I always add it to my screenwash so I can stay fresh during the ride.'

Nik was about to make a comment but Balthasar started the engine and pushed down hard on the accelerator. The car flew forward. They avoided a collision with a truck only because the driver slammed on his brakes. Balthasar then did a one-eighty on the street. Nik clawed at the armrests and frantically tried to put on his seat belt.

'Fucking wanker!' bawled the truck driver, while Balthasar smiled and gave a casual little wave. Before reaching their destination, Balthasar went through three red lights and took a shortcut down a one-way street in the wrong direction. When they stopped, Nik was shaking and only just managed to suppress the urge to make the sign of the cross. At least the drive had woken him up.

'We'll start with the hair.' Balthasar pulled him into an old, beautifully restored block of flats. The entire ground floor was filled with expensive shops and Balthasar pushed open one of the doors, gesturing for Nik to follow him. He found himself in an entrance area made of light marble; the ceiling was covered with small lights that gave off a warm white light. The only dash of colour came from the large flowers placed in gold, thigh-high vases. The look was completed by a Mies van der Rohe-style sofa which sat underneath a shop logo made out of silver. God only knew if it was a hairdresser or an exclusive boutique.

Nik jumped at the sound of a screeching voice. 'Balthasar!' called out a man with the pitch of a teenage girl at a boy-band concert.

'Charles!' Balthasar cried back, equally as excited. He kissed the small, slim man on both cheeks. The hairdresser had long dark eyelashes and brilliantly white teeth and appeared to have the same taste in clothing as the pathologist, but instead of trousers he was wearing a long skirt that went all the way down to his black loafers. He wore a long-sleeved top with a bizarre pattern and a high, tight collar. His short, white, wavy hair had been combed over to the left and his head was shaved at the sides. Below that he had sideburns which snaked down his cheeks before merging into a full dark beard that had clearly been dyed.

'This is Nik,' Balthasar introduced him. 'Your job is to turn this man into a good-looking, well-groomed upstart.'

'I'm the best hairdresser in Munich, my dear, not a miracle worker,' Charles said, inspecting Nik's hair.

'He needs to play a role for a couple of days.'

The hairdresser sighed loudly. 'I hope you've got an unlimited credit card with you. I'll need an Ayurvedic weekend myself when I'm finished with this one.'

'Excuse me. I'm standing right here.' Nik was pissed off.

'Oh! He can talk,' remarked Charles. 'Well, that's a surprise. I was scared for a second he was going to swing from chandelier to chandelier, banging his chest triumphantly.'

'Oh, don't be fooled. He's not far off,' added Balthasar.

Nik straightened up, raising his right index finger. 'If you two don't shut the fuck up, someone's getting a smack in the face.'

'Oh! All these violent threats. How old-fashioned.' Charles placed his own index finger on his lips and shook his head. 'But I must admit, I do like the rough, unrestrained type. Steered back on track, he could really be something. I mean, he's certainly strong.'

'Forget it,' said Balthasar. 'He eats far too much pork and onions for that. And I know how strongly you react to seeping odours.'

'Tragic.' Charles sighed. 'Well, before we start changing his dietary habits, let's get started with the hair.' He pushed Nik into a room with a marble floor and sunlight streaming in through the windows. Six white leather chairs stood in front of large mirrors. Each chair had its own wash basin and individual chandelier. One quick shove and Nik was sitting in one of the chairs.

'Hmm, I think I'll have to use gloves for this bushy undergrowth. I only just had my nails done. Balthasar!' He waved towards a chrome fridge. 'Be a doll and grab a bottle of Prosecco. I won't get out of this alive without alcohol.'

'Got any beer?' asked Nik.

'Excuse me?' said Charles, appalled. 'We are a respectable salon.'

While Charles worked, Nik was forced to endure an almost unbearable monologue about haircuts, care products, styling and various other beauty-related topics. After an hour of torture, as pretty much each hair on his head was being individually wrapped in tinfoil, Nik longed for his old hairdresser across the road from his flat. He was short-sighted, eternally grumpy and drank too much, but at least he didn't blabber on about mind-numbing drivel and only took ten minutes to cut his hair.

It was a further hour before a disgruntled Nik was allowed to leave the salon. A visit to the hairdresser was usually a chance for Nik to think about work but the men's incessant talking, punctuated by effeminate giggles, had almost driven him crazy.

'A new man!' said Balthasar as he got into the car.

'I've no idea why you need two hours for a man's haircut.' Nik folded down the mirror on the passenger's seat. 'Colour, shorter at the sides and a razor to the back of the neck,' said Nik. 'Could've done that myself.'

'Well, you've only ever been to crappy barbers, so you wouldn't know the difference,' said Balthasar with a soft laugh. 'But the professionals recognise the work of a master and that's what counts.'

'Can we just go and buy some clothes so I can get back to investigating?'

'Oh, we're not just buying clothes,' Balthasar said, starting the engine. 'We're going to one of the best men's outfitters in the city.' He waved a platinum credit card in the air. 'So please, try not to bite or shoot anyone.'

'Oh, don't worry. You're first on my list for shooting right now,' Nik retaliated with a smile.

Balthasar slammed on the accelerator and Nik flew back hard against his seat. 'Let's go!' cried the pathologist, going through the first red light of the trip.

There had been no new leads over the last few days. Nik couldn't bring himself to question anyone else for fear they'd suffer the same fate as Roswitha. According to the reports on the CID server, his colleagues hadn't found any more clues. No one in the building had seen or heard anything before Nik had found Roswitha. The majority of fingerprints on the bannister were from the people living in the block and the others weren't in the database. The only DNA on the rope belonged to Roswitha, who was still in hospital in a coma. The only positive thing to happen was that Balthasar had found a contact to get Nik a referral for the rehab clinic. Nik didn't know whether Jon had paid a generous sum to get it but he also didn't care. The Meadows Beauty Resort was the best lead they had and money didn't seem to be an issue for Jon.

It was odd travelling with leather suitcases, packed neatly with made-to-measure suits, designer shirts and brogues. Nik had barely recognised himself when, wearing a dark grey suit, a silk tie and a pocket handkerchief, he'd looked in the mirror in the changing room of the ridiculously expensive shop Balthasar had insisted they buy his clothes from.

Well, you certainly ain't no Tom Ford, but it's an immense improvement for someone who normally looks like a homeless person, had been Balthasar's comment. Jon had also given him a Breitling watch that cost more than Nik's entire yearly wage.

In keeping with his character, Nik was driven to the clinic in a limousine. He attempted to look bored and sipped on a brandy from the mini bar. But as soon as they'd got out of the city, he started mentally recording every detail.

After leaving the A95, they drove for a while along a quiet country road before turning down a narrow track. The clinic owners had probably planned the bumps and twists to deter unwanted guests. The CCTV started after the third bend in the road. Nik spotted a camera hidden in a wire fence that was overgrown with plants and bushes. Only a very observant passer-by would notice it, as it had been painted green and was well camouflaged. Nik knew the camera model. It had a very high resolution, a good zoom and an infrared function that could pick up lots of details even in very low light.

A minute later and they were approaching the beauty resort. There was very little to see from the outside. The place was surrounded by a four-metre-high wall plastered smooth and painted, which, in turn, was surrounded by high trees, cut back on one side to prevent the branches overhanging the wall, while the side facing the forest had been left to grow naturally. It would be impossible to scale the wall without any kind of aid. The only way in and out of the grounds was through a large gate with an intercom system and camera.

The driver said Nik's cover name, Nikolas Kirchhof, into the microphone and the gate opened. Nik had wanted to keep his own forename so that there was no chance of giving himself away if he introduced himself as Nik. And he'd been more than happy to get rid of the 'u' in Nikolaus. He'd taken Jon's surname as that would match the money transfers. Nikolas Kirchhof was a bored, drug-addicted playboy who'd been referred by his parents.

The gate was made of long steel poles staggered vertically one on top of the other so nobody could squeeze between them or see through them. After the gate was fully opened, they went down a walled drive which had space for just one car, until they came to a second gate. The gate opened on to what looked like another world.

The drive was laid with light stone slabs and led past a large fountain, fed with water from a man-made stream that ran from the woods, which was still flowing despite the temperature being well below zero. The clinic building itself was a large manor house with a white façade, elegant plastering and bright red bricks. The walls were adorned with small, warm lights that made you forget about the dreary January weather. A bed of vibrant roses ran alongside the fountain. You could only tell they were artificial if you looked very hard.

As the car stopped at the main entrance, a young woman opened his door, while an Eastern European-looking man unloaded his suitcases from the limousine boot.

'Welcome to The Meadows, Herr Kirchhof,' the woman said, bowing slightly. 'My name is Pia. I'll be making sure your stay with us is as comfortable as possible. If you ever need anything, please don't hesitate to ask.'

Pia was a combination of a model and a fitness instructor. She was about a foot smaller than Nik, with long blonde hair that had been pulled into a neat ponytail. She wore a beige outfit that showed off her sporty figure but was still professionally appropriate. Her make-up was subtle and she wore a very delicate, fresh perfume. Nik guessed she was in her mid-twenties. Her skin was flawless and she had a friendly, genuine smile. Her blue eyes glittered in a way that suggested she was more than just a receptionist.

'Now, if you'd like, I can show you to the check-in area.'

'Thank you, that'd be great.' Nik stepped out of the car. He remembered Balthasar's prep talk: polite but not too friendly, consider the biggest luxuries to be the norm, have special requests but don't be too eccentric, etcetera, etcetera. The lecture might have given Nik a headache but he seemed to know what he was talking about. If only Balthasar had had undercover experience, he would have been perfect for the rehab job.

The check-in area consisted of a marble table and three comfortable chairs. The woman sat down opposite him, opened a folder and took out a Montblanc pen. 'Can I get you anything at the moment?' she asked.

'A coffee with soya milk and something sweet, please,' answered Nik. 'I never got round to lunch. Normally I'm just getting up at this time.'

It was 6 p.m. The patients had probably had hours of aquajogging and Pilates by now but Pia maintained her friendly, neutral face and passed on Nik's order. After just one minute of small talk about Nik's journey from Munich, a silver tray was delivered. On top of it stood a porcelain cup full of steaming coffee, a small jug of soya milk, a mini chocolate croissant, some peeled mango and a macaroon.

'Today we'd like to give you the chance to get to know the resort,' said Pia. 'Your belongings will all be unpacked by staff and your room will be prepared as requested. You will find four bottles of Cape Karoo mineral water in your fridge and our concierge has passed on your preferred coffee brand to our kitchen team. These are the people who will be organising your spiritual food throughout your stay. You can also help yourself to a selection of açaí bowls for breakfast.'

Nik had no idea what Pia was talking about. Balthasar had been in charge of any correspondence before his stay. Pia leaned forward and lowered her voice. 'We've left a colonic cleanser set and some saline solution in the bathroom so you can deal with your faecal blockages.'

'Thank you,' said Nik calmly, while thinking about all the ways he was going to torture Balthasar to death when he left the clinic.

'We'll get started with your treatment plan tomorrow,' the woman continued in a business-like manner. 'We deliberately avoid the use of medication and use a dual approach, which includes spoken therapy with Dr Alois Perlick and physical detoxification, led by Dr Rafael Gawinski and his team of nutritionists and sports physicians. You will feel like a different person by the time you leave,' Pia concluded.

'I can't wait.' Nik had to try very hard not to sound sarcastic.

'Great. Then if you wouldn't mind, I'd like you to sign our agreement.' Pia spread out three sheets in front of him. 'The first one gives us permission to confiscate your mobile phone and look through your luggage.' She gave a brief smile. 'A lot of patients try to smuggle in drugs and alcohol, which are strictly forbidden here.'

'No problem.' Nik took the pen and signed his fake name.

'The second form gives Dr Perlick consent to decide when you have completed the healing process and send you home.'

This was new to Nik. 'You mean I give him . . . ?'

'I hope you understand. Our main concern is your welfare. Your family members have also agreed that we can take you into our custodial care.' She pointed to her folder and smiled even wider. 'I promise, you will have everything you need here. We have swimming pools, massage therapy and a large sauna area. You also have a large selection of streaming services in your room.'

Nik wasn't sure if such a contract was even legal. Reluctantly, he signed the sheet. Jon and Balthasar had gone to a lot of bother to make up a false family background. He wasn't going to waste it all over something so small.

'And by signing the third form, you agree to the treatment methods. All the risks and side effects were sent to you beforehand by email.'

It would've been nice if I'd actually been forwarded the email, Nik thought while signing the third sheet.

'Thank you.' Pia closed the folder. 'Shall I show you to your room?' She gestured towards a corridor that led further into the building.

The splendour of the exterior and the reception area didn't diminish. But Nik wasn't interested in the expensive paintings, the soft background music or the exotic fish in the aquarium. It was the high-grade locks on the doors and the security glass in the windows that were grabbing his attention. It was going to be almost impossible to break open any doors.

As Nik arrived in his room, a stocky man was hanging up a freshly ironed bathrobe on a coat hook. His beer-barrel torso and long arms reminded Nik of a chimpanzee. Going by the size of his biceps, it didn't take much to guess what his job was at the resort.

'I'd like to introduce you to Gunnar,' said Pia. The man shook Nik's hand without looking him in the eye. He had a powerful handshake and his knuckles were scarred. He nodded at the woman and left the room. 'I hope you have a pleasant stay,' said Pia, before closing the door. Despite all the light wood finishes, luxurious carpet and marble wash basin with gold taps, the place still felt like a prison.

'This isn't going to be easy,' mumbled Nik. But he wouldn't leave the resort until he'd found a clue about whoever was behind Olga and Viola's disappearances. What would be easy, however, was pretending to be someone suffering from alcohol withdrawal. Nik was already missing his obligatory evening beer and it was only the first night. He padded restlessly around the room and searched the TV channels. He even tried to read a book. But it was no good. He couldn't relax. His hands were trembling and he had the urge to fight. He got down on the floor and did push-ups until his arms hurt, but that didn't help him fall asleep either. It was three o'clock in the morning before he finally managed to fall into a restless sleep. When he woke up for a second time, his pyjamas were sodden with sweat. Nik couldn't take it anymore and forced himself to get up to dry himself off in the bathroom. He put on some fresh pyjamas and was making his way back into the bedroom when he heard a faint noise coming from the corridor. He put his ear to the bedroom door and heard lots of people walking around. Nik wasn't surprised so much by the fact there were people up and about, but he couldn't understand why they seemed to be moving around so quickly.

'Hurry up!' he heard a man say. And then there was the sound of a defibrillator being charged up. A man swore and something was rolled past Nik's room. He waited until the noises had faded and opened the door. Three doors down the hall he saw a nurse pushing a trolley with a man lying on top. Nik guessed the patient was around forty. His eyes were closed and his head had flopped over to the side. He was wearing an oxygen mask and a light liquid was running from a bag through a tube and into his arm. Still pushing the trolley, the nurse pulled out a card from his pocket, then stopped and held up the card to a reader that was embedded in the wall. A lift opened. It blended in so perfectly with the walls that you wouldn't know it was there unless you'd seen it in use.

'Don't worry, Herr Kirchhof,' Pia said out of nowhere. She was wearing jeans, a polo shirt and sandals. She obviously wasn't on the clock. 'The guest just had a dizzy spell. We're taking him to the hospital just to be on the safe side but I'm sure he'll be feeling better very soon.'

'Did you give him something?'

'We don't administer any medicine here.' Pia opened her hand and gestured to Nik's room. 'Get some rest. You've got a busy day ahead of you tomorrow.'

Nik had no desire whatsoever to step back into his room. He was desperate to know who the man was and what had happened to him, and if that kind of thing happened a lot at the resort. But it would be fatal to risk his cover on the very first day. He'd need to play the wealthy alcoholic for a bit longer and that involved being uninterested in fellow human beings.

'I see,' said Nik. 'Good night.' He stood back and closed the door before lying down on the bed. There was no chance of sleep now, but there was nothing else he could do. He'd just have to wait until morning and then he could get on with the investigation.

Chapter 9

Nik's T-shirt was dripping with sweat and he had to fight for each painful breath, but he kept running towards the barrier. An ambulance flew past him with its piercing siren and he could hear the helicopter's rotor blade chopping at the air above him. A strange, hazy glow had been painted over the street and there were millions of glass shards lying on the ground, sparkling in blue and red as they reflected the police lights. He heaved himself through the gawking masses and ducked under the barrier tape, ignoring the police officer's orders to get back. He started to run, and with every stride, his screams got louder. Everybody was staring at him as he ran past the massive truck, lying on its side like a sleeping giant. The glass from the clinic's loading area had spread out over the road like a lake. As Nik crunched his way across the top, shards of glass pierced his boots and cut the soles of his feet, but he ignored the pain and kept running. He kept screaming and tears streamed from his eyes.

And then he woke up.

◆ ◆ ◆

Alois was the stereotypical psychologist. His hair was blonde and thinning, he wore a pair of steel-framed glasses and was very scrawny. He expertly balanced a pad of paper on his lap and held a pencil in his left hand. Whenever Nik said something, he would nod understandingly, always maintaining full eye contact, until it was his turn to talk. Then he would raise his right hand to his chin and look up, as if he was talking to some higher power.

'Do you feel in any way distressed after seeing that man last night?' He spoke slowly.

'Well, yes,' Nik replied. 'It doesn't exactly make a great impression when a patient dies the day you get here.'

'He didn't die.' Alois waggled his finger. 'He just fainted. Wouldn't want to start any rumours.'

'Nobody just randomly faints in the middle of the night.'

'I promise we do everything we can for our patients' physical and mental well-being.' Alois was trying to steer the conversation towards meaningless chat. 'That must have been obvious when you went to breakfast today.'

'Oh, absolutely,' Nik replied, battling with his own sarcasm. Breakfast had been a health-food nightmare. No eggs, no bacon. In general, nothing fatty. Just heavy slabs of wholemeal bread that would lie in his stomach for hours. Then the weird açaí bowls Pia had mentioned and some purple mush, which was apparently bursting with all the vitamins you needed to start the day off well. And then there was the juice, which looked and tasted like spinach that had been regurgitated by a baby. The only half-decent thing was the coffee, but even that was limited to two cups per person. 'I've never had a breakfast quite like it,' Nik said, thinking about how much he missed his waffle machine. 'I can particularly recommend the juice I was told to drink.'

'Ah, that's not just a juice,' explained Alois. 'It's the liquid result of all our knowledge on nutrition and superfoods. Has a wonderfully revitalising effect. You must have noticed?'

'If you mean half an hour on the toilet with brown water gushing from your backside. Then yeah. Never felt so revitalised.'

'Well, there you are then!' The psychologist clapped his hands together. 'You've already solved the blockage issue your brother told us about in so much detail.'

'Ah, yes, Balthasar. Such a great support,' responded Nik enthusiastically, thinking about how desperately he needed a beer.

Alois looked up again. 'Now, let's talk about you. What do you think is the reason behind your alcohol addiction?' He looked down at his notepad. 'The state of your liver is very concerning.'

'It just somehow caught up with me, I suppose. You start drinking in high school, then you're at all the uni parties. And later on there's the stress at work. That's it really. And before you know it, you're addicted.'

Alois nodded patiently. 'And have you ever thought about how you could get rid of your addiction?'

'I just thought you'd ply me with drugs and then I could go home two weeks later all recovered.'

Alois gave a short and powerful puff out of his nose and throat. Nik took it as a laugh but it sounded more like a choking sheep. 'If somebody could invent a drug like *that*, they'd be a very rich person. They'd be able to rid the world of alcohol addiction.'

'A friend of mine told me about some drug that kills the craving to drink,' Nik explained. 'Diso . . . disulfate or something like that?'

'You mean disulfiram?' asked Alois.

'That's the one.'

'Disulfiram is a substance that's very hard to control, and it doesn't suppress the urge to drink alcohol, it causes poisoning when it's mixed with alcohol. The reactions are very dangerous and in the worst cases it can cause a heart attack.' He shook his head. 'Disulfiram can only be used to treat alcohol addiction with the most disciplined of patients because any relapse could mean death. Not only does that kind of treatment go against our principles, there are very few people who would be willing to take such a risk. And anyway, since there is no alcohol on the premises, the use of such a medication would be in vain.'

'Right, of course,' Nik said sceptically. 'Anyway, about my neighbour from last night . . . the one who fainted or had a heart attack or whatever it was . . .' Nik winked. Alois took off his glasses and examined him more closely, evidently unsure what to make of him. 'Is he OK?' Nik asked. 'I never saw an ambulance leave?'

'Everything's fine,' Alois said calmly, playing down the question. 'We took the patient to our sickroom, where he was stabilised.' He made a note. 'And now to you,' he said, changing the subject again. 'How do you feel when you drink alcohol?'

'Strong and confident.' Nik had read enough on the typical alcoholic to pass the test. 'I feel less inhibited around others.' Alois nodded and wrote down something else. 'Like, if I have a meeting, I'll have a drink beforehand. It calms my nerves and I feel like I can face anything.' Nik was rolling out all the clichés. But as Alois got to the end of a second page on his notepad, Nik realised that was probably enough. He also didn't want to exaggerate. 'Oh God.' Nik stood up and put his hands on his stomach. 'Something's not quite right here. Back in a sec.' Nik ran out the room and slammed the door shut, but instead of heading to the toilet in his room, he put his ear up to the psychologist's door. Alois was on the phone. The door was so well insulated, he could barely hear a thing, but he still made out the words 'Nikolas Kirchhof' and 'disulfiram'. Nik smiled and went back to his room. The foundations had been laid and it would be interesting to see whose feathers he'd ruffle.

◆ ◆ ◆

Lunch at the resort was also the opposite of what Nik would describe as a good meal. A piece of white fish, some steamed potatoes and carrots, and a spoonful of pickled beetroot and kohlrabi. No sauce. No fat. Just a small side salad, two apples for dessert and a glass of water to wash it all down. And as if the food wasn't bad enough, the staff were continuously going on about how well balanced it all was. When Nik asked for some salt and ketchup, the employee laughed sincerely, as if he'd heard a really good joke, and went on to give Nik a lecture on how vital it was to avoid saturated fats, sweeteners and flavourings. By the time Nik had finished everything on his plate, he was hungrier than when he'd started. He picked up an apple and took an unsatisfying bite while simultaneously scrutinising his fellow inmates. There was a strict daily routine at the clinic and meals were only provided within small time slots. If you turned up late, you didn't get any food. So Nik could be pretty sure all the guests were at lunch.

Nik's first analysis didn't reveal much. Other than him, there were twenty-two patients in the clinic. Seventeen men and five women. The youngest one only looked about eighteen and the oldest, around sixty. Most of them were alcoholics, evident from the tell-tale spindly red blood vessels on their faces and the shaky, clammy hands that come from withdrawal. He also noticed a few coke and heroin addicts. But none of these people were going to help him solve the case. He finished off his apple and was about to leave when he heard a couple of men behind him.

'Leo!' one of the men called as he plodded into the restaurant. He was extremely overweight and sweating profusely. His face was bright red and he wheezed with each breath. He arrived at his friend's table next to Nik's and wiped his forehead with the back of his hand. The friend smiled and stood up. He was about forty, with blonde curly hair and very tanned skin. He looked like he'd just got back from a holiday in the Caribbean. His smile revealed a set of dazzling white teeth and his eyes were a piercing blue. His designer stubble softened a sharp jaw line. Leo would have looked more at home on a sunny Australian beach than he did in a Bavarian wood in winter.

Unaffected by the sweat, Leo hugged the man like they were old pals. At first it appeared completely harmless but on closer inspection, Nik spotted Leo's hand sliding into the big guy's trouser pocket. The move was fast and discreet, like he'd done it on many occasions. Leo scanned the staff to see if anyone had noticed, but they all appeared to be doing something else. Nik made a start on his second apple and observed the two men from the corner of his eye. There weren't very many things someone could hide in the palm of their hand. Mobiles, alcohol and sweets were out of the question. Money wasn't an issue for these people and even a USB stick would have been too big. So the only feasible thing was a tiny bag of drugs. Leo and his friend chatted a little while longer until finally, Leo left the restaurant and the overweight man sat down to eat. Nik followed Leo into the corridor.

'Excuse me!' Nik called. Leo stopped. An inexperienced criminal would have lost their cool if they thought someone might be confronting them about a crime. But as Leo turned around, he was the perfect salesman: open, friendly and utterly confident.

'Yes,' he said with a smile.

'Hi. Sorry to bother you,' Nik began. 'My name's Nikolas. I just got here yesterday and, well . . . God, I'm bored. D'you know if there's anything to do around here that doesn't involve talking about your childhood, or eating shitty food or being healthy?' An untrained eye would have missed the slight change in Leo's smile, but Nik could tell he'd made the man stop and think. He looked Nik hard in the eyes, like he was trying to examine him internally, and considered how to answer the question.

'Did you have anything in particular in mind?'

Asking for drugs would have been far too obvious. Leo would know Nik had seen the handover. He moved in closer to Leo and glanced around the corridor as if he was trying to make sure nobody was listening. 'You know, maybe a bit of harmless fun with a young lady? The guests in here are far too old for me.'

Leo looked Nik up and down once more, still unsure what to make of him. 'Then today's your lucky day, my friend,' he said at last. 'Every second Wednesday we organise an informal little party in the yoga room.'

'A party?' Nik asked, impressed. 'I thought drugs were banned here.'

'Well, loud music isn't a drug,' Leo explained. 'And none of the patients here are sex addicts, so the staff kind of turn a blind eye for the night and let a select group of . . . ladies come to the party.' He shrugged his shoulders, proud of his little venture. 'There'll be virgin cocktails, milkshakes and tasty finger food.'

'Sounds perfect.'

'Kicks off at eight. So see you then.' Leo patted Nik on the shoulder and walked away. Nik waited until his new friend was out of sight before going back to his room. He now knew how Olga had ended up in the clinic and was intrigued to see what else he'd find out at the party.

Nik had never been to the yoga room before, but he assumed the loud music was coming from there and followed the noise. The bass was booming, making the windows vibrate and there was a DJ in the corner of the room. He was wearing headphones and playing with knobs on a mixing desk. Next to him was a table filled with Spanish tapas, Greek olives and bitesize wholegrain canapes. Another man stood behind a small bar cutting up fresh fruit, which he then used to mix bright red drinks. A young woman was assisting him. She would collect any empty glasses, wash them and hand out fresh drinks. There were male guests standing in the middle of the room talking to young women. Going by their tight-fitting clothes and high heels, there was no question why the women were there. At the side of the room was a dark, handsome man talking to three of the female residents. He looked like a Spanish bullfighter: tall and strong, with long dark curls that fell past his shoulders. You could see his well-formed, hair-free chest under his white see-through shirt. Nik counted sixteen patients but no staff. No Alois to monitor their behaviour, no Gunnar to keep the peace and no Pia . . . being Pia.

'Nik!' Someone called his name over the music. Leo came over to him and hugged him. 'It's cool if I call you Nik, isn't it?' He was back to his usual self again and didn't give off a hint of distrust as he went to shake Nik's hand. 'My name's Leopold von Waldbach but friends call me Leo.'

'Nice to meet you.'

Leo passed him one of the red drinks. 'Tastes like a strawberry margarita, just without the tequila.'

They said cheers and Nik took a sip. The strawberries were deliciously fresh despite the time of year and the drink had just the right amount of syrup. But without the tequila, it lacked that all-important kick.

Nik noticed one young woman in particular. She was barely eighteen, with dyed red hair, and she towered over most of the guests in her high-heeled boots. She was wearing dark blue lipstick and a very light foundation. Her full backside curved perfectly, and was enhanced further by her short black leather skirt.

'Our number one product,' said Leo as he caught sight of Nik's face.

'How d'you get the girls in?'

'Got a little deal going with the management,' explained Leo. 'Patients were pouncing on each other, you know. Wasn't exactly making for the best atmosphere and took a toll on the success of the treatment.' He took a sip of his drink. 'So now they let in a group of prostitutes every fortnight to deal with the urges. The female patients seem pretty content too.' He gestured with his head towards the bullfighter.

'And how does it work?' Nik asked. 'Do I need a number or something?'

'It's done according to how long you've been staying here. My fat friend over there, Waldemar, he's always here. Last time he came in, he'd been found in a champagne bath with a blood alcohol level of three point one. Had to be resuscitated. That was four months ago.'

'Long time to be in rehab.'

'Yeah, you'd think so. But Waldemar's only in sixth place.' He turned back to Nik. 'So, why you here then?'

'Too many parties, too much alcohol and too many exceptions,' Nik began. 'Or at least that's what my dad said. So he gave me a choice. Either I go to rehab or he pulls the plug on my inheritance and his local Bavarian folk club gets enough money to buy lederhosen and dirndls for all eternity.' Nik took a sip of his cocktail. 'And you?'

'Repeat offences for driving without a licence under the influence of drugs,' said Leo. 'Even my well-paid lawyer couldn't save me from jail last time after I hit a school bus at a hundred and twenty.'

'Hundred and twenty? That's not that fast.'

'In a pedestrian zone it is,' added Leo.

'Oh.'

'Been here for four weeks and I'm still waiting for the doctor to say I'm good to go home.'

'Nothing you can do? Say you'll donate a load of money for another yoga room or something?'

'Already tried,' replied Leo. 'As well as loads of other things. But nobody gets out of here unless you play along.' He took Nik's glass. 'These strawberry smoothies are boring.' He changed the subject. 'The bartender's made something new for us.' He went over to the bar and spoke to the young man, who handed over two glasses. Leo passed one to Nik.

'Champine,' explained Leo. 'A non-alcoholic champagne made from fizzy water and pine needles.' He raised his glass to Nik's and downed the drink in one. Nik did the same. It tasted awful, like pressed tree bark. It took all his effort not to spray the whole lot back out again. 'And? What d'you think?'

'Disgusting.'

Leo laughed and patted him on the shoulder. 'Don't worry. I've got two hours until the redhead's taking me to my room. We'll find something you like.'

Nik's next drink was called Seedlip, a clear water that had been infused with herbs and spices. And the one after that, a mixture of vegetable juice and woodruff vinegar. And it was while drinking the vegetable juice that Nik noticed his knees start to shake.

'You all right?' asked Leo.

'You sure there's no alcohol in these?' Nik asked. The room started to spin and the bass got deeper and slower. He tried to lean on the wall.

'Can I get some help over here?' Nik heard Leo say. 'Our newbie's not doing so well.' It was the last thing Nik heard before he sank to the floor, unconscious.

◆ ◆ ◆

Nik woke up in his bed still in his clothes from the night before. His head ached, and he still had the awful taste of pine needles in his mouth. His eyelids were stuck together with a layer of gluey sleep. His watch said 9.23 a.m., which meant he'd missed breakfast. But that wasn't a problem. The thought of food made him retch. He staggered slowly into the bathroom and turned on the cold tap. He let the cold water run over his head until he could think again. He picked up the towel and dried his hair while looking at himself in the mirror. Despite the extortionate haircut, he looked terrible. His eyes were red and swollen and there was a large patch of saliva on the arm of his crumpled shirt. His top button had been ripped off. Nik chucked the towel in the shower and went over to his cupboard, where he pulled out his metal suitcase. Down beside the wheels was a tiny hidden compartment. He used a thin nail file to open it and pulled out a mini folding phone. The X-ray machine in the clinic wasn't as powerful as the ones at airports, so a little lead covering had been enough to get it past the staff. He turned on the phone and was surprised at how good the reception was. There had to be a radio mast not far from the clinic. He looked up Jon's number and pressed call.

'Morning,' Jon said after the second ring.

'Hello,' Nik growled. His voice was coarse.

'If you weren't currently sitting in a rehab clinic, I'd swear you'd pulled an all-nighter.'

'That's basically what happened. Except this time it wasn't down to me. Someone spiked my drink.'

'What? Did you ask the wrong questions or something?' asked Jon.

'Didn't even get that far but whoever it was searched my room while I was asleep.'

'And you noticed that even though you were drugged?'

'No,' Nik barked. 'I used the hair trick.'

'No idea what you're talking about.'

'You should watch more old Bond films.' Nik grabbed a bottle of water from the fridge and took a swig. 'You stick a hair over the gap between the cupboard door and the frame. If you do it down at the bottom no one can see it. And when the door's opened, the hair falls to the ground.'

'And was there a hair on the ground under your cupboard?'

'Yes,' said Nik before downing the rest of the water. 'But it's actually a good sign someone drugged me and searched the room. Means they're wary of nosy patients and trying to hide something.'

'Who was it?'

'A new friend. But I don't know if he's got anything to do with our case or if he's just afraid I'll blab to someone about his drug business.' Nik started a new bottle. 'Did you link Viola to the clinic yet?'

'No,' answered Jon. 'I know how Olga ended up inside but I've got no idea what Viola's got to do with it. Maybe she's got a file in there.'

'Doubt it, but I'm gonna have to speed things up in here. I'll start dropping her name. Maybe someone will react to that. And in the meantime I'll see if there's a file for Kathrin.'

'I tried all night to access clinic data but didn't get anywhere – it's like the clinic isn't online.'

'It isn't,' Nik confirmed. 'My therapist's got an old-fashioned hanger file for me and writes all his notes by hand. And he's got two cabinets in his room with enough space for hundreds of files. The computer in his room is either just for show or used for other things.'

'God, that *is* old-fashioned,' mumbled Jon.

'Yeah, but secure,' said Nik. 'Means hackers like you or journalists can't download the data.'

'True. So how d'you plan on checking to see if Kathrin was there?'

'The old-fashioned way too. Pick some locks.'

'I put your lock pick in the secret compartment,' said Jon.

'It's no good. All the doors in here are electric. The staff use personalised key cards to open the locks. I'll need to use my nimble fingers.'

'You've got nimble fingers?' Jon sounded astonished.

'You'd be surprised,' said Nik. 'You learn a lot dealing with hundreds of break-ins and thefts at the CID.' Nik was exhausted and sat down on the bed. 'When everyone's asleep, I'll go and look at the filing cabinet. Let's hope I find something.'

Chapter 10

Nik couldn't think of a worse way to start the day than a conversation about addiction, his childhood and what he imagined himself doing in five years. There were all those patients in the clinic and it was actually Alois who needed therapy the most. But Alois had a doctorate in psychology, so he got to sit on the other side. And despite all his self-assurance, he wouldn't have realised Nik was a police officer if Nik had gone in with his badge stuck to his forehead.

But it was Alois's self-adoration that gave Nik time to study the room. There were neither motion detectors nor cameras and the lock on the filing cabinet was very basic. The windows were made of security glass and the brackets on them were burglar proof. Not even a crowbar would break the window out of its hinges. Nik would have to get one of the employee's key cards.

The fact that the filing cabinet was locked was a good sign, as it meant other people probably had access to the room. And since all the locks in the clinic were identical, that was certainly a possibility.

After an hour of chat, Nik made his way past the yoga room, towards the relaxation area. The yoga room was now completely void of any signs from yesterday's party. He lay down on a massage table and let a robust young woman push him around for an hour. She squeezed out all the tension that had built up from the night before, while he sipped peacefully on a freshly squeezed orange juice. The essential oils were just the right strength, and for the first time since he'd arrived at the clinic, Nik was able to enjoy the perks of having bucketloads of money. Even if it wasn't his own.

After his massage, he wandered over to the swimming pool. It was twenty-five metres long, heated and situated in a lavish conservatory. All around the pool were loungers with thick cushions where guests could nap.

Leo's friend Waldemar was sitting on a chair reading a newspaper. There was a plate of sliced fruit and a large jug of water on a table beside him. The dressing gown barely covered his belly. He had short, thinning hair and long sideburns. All in all, with his wobbly chin, small protruding ears and pale skin, the man reminded Nik of Porky Pig. The only thing missing was the red bow tie. He was breathing heavily and scrunching his eyes up, as if he'd forgotten to put in his contact lenses. But his general demeanour was like that of a contented old man who'd just done a line of coke and had sex with a prostitute.

'Good morning,' Nik said, sitting himself down on a chair opposite Waldemar. The man looked up from his paper and squinted. He blinked for a couple of seconds while trying to work out if the face was familiar.

'Name's Nik.' Nik offered his hand to Waldemar. 'I'm a friend of Leopold's.'

'Ah, yes. Good old Leo.' He put down his paper and shook Nik's hand. 'What would we do without him!'

'Be high and dry, I assume,' replied Nik. 'Thank God for his contacts though. Staying off the booze is bad enough for me. Kicking anything else would be hell.'

'You said it.' Waldemar nodded in agreement.

'How the hell does he do it?' Nik began. 'Getting all that stuff past security. Everyone's luggage is screened.'

'Wouldn't want to know,' Waldemar said, trying to move the conversation in a different direction. 'As long as I get my stuff, I couldn't care less.'

'Yeah, you're right.' Nik caught on and changed the subject. 'Great place though. So many things to do. It's a blessing really.'

'Who managed to get you in?'

'Viola Rohe,' said Nik. 'She was here last year. Maybe you know her?'

'Name doesn't ring any bells,' replied Waldemar genuinely. 'And I've been here a lot.'

'Nice woman,' said Nik. 'I'd love to tell you more about her but I've actually got an appointment in a minute. Maybe another time.' He stood up and shook Waldemar's hand again. 'Was nice meeting you.'

For the remainder of the morning, Nik roamed the clinic grounds, sat in the library and got roped into a game of shuffleboard. Everywhere he went, he'd start a conversation. He even told his cleaner a story in his room. By lunch time, he was losing his voice but he'd managed to drop Viola's name into every conversation. Sometimes she was an acquaintance, sometimes a friend, and at other times just a distant relative. No one he spoke to knew her name but the seed had been planted and he was desperate to see if someone would react. After that, it was time to check out the security in the clinic. He wandered around, seemingly aimlessly, until he came to the back door. This was the door that the staff used to enter and leave, and out of bounds to patients, but Nik was new, so he was counting on the fact that nobody would think twice if he got a little lost. Beyond the back door was a room where the employees picked up their ID when they started their shift and dropped it off again before heading home. It was a procedure that exposed a sense of paranoia among the management. A fear that an ingenious hacker could get their hands on a card and make a copy. They wouldn't be the first employers to stop staff taking their key cards home, but it was exactly this safety precaution that would help Nik with his investigation.

He went inside the building and looked around, acting confused. A muscular young man was standing behind a high counter, a bit like a reception desk. The man, who had a military haircut, wide shoulders and a straight back, appeared to be responsible for taking in and giving out the cards. He had hardly any facial hair and his cheeks were dotted with freckles. He clearly had nothing to do with looking after patients and was just a member of security. Behind him was the room where all the cards were stored. From where he was standing, Nik could just make out a man sitting on a chair watching a monitor, but nothing else.

'Can I help you?' asked the young man in a friendly manner.

'I'm afraid I'm lost,' said Nik, playing the confused patient to perfection.

'No problem,' replied the man. 'Just go down the corridor and you'll come to a glass door. Ring the buzzer and I'll let you in. Then you're back in the patient area.'

'Great.' Nik raised his hand to say thanks and goodbye. Now he knew where he could get his hands on an employee key card, his job here was done. For now.

Nik wasn't exactly heartbroken that he'd have to skip lunch. Having studied the menus for the week, he knew that Thursday's lunch would consist of broccoli and red cabbage bake. The hour between twelve and one o'clock in the clinic seemed to be a sacred time. A time when everything came to a standstill. There were no therapy sessions, you couldn't book a massage and even the cleaners parked up their trolleys. It was only in and around the kitchen that a few people were still working. The staff had a separate dining hall, which could be seen from a specific spot in the east wing.

Just before twelve, Nik walked over to a small, private room where the cleaners left their trolleys. He squeezed himself into a bend in the corridor and closed his eyes, concentrating on the fast-approaching steps. The thick carpet made it difficult to hear, but he could tell it was a pair of women's shoes. They squeaked with every step. Just before the person went to turn the corner, Nik took a step. His timing was perfect.

'Oh, excuse me!' he said as he collided with the woman. He raised his hands in front of him, as if trying to reduce the impact. He then put his left hand on the cleaner's shoulder while his right went down to her hip, where her card was hanging. It was attached to her trousers by a carabiner. Nik pushed the lever with his thumb and lifted it upwards quickly. At the same time, he applied some pressure to the woman's shoulder, distracting her attention away from her hip.

'Excuse me,' said the woman in a delicate Eastern European accent. She took a step backwards and let her head fall submissively.

'Oh no, please.' Nik raised his left hand in a motion of peace while he quickly put his right hand behind his back. 'Really not a problem.' He smiled at her. He felt terrible that he'd had to use the weakest link in the clinic's hierarchy, but in his experience, cleaners had access to most rooms.

Nik moved on. Even if the woman *did* notice her card was missing, she'd never dare blame a patient, so Nik would have enough time to get on with his plan. Even assuming Alois used up the whole hour for his lunch break, it still wouldn't be enough to crack open the cabinet, look through hundreds of files and lock the cabinet again. He needed more time. And this was where some of Nik's previous preparation would come in handy.

Beside the door in Alois's room hung a large whiteboard with an overview of employee shift times. Alois had completely forgotten to cover it up on Nik's first visit, so he'd had plenty of time to study it. He'd gone down the list of employees until he'd found the word 'holiday'. It was beside the name 'Silke Tinz'.

As soon as security were all sitting down in the canteen, he went around to the back entrance again. There was a sign on the counter that read 'Back at 1 p.m.'. Obviously, the room with all the cards was locked but even this room had to be cleaned sometimes. Nik held the cleaner's card up to the reader and a green light blinked. Smiling proudly, he went into the room. There were lots of named cardholders. Some of them had cards in them, others had letters or little notes. He took Silke Tinz's card out of the holder and replaced it with a piece of paper folded to the same size as the card. Silke would be on holiday for another eight days, so this way, it would take longer for anyone to notice the card was missing. As long as the cardholders weren't checked regularly, he'd be able to use it for the whole time she was away.

Nik left the room and hurried back towards the patients' area. When he got there, he hid behind a cleaning trolley, washed his fingerprints off the cleaner's card and put it on the floor to make it look as if she'd dropped it there. He then headed back to his room and ate a highly nutritious cereal bar. He lay on his bed and closed his eyes. He needed to rest before the busy night ahead.

There was no curfew in the clinic and as long as the patients didn't leave the premises, they were allowed to walk around freely at night. Nik had uncovered three cameras inside the building. One at the front entrance, one at the staff entrance and one at the main reception. He hadn't seen any in the corridors or in front of the rooms, but knowing how easy it was to hide them, he would just have to hope the corridor in front of Alois's room wasn't being monitored.

It had just gone two in the morning. Most patients were normally sleeping at this time and in terms of staff, it was just the reception that was covered. Nik put on a warm jacket, a thick scarf and a hat, as if he was about to go out for a walk in the snow. He didn't meet anybody on his way to Alois's room and couldn't hear any footsteps or voices. He took out Silke Tinz's card and opened the door to Alois's room. All the blinds were down and barely any light was getting through from the hallway, so Nik turned on a table lamp. He took out his lock pick and opened the cabinet.

Thankfully, the psychologist was pedantic. He'd labelled all the files and arranged them alphabetically. Nik rifled through, looking for the Gs. Bingo! He grunted in satisfaction. They'd been right. Kathrin *had* been a patient here. Using his phone and the light from the lamp, he took a photo of every document. He then browsed through them to see what was there.

Kathrin Glosemeier had been in the clinic between 19 April and 14 May. On two occasions she'd been caught driving under the influence of alcohol, and on another the police had found her in a confused and drunken state near to Marienplatz. Alois had concluded that Kathrin was highly unstable when she arrived. Her first few days in the clinic had not gone well. She refused all treatments, lashed out at nurses and threw a plate of food on the floor in the dining room. After that, she suffered a nervous breakdown and had to be under twenty-four-hour observation.

Alois's notes were extensive and exposed the inner conflict Kathrin had experienced. She had moments where she would blame others for her problems and moments when she simply sat and cried. Sometimes she blamed her mother, or ex-boyfriends, or teachers or business colleagues. But it was mostly her father who she saw as the source of all her issues. And it wasn't only her mental health that had suffered; her body had also taken badly to the alcohol withdrawal. For two days she was too weak to even leave her room and was made to drink a high-calorie shake every day so she didn't lose any more weight.

In the end, Alois administered disulfiram beta 3, which Kathrin took daily with her breakfast shake. There was nothing written to say the administration of the drug had been discussed with the patient, indicating the substance was being mixed in her food without her knowledge.

Nik let out a quiet whistle of disbelief. But that wasn't everything. After Kathrin broke down physically and mentally, Alois wanted to test the effects of the disulfiram beta 3 when taken with alcohol, so he started adding that to her shake as well. Although he'd used a very small amount, the effects were disastrous. After just a couple of minutes Kathrin was complaining of hot flushes and itchy arms. Her face went red and sweat started pouring down her forehead. She was sent to the sick room, where staff discovered a significant increase in blood pressure and an abnormal heartbeat. She suffered a panic attack and threw up on the floor but four hours later she was stable again.

The results were collected in a scientific summary, which, considering Kathrin had almost died during the experiment, came to a very positive conclusion.

Nik put back the file and closed the cabinet, making sure he left no signs he'd been there. All set with the photos on his phone, he left the room. As he started walking along the corridor, he saw Gunnar coming towards him, his shoulders and head hanging down like a gorilla's. Nik raised his hand to wave hello and as he did, Gunnar took a swing at his chin, hard. It felt like he'd been hit with a hammer. Nik fell to the floor and concentrated on not losing consciousness. He hadn't expected Gunnar to attack him.

'What the hell . . . ?' he began, as Gunnar grabbed him powerfully by the throat, stopping any air from getting in. Nik tried to free himself, but the man held him down with the ease of a freestyle wrestler. Nik elbowed Gunnar in the head but it only made him grunt faintly. Nik stuck out his leg and used every last bit of strength to try and stand up, but it was no use. It was like trying to push a mountain. Gunnar kept him down on the floor and tightened his grip.

Everything went blurry, and finally he lost consciousness.

◆　◆　◆

As Nik opened his eyes, he felt the ties on his wrists. He was sitting on a chair in a room with no windows. Apart from two white cupboards and a shelf with some towels, the room was empty.

'Beginning to get used to this,' Nik mumbled, his voice raw from being strangled. Gunnar was standing beside the door talking quietly to Leo, who was watching Nik closely, waiting for him to try and escape. His usual casual, charming manner was gone and he now seemed more like a judge preparing to charge the accused.

'OK, Leo,' said Nik. 'What the hell?'

Leo moved away from Gunnar and sat down on a stool in front of Nik. 'What are you doing here?'

'Well, this is a rehab clinic,' replied Nik, 'and I'm an alcoholic. So . . .'

Leo smacked him hard with the back of his hand. 'Can do that all night,' he said. 'The room won't be used until tomorrow morning and no matter how loud you scream no one can hear you in here.'

'Afraid I might tell someone about your drug business or someth—?' Leo smacked him again, throwing his head to the side.

'You clearly don't get it, do you?' Leo remarked. 'It's not a question of whether you tell me why you're here. It's a question of how much pain you can handle until you do.' He spoke calmly and with conviction. He was prepared to beat Nik up until he gave him an answer he was happy with. Leo lowered his head until their noses were almost touching. He looked at Nik penetratingly, without blinking, as if trying to hypnotise him. 'Why . . . are . . . you . . . here?'

'OK, OK,' said Nik, trying to placate him. He inhaled deeply and rammed his forehead into Leo's face. Leo stumbled backwards and put his hand up to his face. Blood streamed between his fingers. Nik's grin was swiftly put to an end by another smack from Gunnar, which sent him crashing to the floor, taking the chair with him. His chin was throbbing but hearing Leo swearing made up for the pain. Gunnar pulled Nik and the chair back up. The tissue Leo was holding up to his nose was already red with blood.

'Why don't you untie my wrists and send the gorilla outside?' Nik suggested. 'Then we'll see what you can get out of me.' He spat on the floor.

Gunnar came closer, getting ready to hit him again, but Leo lifted his hand. 'Then I'll begin, shall I?' He sat back down in front of Nik. 'I spiked your drink at the party and while you were sleeping I searched your room. I didn't actually find anything interesting, but, you see, I've got a couple of mates over at the police station and, with Gunnar's help, I managed to get your fingerprints over to them. And guess what they told me?' He smiled. 'Your name's Nik Pohl and until not that long ago, you were with the Munich CID. But then you got suspended. And that brings us right back to the start.' His smile disappeared. 'So what's a CID agent doing in a rehab clinic where one month costs more than his yearly salary . . . with a false name?'

'I'm working undercover.'

'Undercover?' repeated Leo.

'I'm investigating illegal medical trials in the clinic.'

Leo signalled to Gunnar. Nik and the chair were smacked on to the floor again.

'Why are you making this so difficult?' asked Leo. 'My police mates told me about your work and there was no mention of any cases involving substance abuse. Plus, you never worked undercover. And yesterday you spent the whole day asking about Viola Rohe. Viola never worked here, she was never a patient here, and she never worked in the pharmaceutical industry. So I'm having trouble linking your questions to illegal medical trials in the clinic.'

'Did you know Viola?'

'Yes, I did.' Leo's hands were clenched together and his eyes were squeezed shut. 'And I swear to God Gunnar will throttle you until I know why you're asking about her.' Leo seemed determined to find out what Nik was hiding and had become twice as tense at the mention of

Viola's name. Nik could tell it was the kind of anger that would only diffuse when he'd been told everything.

Nik considered the situation. Leo was basically a businessman who enjoyed overstepping his boundaries and getting what he wanted. But Nik could tell he lacked the typical attitude of a cold-blooded murderer.

'So, all this isn't about your drug business. It's about Viola?' asked Nik.

'Correct.'

Nik bit on his lower lip and thought for a moment. Apart from this conversation, he'd got nowhere in linking Viola to the clinic. Nobody knew of her or flinched at her name. Maybe it was time to take a risk.

'I'm investigating Viola's disappearance.'

Leo stood up and took a step back. 'Undercover?'

Nik shook his head. 'I got suspended because I stuck my nose too deep into the case. There are people at the police doing everything they can to stop the case being investigated any further and I want to know why.'

Leo kept his eyes fixed on Nik and took a deep breath. He was unsure what to make of the information but something in his manner had clearly changed. After a moment of silence, he moved behind Nik and untied his wrists.

'I knew something'd happened to her.' His anger was dark. He seemed upset, almost distraught.

Gunnar gave Nik a glass of water and left the room.

'I met her at one of our Wednesday parties,' Leo explained, sitting back down on the stool. He was looking at the floor, as if he'd find the memory of that day down there. 'She didn't stand out next to the hot prostitutes, but she had something special. Don't know if it was her posture, or the way she laughed. Or how she politely hid her intelligence from the customers. She was pretty wary and shy at the start. Didn't want people to think she was a hooker. But when I left that night to go back to my room without making any moves on her, she started to trust me. I even helped her out with the dishes at the second party, just so I could be near her.' He looked at the tissue he'd been using for his nose. The bleeding had stopped. 'It was a mild October night. Already late. Most of the patients had gone to bed or headed off with a girl. She stopped clearing away the glasses and went outside. It had started to rain a bit and there was this cool breeze because a storm was coming. Felt fantastic after the stuffiness of the room. She took off her shoes and started walking on the grass with her hands up in the air. She was swaying softly . . . like she was doing a slow dance . . . and humming a tune.' Leo closed his eyes. It was clearly painful for him to think about the night. 'She was so beautiful,' he whispered. 'Her hair got wet and it started sticking to her back. And her dress was clinging to her body. And that smile . . . My God, that smile was beautiful . . .' He shook his head. 'I asked her what she was doing, and she said, "Don't you hear the song?" And I said, "No, which song?" And she said, "The rain's singing a litany. About its journey down from the sky to earth, along the rivers into the sea." She waved me over to her and when I closed my eyes, I really did hear it. At first it wasn't loud . . . more like a large crowd of people whispering. And then . . . all the voices kind of came together and started to sing.' Leo wiped away a tear. 'She was at one more party after that. Told me about uni, her plans for the future, her dreams. But then two weeks later, another woman had taken her place at the bar. I asked where she was, but nobody knew. And that was it. We never saw her again.' He looked up. 'Do you know anything about her?' he asked hopefully.

'Where do I start?' Nik answered, before taking a sip of water and telling Leo everything he knew about Viola, including the similarities between her and Kathrin's cases. It took a long time and it was warm and muggy inside the room, but Leo listened intently until Nik had finished.

'I can't believe it,' Leo said. 'Who the hell is powerful enough to get three investigations completely wiped?'

'Isn't necessarily just the one person. Might be a group,' Nik replied. 'How much d'you think you could make from a drug that got rid of alcohol addiction and didn't have any bad side effects?'

'Oh, you're easily into the double-digit millions. Definitely enough that lots of people would be willing to harm three women. Can't believe the police are in on it too though. Never would've expected that.'

'You can get people to do whatever you want if you've got enough money,' said Nik. 'Whether through paying them, or blackmailing them or threatening to hurt their family.'

Leo sighed loudly. 'So what can I do?'

'I need to find out more about these tests,' Nik replied. 'They might be the key. And to do that, I need to get on the computers.'

'I thought Alois wrote everything by hand?'

'He does. All the notes from the sessions are done by hand. But basic details are put into the system at the reception.'

'Makes sense,' said Leo. 'Staying in a beauty resort isn't exactly a big deal, but nobody wants a treatment plan for alcohol addiction on their record.'

'Exactly. But if the clinic is producing or testing a new drug, then there have to be some digital records. They can't be working on a project this size with a slide rule. But I've been walking around a lot and the only computers I found were the one in Alois's room, the one at reception and the one in the key card room.'

'That's because they're in the basement,' Leo remarked.

'The basement?' Nik repeated. 'I thought it was just the loading dock and sick room down there.'

'Yeah, well, I was down in the sick room three months ago when I fainted. Looks like an intensive care ward. All the latest high-tech equipment . . . and a medicine cabinet that would make a junkie's eyes water. And then, when it was time for me to go back upstairs, we were waiting for the lift and I saw this door open. Behind it was a long corridor with four labs. All made of glass and full of massive, state-of-the-art pharmaceutical machines. There were two men in lab coats standing in the corridor pointing to a tablet.'

'Who were they?'

'I only knew one of them. Dr Rafael Gawinski. Specialises in treating alcohol addiction. He's pretty much Alois's counterpart. And you only get out of here when both of them say you can.'

'I've never seen this Gawinski.'

'Yeah, nobody ever does, because his staff do all the tests. He just interprets the results. Apparently, he doesn't like being around patients.'

'Maybe because he's illegally pumping drugs into them.'

'Sounds about right,' Leo agreed. 'But anyway, we need to get into the basement.'

'I can use the card I stole to get in there but I've no idea how we're supposed to get at the computer data.'

'Don't look at me,' said Leo. 'I'm pleased if I can save a number to my contacts.'

'I know a computer guy. I'll get hold of him on my mobile and he can put something together. But we'll need a way of getting whatever he makes into the clinic. How d'you get your drugs in?'

'With the catering service,' said Leo. 'The driver gives Gunnar a small package and Gunnar puts it in my room. But the next delivery isn't for another week.'

'Yeah, that's too late.'

Deep in thought, Leo rubbed his index finger over his lips. 'How big d'you think the package will be?'

'No idea. About a kilo in weight and maybe about the size of a small shoebox.'

'My nephew asked me for a drone for his last birthday so he could drop water bombs,' Leo explained. 'I had no idea what I'd bought but two days later, he sent me a video of his first attempt. He'd used GPS to drop the bombs on a neighbour's conservatory . . . right to the centimetre. And I doubt your friend'll have any issues with the technology considering my nephew's only eleven and not exactly the sharpest tool in the shed.'

'Don't really know much about drones. Aren't they pretty loud?'

'Yeah, but some things around here are much louder,' said Leo. 'It'll just be a matter of timing.'

Chapter 11

The morning darkness and heavy snow made it easy for Nik and Leo to hide. Fighting their way through some heavy undergrowth, away from the main driveway, they made their way over to a small storage shed. As they arrived, they saw a man pushing a wheelbarrow loaded with shovels. He was wearing old dungarees and a dirty, thick winter jacket. His wispy grey hair was sticking out from underneath his woollen hat and his full beard sparkled with drops of melting snow. His boots crunched with every step.

'That's Hans Ziemer,' Leo whispered. 'Plumber by trade but looks after all the outdoor grounds here and the drainage system. Doesn't exactly fit the clinic's desired image, so he's not allowed inside the main building, which doesn't seem to bother him in the slightest.'

'And what use is he to us?'

'Well, good old Hansi's work might not be the best when it comes to quality, but in terms of efficiency, he works like clockwork. Starts every day at 8 a.m. when he clears the driveway – in autumn it's the leaves and in winter the snow.' Leo pointed to a machine that looked like a lawnmower, with a large shovel attached to the front. 'That's his petrol-powered snowplough,' explained Leo. 'Loud as an old tractor. We don't hear it inside the clinic 'cause the windows are triple-glazed. But if you go outside at eight in the morning, you can't hold a conversation.' Leo pointed up to the sky. 'It's going to snow again tonight, so we can be pretty sure that Hansi will be at work on time tomorrow to clear away the snow. And believe me, you wouldn't notice a plane landing in that racket.'

'Or a drone,' added Nik.

Leo nodded proudly. 'As well as drugs, I also smuggled in a smartphone. I've got this app I use when I go hillwalking in case I get lost. We could use it to send your friend the exact GPS coordinates of the little forest clearing behind the building. Then he can land the drone there just after eight tomorrow and no one will notice. After that, we grab the package, and the drone can start back up after one minute.'

'Sounds like a plan,' said Nik.

'Great. Let's get going then,' said Leo, taking out his phone. 'I'll get the coordinates for the clearing.'

Nik got up impatiently the next morning at seven o'clock. Having to wait twenty-four hours before he and Leo could kick-start their plan had been torture. He put on some clothes that were suitable for a walk in the snow and went for breakfast. It was a sunny, still morning. Perfect for flying a drone. Jon would be nearby already, somewhere on a woodland path. Jon was still raging at Nik and his demands from the day before. Not only did he have to find a drone, he also had to build a mini computer with hacking software that would establish a connection with Jon's computer from inside the clinic. He'd worked all day and night. Nik had known he was asking a lot, but he saw it as a way of getting even for having to suffer the clinic's high-fibre vegetarian meals.

At one minute to eight, Hans came around the corner pushing his snowplough. Nik said hello as he walked past him on his way towards the clearing. Shortly after, there was a thundering roar. Nik took out his phone and called Jon. As planned, he let it ring once before hanging up. As Nik was forcing his way through layers of snow-covered spruce branches, he bumped into Leo. The plaster on his swollen nose made him look like a hardened boxer, but his mischievous grin gave away his excitement. They had only just arrived at the clearing when they heard a high buzzing sound, barely audible over the snowplough. Seconds later, a white drone landed in front of them, exactly where it was supposed to. Snow sprayed out from underneath, forcing Nik to look away until the four rotor blades had stopped spinning. A box, barely bigger than a mobile phone, was attached to the underside of the drone. Nik ran over, removed the package and put it under his jacket. The humming of the rotor blades started up again as he walked back over to Leo and a couple of seconds later, the drone was gone.

Leo hit Nik jovially on the shoulder. 'That went well,' he said. 'What do we do now?'

'If I understood Jon correctly, I have to connect the device to a computer inside the clinic. The built-in radio module means Jon can access everything without having to be anywhere nearby.'

'And how are you going to attach it?' Leo asked as they made their way back to the clinic.

'Alois's computer sits underneath his desk, beside a shelf. I'll stuff the thing between the cables and no one will notice it's there.'

'You're gonna break into his office again?'

'No need. I've got my session today,' said Nik. 'And we always start off with Alois fetching me a fresh coffee from the machine in the staff room. All the filing cabinets are locked and the computer's password protected, so he feels fine leaving me alone in there. And while he's out, I'll link up our little magic box.' Nik moved a bit closer to Leo. 'And then later tonight, we'll take a trip to the basement. God knows what we're gonna find down there.'

Nik put on some jogging bottoms, a T-shirt and some trainers. If he bumped into anyone, they'd think he was on his way to the twenty-four-hour gym. His phone was tucked into the elastic of his trousers and he was wearing headphones with a microphone in his right ear. The clinic was quiet at this time of night. No conversations, no patients in the corridors and even the reception was unoccupied. The night porter was lying on a lounger in the room behind the reception, snoring softly. The carpet absorbed Nik's steps as he walked over to Leo's door. He knocked lightly. Leo came out instantly, also dressed in sports clothes. He looked up and down the corridor, like a thief on his way to a robbery. 'Everything OK?' he whispered.

'Almost,' answered Nik. 'We just need to wait for Jon to get us access to the lift.'

'But you've got a staff card.'

'Luckily, Jon checked it before I set off and it wasn't programmed to get in here,' explained Nik. 'Jon needs to copy someone's profile to get us access.'

'Not just *someone's* profile,' Jon's voice suddenly sounded on the headset. 'Dr Gawinski's. He has access to everywhere.'

'How long?' asked Nik.

'Almost there,' Jon replied.

Nik moved towards the lift and waved Leo over. The door fitted seamlessly into the wall. If it wasn't for the small reader at the side, you wouldn't even know it was there.

'That's it,' said Jon.

Nik held the card to the reader. A green light blinked and they heard the lift start up. 'Hopefully, no one will hear it,' remarked Leo. He was moving nervously from one foot to the other.

'It's three in the morning. Most people are in a deep-sleep phase at this time of night. I'm more worried someone will be working downstairs. As soon as we're down there, it's not as easy to say we got lost on our way to the gym.'

'Gunnar told me nobody's been brought downstairs recently. The sick room is empty. But he didn't know anything about the research lab.'

The door opened. Nik went in first, with Leo behind. He pressed the button for the basement. The door closed and the lift started to move. Nik squeezed his fists together. Entering highly unpredictable areas was standard when he'd worked for the CID, but the difference then was he'd always been armed. And he'd been on the right side of the law. Now he was the burglar.

The door opened and a gust of cold air and the harsh smell of cleaning product hit the men. Everywhere was lit with long neon tubes that were set into the ceiling. They stepped out of the lift into the lower level of the building. It looked just like a hospital. Sterile and white with laminate on the floor. Nik could see two mobile beds and two surveillance monitors on the wall. Next to that were two cupboards full of medication and a sink. In front of the beds was an ultrasound machine and a heart-lung machine.

'That's the toilet.' Leo pointed to a side room. 'If we keep left, we should come to the lab.' Nik led the way. After three metres, the corridor came to an end and they arrived at a large, unlabelled metal door. Nik held the card to the reader and the door slid to the right with a soft hiss. The rooms were just as Leo had described them: four laboratories with glass walls and lots of expensive, complicated machines. Nik also noticed a microscope, piston pumps for drug production and numerous computer screens. The larger machines looked like photocopiers. At the end of the corridor was another lift.

'What now?' asked Leo.

'First of all, we need to connect the USB device to a computer.' Nik took the stick out of his pocket. 'Jon said something about an isolation unit or something . . .'

'It's called an isolated solution,' Jon corrected him over the phone. Thankfully there was still good reception downstairs. 'Basically, it means the clinic computers are not connected to the lab computers.

The USB stick downloads everything and we have to organise all the data ourselves later on.'

'OK, so it means someone's trying to hide something?' Nik asked.

Jon laughed. 'It's what you call paranoia to the highest degree. It doesn't matter what you find, the clinic doesn't want it going public.'

Nik turned on a computer and put in the stick. 'How long does it take?'

'Should say on the screen.'

The screen had gone green and a progress bar with the words 'Copy in Progress' appeared. 'Fourteen minutes,' Nik told Jon before turning to Leo. 'I'll take the two rooms to the right. Look for anything interesting that's not on a computer. Handwritten patient files . . . or experiment records. And anything that shows what the lab's used for.' Leo nodded and went to start searching.

The computer room was packed with cupboards and tables. A maximum of two people could fit in there to work. Most of the cupboards were unlocked but all Nik found were flasks, test tubes, Bunsen burners, centrifuges and instruction manuals. The room next door had a mortuary fridge. Nik opened it but all the stretchers were empty. Next to that was a fridge with a glass door. Inside were hundreds of test tubes, all dated and labelled 'Disulfiram Beta 4'.

'I've found something,' Nik said into the mic. 'Samples of disulfiram.'

'Take some with you,' said Jon. 'Along with the test records and patient files, the evidence is indisputable.' Nik filled three unused test tubes with the samples and put the empty ones back in the fridge. That way it wouldn't be so obvious samples were missing. Just as he was putting them in his pocket, he heard a loud beeping from the room next door.

'Nik!' Leo called loudly. He found his new partner in crime standing in front of a large cupboard. On the outside of the cupboard was an electric display with four little lines, blinking in red. It needed a code. 'It only came up after I tried to open the cupboard.'

'What's inside?'

'No idea. It's locked.'

'Jon, can you get the code?'

'Not from here,' replied Jon. 'An alarm is probably about to go off.'

'Then we need to go.' Nik ran to the computer room and a piercing ringing started. It reminded him of school fire drills.

'How long has it got?' Leo called through.

'Fifty seconds,' Nik answered, looking at the screen.

'That's too long!' cried Leo.

'Do *not* take the stick out before it's finished,' Jon said over the phone. 'The files are compressed. If one is damaged, they're all worthless.'

'Security'll be down any second,' Leo said.

Nik held his fingers in preparation around the stick. 'Hurry up, for fuck's sake.' Thirty seconds.

'We need to go!' Leo shook Nik's shoulder.

'We won't get a second chance, Leo,' Nik said. 'When Gawinski finds out about the break-in, they'll close the lab. He might even delete all the data and move the lab somewhere else.'

'We're getting visitors.' Leo pointed to the lift. A green arrow-head above the lift signalled it was going upstairs. The progress bars disappeared. 'Finished.' Nik pulled out the stick and the men ran out of the room.

'Hide over there.' Leo pointed to a column beside the lift. 'When they've got far enough down the corridor, get in the lift and go upstairs.'

'They'll see me!' cried Nik over the alarm.

'Not if I distract them.'

'No, we're both going!' said Nik, pointing to the lift they came down in.

Leo shook his head. 'They'll turn this place upside down until they find someone. I'll be fine. They'll interrogate me and I'll just spew out some alcoholic's adventure story. That way nobody will suspect anything from you and you can get those samples and that USB stick out of here.' Leo grasped Nik firmly on the back of his neck and looked him in the eyes. 'Find out what happened to Viola,' he told him forcefully, before giving him a shove and pointing at the column. Leo went to the other end of the corridor, where he would still be visible from the lift. He untucked half his shirt, gave his hair a ruffle and kicked off a shoe into the corner of the room. Nik threw himself behind the column just as the lift opened.

'I need another drink . . .' he heard Leo shout over the wailing of the alarm. 'Must be some around here somewhere,' he went on, slurring his words. Three men came out of the lift and rushed straight for him. Not one of them looked to the side and Nik jumped into the lift before the doors closed and pressed himself tight up against the wall. The last Nik saw of Leo was him staggering towards the men, gesticulating wildly and slurring some drivel about how much he missed the booze. As soon as the lift doors closed, the sound of the alarm became very faint.

Up on the next floor, the only sign that something was going on was a small red light beside the lift. Other than that, there was no way anyone could know about the commotion just one floor below.

In no time at all, Nik was back in his room. He put the samples behind the water bottles in the fridge and hid the USB stick in the secret compartment in his suitcase. It was almost impossible not to go and look for Leo, but he had no choice. He had to play the role of uninvolved patient, or all their efforts would be wasted. But he'd never be able to sleep. The few hours left until the morning would be some of the longest Nik had ever endured.

Nik made his way to breakfast at the first possible opportunity. He couldn't bear the uncertainty any longer. He took some muesli and orange juice and sat down at the rear of the canteen with his back to the wall. That way, he could see all the tables and the corridor outside. The room started to fill up slowly. He wasn't hungry, so he poked at his muesli, watching the staff closely out of the corner of his eye, but nobody seemed to be taking any notice of him. No hidden signals with the fingers, no whispering. Nobody appeared to have seen him last night and Leo must have kept his mouth shut. Fifteen minutes later, all the tables were full and Nik's impatience had become unbearable. He nodded at a member of staff to clear away his plate and headed over to Leo's room. He managed to force a smile, like he was looking forward to spending a relaxed day with his friend.

The corridor was empty. He knocked on Leo's door. 'Leo!' he called. 'Everything OK?' He waited but the door didn't open. He knocked again. This time a bit louder. Nik put his ear up to the cool wooden door but there was nothing. No steps, no running water or any other noises to suggest Leo was in his room. He went to the exercise area, the yoga hall and the swimming pool, but still no sign of Leo anywhere. As Nik was making his way back to the restaurant, hoping he'd see Leo at the buffet, there was a public announcement.

'Dear guests,' a female voice said over the speakers, 'we regret to inform you that our patient, Leopold von Waldbach, died last night. Despite all resuscitation efforts and his immediate transfer to the nearest hospital, Herr von Waldbach suffered a heart attack.' The woman cleared her throat. 'He was a very well-loved guest and our thoughts go out to his family. He will be dearly missed.'

Nik ran to the nearest toilet, shoved open the door and threw up. The muesli, the orange juice, yesterday's salad – and probably a whole load of disulfiram – came up. His stomach cramped in excruciating pain and he threw up until it was empty. He stood up and kicked the toilet tank as hard as he could. The plastic cracked and water ran on to the floor, but he kept kicking until the toilet was smashed to bits. Without even thinking, he put his hand up to his neck. But his locket was at home. No cyanide. Ending it all right there and then in the clinic wasn't an option. He turned around and left the toilet and, walking past two gawking men, made his way to the exercise area. At this time of day most of the carers were there, supporting guests with exercises, helping group leaders or just cleaning up used towels.

Nik saw Gunnar pushing a laundry trolley towards the staff area. He walked towards him. Gunnar was taller and stronger than Nik but in his blind rage, Nik managed to push him into a changing room and hold him on the ground. The man clearly hadn't expected the attack.

'What happened last night?'

'I don't know,' replied Gunnar.

'Tell me what fucking happened! Leo was fine when I saw him last.' He pulled Gunnar's head up by his collar. 'What happened to him in the basement? And if I hear the words "heart attack" one more time, I swear you'll be the next patient down in the sick room.'

'I warned him,' said Gunnar. 'I told him not to go downstairs.'

'What's so fucking important about a drug for alcoholics that it's OK to go around murdering people?'

'It's not the drug that's the issue, it's the illegal tests,' said Gunnar. 'If that gets out, the clinic will close, the medication won't get authorised and half the staff will go to jail.'

'And Leo had to die for that?'

'Dr Gawinski is insane. This isn't a clinic. It's his lab, complete with slaves and test objects. Anything else is a cover.'

'And that doesn't bother you?'

'Look, I'm divorced, and I've got three kids with two different women. I earn twice as much here as I would in any hospital.'

'So you're doing it for the money?'

Gunnar puffed out his nose. 'Easy for all these rich bastards, isn't it!' Gunnar replied. 'Five houses, three sports cars, parties every day and enough money to supply an army with coke. Yeah, then it's pretty easy to judge. But when you don't know how you're gonna pay the rent or get your son the trainers he wants, then taking money from someone like Gawinski is pretty fucking easy. So when he tells you not to ask any questions, you don't. You smile, you nod and you enjoy the look on your son's face when he opens up his birthday present.'

Nik let go of Gunnar and stood up. It wasn't easy holding back his anger. He was fuming and dying to thrash someone just to feel the pain in his fist. 'Listen, Leo was a lazy toff who pushed drugs for a living. But he still didn't deserve to die for their sakes or for some stupid trials.' Nik turned around and got up without helping Gunnar off the floor. 'Nobody does.' He went back to his room. He needed to get out of the clinic and tell the public what was going on in here. Leo had to be the last victim.

◆ ◆ ◆

'Getting out of there isn't easy,' said Jon. 'You need permission from Gawinski and Alois.'

'You're trying to tell me those forms we filled in are legal? I never saw any legal order appointing a legal guardian, so as long as I'm not declared mentally incompetent I can leave here whenever I want.'

'Do you want a lawyer?' asked Jon. 'The clinic has been through this before and thanks to those prices, they've got mountains of money at their fingertips. They'll take it to court, and until then they'll hold your arse down under a microscope and find the samples you nicked in your fridge. And after finding Leo down in the basement yesterday, you can be sure they'll be checking everything down there. At some point they'll notice samples of disulfiram are missing and then it's just a question of time before you get caught. We need that USB stick. The photos you took of the paper files aren't enough.'

'OK, so I need to get out quick,' confirmed Nik.

'Yes.'

'And what about Leo's murder?'

'What can you do?' asked Jon. 'It's not like you can nip down to the basement and ask someone where he died or where his body is.'

'But he sacrificed himself for me,' said Nik. 'I'd be dead if it wasn't for him. I owe him something.'

'He sacrificed himself for Viola,' Jon said pragmatically. 'So that you could get everything out of the clinic and find out what happened to her and all the other women.'

Nik punched the wall. He wanted to run out of his room, grab Alois and beat the truth out of him. But Jon was right. If he did that, it would all have been for nothing. Including Leo's death.

'You're right,' Nik agreed. 'So how do we go about getting me out of here?'

'As correctly as possible. Normally Pia gets a letter from Alois and Gawinski saying the patient can be released. And after that she puts everything in motion.'

'And how should I get the release letter from the doctors?'

'It's a standard letter. I've got access to the file and I can get the signatures forged. It will only turn into a problem if Gawinski or Alois notices.'

'Any ideas?'

'Gawinski was in Geneva yesterday giving a speech on alcohol addiction. I found his mobile number in a computer file and saw he was in a small village near Geneva. I hacked the network provider, which means I can block his phone and no one will be able to reach him.'

'Sounds good,' said Nik.

'Only problem is . . . he apparently left for Geneva airport early today and the calendar on his phone says he travels back to Munich today. As soon as he gets back to the clinic, a block on his phone is useless.'

'How long till he's here?'

'Hard to say,' said Jon. 'The flight is about an hour. If he checked in a suitcase, he'll be a bit longer, but if he's only got a carry-on, he'll pretty much walk right out the airport. I'd say about two hours . . . if we're lucky.'

'Not a lot of time.'

'No. And don't forget you'll need to keep up your cover. Have your suitcase packed but don't appear panicked. After last night the staff are going to be tense. They'll look through your bags and frisk you and ring the alarm at the slightest thing. I'll backdate the release letter to yesterday so it's not so conspicuous.'

'And what about Alois?'

'I've actually got no idea how you can get him to release you,' Jon admitted.

'It's OK. I've got an idea,' said Nik. 'Won't be a goodbye he'll easily forget.'

Chapter 12

According to Alois's calendar, he had sessions the whole morning. The next free spot would be two o'clock, which was far too late for Nik's getaway plan. But Nik knew from experience that Alois ended his sessions after fifty-five minutes. He always made use of the time to go to the toilet, finish his notes or make a call. And today, Nik would also make use of those five minutes. He stood next to Alois's door, crossed his arms over his chest and gave a little smile. The door opened at thirteen minutes to nine. A woman in her late forties shuffled out of the room. Her face was lifeless, and it was clear she hadn't got much sleep the night before. Her arms hung hopelessly from her slouched shoulders as she walked past Nik, not even noticing he was there. She had bright blonde hair and dark tanned skin, like she'd fallen asleep on a sunbed. Going by the rings on her fingers, there was no doubt she could afford the stay at the clinic.

'Have a nice day, Petra,' Alois called as she walked away.

As Nik came in, the psychologist was sitting behind the desk staring at his computer screen. 'Do we have an appointment, Herr Kirchhof?' he asked, leaning back in his chair. He looked up to the ceiling and laid his finger on his lips, trying to visualise his schedule. Nik closed the door and went over to Alois.

'I just wanted to ask your permission to leave the clinic,' Nik said.

'Excuse me?' said Alois, bewildered by Nik's request. 'We haven't even got through ten per cent of our session plan, and that's not including the physical side of treatment. I'd suggest you . . .'

Nik's right jab made Alois cry out and fall off his chair. He opened his eyes widely and rubbed his chin. Nik turned him on to his front and forced his knee down on Alois's back. He twisted his arm painfully behind him.

'This is what's going to happen,' Nik began quietly. 'You're going to call the delightful Pia and tell her what wonderful progress I've been making in our sessions. And as Dr Gawinski doesn't have any objections, I'm allowed to leave the clinic. You'll find all the forms you need in your mailbox.'

'How did you—' Alois began.

'No questions.' Nik interrupted him with a shove.

'Nobody has ever been released this quickly,' Alois moaned.

'Then find an excuse. 'Cause if you don't . . .' Nik twisted his arm further.

Alois cried out as tears started to collect in his eyes. He kicked his feet on the floor and tried to escape, but Nik's hold was too tight. 'OK!' he shouted.

Nik bent down to speak in his ear. 'I'm going to let go now so you can make the call. One stupid remark and I'll break every bone in your body.' Alois nodded. Nik pulled him up on to the chair and kept his hand on his shoulder, just in case he got any ideas. Alois dialled a number.

'Hi, Pia. Yeah, it's Alois.' His voice was friendly. 'I just wanted to say that our patient Nikolas Kirchhof will be leaving the clinic today.'

'Ah, yes, I was just going to call you.' Nik could hear Pia's voice on the line. 'The forms came through for Herr Kirchhof saying his therapy is finished . . . even though he's only been a patient with us for a few days . . . ?'

Alois looked nervously at Nik, not sure what to do. But Nik just smiled at him and tightened his grip on Alois's shoulder. 'I'm afraid Herr Kirchhof is suffering from weak kidneys and as a result we can't proceed with the treatment.'

'Weak kidneys? There's nothing in—'

'It's fine, Pia.' Alois interrupted her. 'You can discharge him.'

'OK . . .' she replied, her voice brimming with suspicion.

'Herr Kirchhof will be down shortly. Can you call him a taxi, please.'

Alois put down the phone and turned to Nik. 'The clinic belongs to Dr Gawinski. I'm just an employee.' Nik punched Alois in the solar plexus, silencing him instantly.

'That was for Leo,' said Nik, taking a roll of tape that he'd stolen beforehand out of his pocket. He started wrapping up Alois's hands, then his feet and finally his mouth. Nik grabbed him under the arms and dragged him behind the couch before attaching his arms to the chrome legs. He wouldn't be able to free himself on his own. Nik took a piece of paper from the printer and wrote on it in large letters, 'Please Do Not Disturb'. He took Alois's key card and left the room, closing the door behind him.

'Time to go home,' Nik mumbled, after hanging the sheet of paper on the door.

Nik couldn't be bothered waiting for the porter, so he wheeled his suitcase to reception himself. 'Good morning, Pia.'

'Good morning, Herr Kirchhof.' She put the phone back on to the charging station. Her smile was more strained than when Nik had arrived at the clinic, and he realised she had probably been trying to get hold of Gawinski. The last SMS from Jon had said Gawinski was in Freising, a small town right next to Munich airport. On a weekday or a public holiday, it would have taken him ages to get to the clinic. But today was neither, so it was unlikely there would be any hold-ups at the airport or on the roads. It was going to be tight.

Now that Nik's phone was back in its secret compartment, he had no idea how far away Gawinski was. At any other clinic, Nik would have just stepped out the door and gone straight to the nearest U-Bahn. But there was no getting over the walls at this place, so he'd have to keep his cover going right to the end. He tried to stay calm but despite the cool air conditioning and his thin cotton T-shirt, he had started to sweat. He did his best to keep his feet still and not let his voice get tight.

'Your taxi will be here shortly,' said Pia. 'But we will have to search your bag before you leave. There was a . . . an incident yesterday and some things were stolen.'

'An incident?' Nik asked, feigning surprise. 'I never heard anything.' Pia's lack of trust in Nik was blatant. But officially, all the paperwork was there and one of her bosses had personally given Nik's discharge the green light. So as long as Alois was tied up and Gawinski wasn't in the clinic, there was nothing she could do. Pia waved over to a member of staff, who had the same powerful figure as Gunnar and rolled Nik's suitcase behind the desk, presumably towards the X-ray machine. The man beckoned Nik into a private room. First of all, he waved a hand detector over Nik's entire body. It was one of the most expensive on the market. Extremely sensitive, with a 360-degree detection sensor and military standards. It beeped when it went over Nik's watch and again with his belt. Then came the frisk. The man had no problem grabbing Nik's groin thoroughly and he even looked at the heels of his shoes. A minute later he led Nik back to the reception and nodded at Pia. For a moment he saw the dismay in her face that nothing had been found. But seconds later, her business smile was back.

'So, that's that!' She rolled Nik's suitcase around to the front of the reception. 'Can I walk you to your taxi?'

'Of course.' They went out the main entrance.

Pia handed the suitcase over to the taxi driver, who put it in the boot.

'I hope we were able to be of some help to you, Herr Kirchhof.' She shook Nik's hand.

He smiled as widely as he could. 'Oh, you couldn't begin to imagine what a help it's been.' Nik got into the taxi.

The driver got in and turned to Nik. 'Where to?'

'Munich Main Station, please.' Suddenly, an alarm started to ring. Nik looked out the car at the building and saw Alois standing at a window. His hands were no longer tied and he was flapping his arms frantically.

'Wait!' called Pia, walking quickly around to the driver's side. A red light was flashing beside the open gate. It would start to shut in a matter of seconds.

'Five hundred tip if you drive *right now*.'

The driver looked at Pia for a second before pulling the car into gear and slamming on the accelerator. He raced between the two gates just in time and sped down the twisting drive. Nik let out an enormous sigh of relief. Before they got to the main road, Nik put down his window and stuck his middle finger up at one of the hidden cameras. He'd made it.

They arrived at Nik's new flat and he paid the driver as promised. He took his phone out of the suitcase and called Jon. 'I'm out,' he said.

'Did you get the samples and the USB stick out as well?'

'Yes. Don't ever tell me I'm not dedicated to the job.'

'What did you do?'

'I transferred the samples into tiny plastic bottles, tied them up in condoms and swallowed them.'

Jon made a noise that showed his disgust. 'So it's gonna be a while before Balthasar can start working then. And the USB?'

'You probably don't want to know.'

'You didn't swallow it?'

'It was too big. So let's just say . . . I shoved it where the sun don't shine.'

'Jesus,' said Jon. 'You know I still need to get files off that, don't you?'

'That's why it's also wrapped in a condom.'

'Oh, that makes me feel a lot better,' replied Jon.

'I'll let you know when everything's . . . turned up.' Nik hung up and put the phone in his pocket. He closed the main entrance door and went upstairs with his luggage. When he got to the second floor, he heard music. It got louder the further upstairs he went. Just as Nik was thinking how much he detested 'Dancing Queen', he realised the music was coming from his flat. Perplexed as to why a burglar would listen to ABBA, and at such a loud volume, he then heard a high voice loudly joining in the chorus, not hitting a single note.

'Balthasar,' mumbled Nik as he opened the front door. The pathologist was wearing bright red jogging bottoms and a matching hoody. He was also wearing a white sweat band on his head and white trainers. He was dancing on the spot and reaching his hands up in the air like he was trying to touch the ceiling. When he noticed Nik, he stopped dancing mid-move, reached for the remote and turned off the music.

'Nik!' He walked over, arms wide, his expression joyful. 'Jon told me you'd be coming back. Perfect timing. I just finished my workout.' He pointed to an exercise mat on the floor.

'What are you doing in my flat?'

'Jon's flat.' He reached for a towel and wiped the sweat off his forehead. 'My current partner and I had some um . . . differences of opinion, so I set myself up here for a while.'

'How did you get in?'

'Oh, that lock wasn't a problem.'

'You can pick locks?'

'Oh, yes. Ever since my nanny put a padlock on the biscuit tin. I was only five at the time. But don't worry' – he pointed to three suit-cases and two bags in the corner of the room – 'I only took the bare necessities. And I'm going out in a minute.'

'Why does it smell so weird in here?' Nik walked around sniffing at the air.

'It's lavender,' said Balthasar, beaming. 'From Provence.'

Nik noticed a small sachet of it on the coffee table.

'I also put some in your laundry cupboard.'

'In my laundry cupboard?'

'You know' – Balthasar spoke softly, as if he didn't want to be overheard – 'you should use more softener. Less rubbing at the groin.'

'OK! OK!' Nik got Balthasar in a headlock and dragged him to the door under his arm.

'Let me go, you brute.' The pathologist tried to free himself and hit Nik in the stomach. But the punch was weak and did nothing to deter Nik.

'And I still owe you one for your little constipation gag.' Nik pulled the door open and pushed Balthasar on to the landing. Ignoring Balthasar's offensive language, he threw his luggage into the hall and slammed the door shut, then steadying himself against the back of the door with his hand, he let out a sigh of relief. 'I need a beer.'

'You hooligan!' Balthasar shouted through the door. It was bad enough he hadn't showered after doing his exercises, but Balthasar wouldn't normally be seen dead outside the house in a jogging suit. Just as he went to start searching for his phone in one of his bags, Nik flung the door open again.

'Why is the fridge full of Prosecco?'

'So it stays cold,' replied Balthasar, screwing up his face at the stupid question.

'Eighteen bottles?'

'One must always be ready for guests.'

'Which guests drink eighteen bottles of Prosecco?'

Balthasar started to answer but Nik put up his hand. 'Actually . . . I don't want to know. Where is my beer? It was in the fridge.'

'I poured it all out.'

'You poured it out?!' Nik was furious.

'Nik, are you not aware how much flatulence is—'

'Stop!' Nik cried. 'I need to make some space in the fridge.' He slammed the door again.

'OK, but don't throw it away! It's a special delivery straight from Italy!' Balthasar called from the landing. He put his ear up to the door and heard a window being opened. Swiftly followed by a series of smashes, then car brakes, a horn and the harsh clatter of metal.

'Oh well, karma is a bitch, I suppose,' said Balthasar, smiling and rounding up his bags. It looked like he'd have to spend a few nights in a hotel. Thankfully, he'd only packed the bare necessities. He stopped for a moment. 'Feels like I've forgotten something.'

'Oh my God, that's disgusting!' Balthasar heard Nik shouting from inside the flat.

'Oh, that was it!' said Balthasar joyfully. He put his head up to the door. 'Now be careful, Nik,' he called. 'Latex is delicate!'

Chapter 13

The sunny weather matched Nik's mood perfectly and the snow had a calming effect as he walked through the English Garden, newspaper in hand. 'Haven't seen you this happy in a long time,' remarked Mira. Despite it being milder, she was still wearing her winter jacket, a scarf and a woollen hat. Nik pointed to the front page. Underneath a photo of the clinic were the words 'Medical Trial Scandal' printed in large letters. And underneath that was a photo of Dr Gawinski.

Mira nodded approvingly. 'How did you pull that off?'

'With a mixture of evidence and forgery,' Nik began. 'Thanks to the files, samples of my blood and the stolen samples, there was no doubt Gawinski was testing out disulfiram on people without their knowledge.'

'And why?'

'To treat alcohol addiction. If taken together, alcohol and disulfiram can be deadly. The side effects are horrific. But if someone could alter the substance to limit the side effects to feeling unwell and throwing up at worst, it would be a fantastic way to treat alcohol addiction . . . and it would rake in billions.'

'Actually sounds like a good thing.'

'Well, yeah, but Balthasar reckons if Gawinski hadn't tested it like he did, on patients who were clueless, he'd only have made minimal progress.'

'Why didn't he just go about it legally and test it on willing people?'

'Because it never got approval. So instead, he just used his patients as guinea pigs. All that money he was making at the clinic went towards researching and refining the substance.'

'Did anyone die?'

'Balthasar thinks there were two cases where the interaction between the medication and alcohol led to death. But it'll be up to the public prosecutor to decide that. We gave the press all the bits of evidence that make for sensational headlines. We had to ruin Gawinski's reputation.'

'And what did you fake?'

'The report on Leo's death,' said Nik. It still hurt to think about him. The way he'd faked being drunk so Nik could get away. 'We forged a letter from Gawinski to Alois and the clinic's security manager where he recommends Leo should be dealt with because he'd found out about the trials. They killed Leo *after* I got the files off the computer, so there was no mention of him anywhere. We needed something that would give the investigators a prod in the right direction.'

'And what really happened to him?'

'His death certificate says he had a fatal fall, but the public prosecutor has ordered an autopsy. And now, because of the press leak, there's so much attention surrounding Leo's death that nobody would be able to cover anything up. Not like Kathrin, who just had to disappear silently.'

'And what *is* the deal with Kathrin? And Viola and Olga for that matter?'

'We found files on Kathrin's stay in the clinic but nothing whatsoever about Viola or Olga. Them going missing had nothing to do with the medical tests.'

'So it was just a coincidence that all three were in the clinic?'

'God no,' said Nik with complete conviction. 'That's the only connection we have. Just because we can't link those two to the tests, doesn't mean there isn't a link to the staff or patients. We just need to find out who.'

'And how are you going to do that? You're suspended, so it's not like you can just interrogate Dr Gawinski or the patients.'

'With a timeline,' Nik explained. 'We know when Kathrin stayed at the clinic. And we know the days of the parties when Olga and Viola were working. So now we need to get the names of the staff and patients who were in the clinic at the same time as Kathrin and compare their photos with the people at The Palace on the night Viola went missing.'

'Sounds like a lot of work.'

'It is.' Nik smiled. 'But not for a computer whizz.'

'Looks like you've grown quite fond of this Jon bloke.'

Nik gave Mira a sharp look. 'Jon threatened and blackmailed me into doing this case. I've been beaten up twice, tortured . . . and I was almost shot! And he's the reason I got suspended!'

'But he did uncover a medical scandal.'

'By accident,' Nik reminded Mira.

'But isn't it nice to know you caught a ruthless doctor who would've just carried on killing . . . or getting to expose all that corruption at the CID?'

Nik groaned stubbornly.

'He even got you enjoying your job again. Can't remember the last time you were this chatty.'

'Now you're just exaggerating.'

Mira laughed. 'OK, so Jon's way of getting you on the case might not have been the most orthodox, but one thing's for sure, he definitely knew you were the right guy for the job.'

Nik's phone started to ring. He looked down at the screen. 'Speak of the devil,' Nik mumbled, answering the call. 'Yep?'

'I'm finished,' said Jon, sounding relieved. 'That was torture but we've got two new suspects. Both were at the clinic while Kathrin was there, and both are on the club footage. Crappy quality, but you can see their faces.'

'Great.'

'Jump in the hire car and drive towards Obergiesing,' said Jon. 'I'll send you the first suspect's details in a minute.'

The flat could have been bachelor-pad heaven. A two-hundred-square-metre loft-style apartment with dark parquet flooring scattered with light grey rugs, and a large white sofa. It also had a modern kitchen, a large LED TV and a Jacuzzi on the patio, which looked on to a back garden full of apple trees. But currently the place was a rotting mess. Completely neglected by whoever was staying there. The floor was hidden under a sea of unopened letters, newspapers, empty champagne bottles, old takeaway boxes and dirty clothes. The white couch was covered in large coffee stains and dirty plates were stacked high on top of the hob. The curtain at the patio door had been ripped down and left draped over a broken stool.

'This is what you normally see with junkies,' Nik said into his phone as he peeked through the living room window. 'Not your typical junkie hideout though.'

'Belongs to Silvio Verbeck. The son of a property mogul who owns buildings on Marienplatz and Kaufingerstraße. Silvio inherited one of those buildings from his dad and gets a healthy income from the rent.'

'And what does he do?'

'He's got shares in a bar and two restaurants. You can see him on every other photo on their social media sites.'

'Anything else?'

'Thirty-four years old. Born in Munich. Picked up twice for drug consumption – so no driving licence. But he's never been to jail.'

'Any violent offences?'

'No,' Jon answered. 'He's been a resident at Gawinski's twice. The first time for six weeks, the second for three months. He must have had contact with the women during that time.'

'I'll knock.' Nik went to the front door, which was covered by a small awning, and saw two cameras. One directly above the entry system and the other at the edge of the awning. There was a small, well-kept garden in front of the entrance area, which itself had been laid with light-coloured paving slabs. Silvio clearly wanted to keep up appearances on the outside of the building. Nik pressed the buzzer. He heard a loud gong from the front door. There was a long silence. He was just considering whether he should break into the flat when a man's voice came over the intercom.

'Hello?' He sounded like he'd just woken up.

'Hello, Herr Verbeck. It's Inspector Pohl from the Munich CID.' Nik held up his fake badge to the camera. 'I need to talk to you about your stay at the Meadows Beauty Resort.'

'Don't know it,' said the man.

'Maybe you haven't read the news, but the clinic's been shut down and all files have been passed on to the public prosecutor's office,' Nik lied. 'Your files are there too.'

'That's private information,' Verbeck replied. 'And I don't have any time. Call my lawyer.'

'Herr Verbeck,' Nik went on, 'I just need to speak with you for a few minutes. A couple of questions, and then I'm gone. Or . . . I can just get my colleague from the drug squad to come down with a search warrant for your flat. Whatever the case, you'll have to talk to me at some point.'

Verbeck said nothing. Then the buzzer sounded, and Nik pushed open the door.

The smell inside the flat was even worse than the mess. The living room window hadn't been opened in days and the air was warm with the sour smell of booze and mouldy food. Verbeck met all the criteria of a well-to-do drug addict. His brown hair was greasy and dishevelled, he hadn't shaved in days and his skin was a sickly pale tone. He had a small cut above his left eye, probably the result of a fight. His tailored white shirt was creased and stained and the top two buttons were undone. As was the fly on his Karl Lagerfeld jeans. He was wearing Bugatti sunglasses and an ostentatious gold ring on his index finger. His hands were shaking and sweat beaded his brow. He forced out a quick and grudging 'Hello' as Nik shook his hand. He stank and clearly hadn't washed in days. His mouth let out a heavy stench that mismatched his bleached teeth. Nik gestured towards the couch and they both sat down.

'Herr Verbeck, why did you stay at the Meadows Beauty Resort?'

'Well, it wasn't for the manicures,' he answered snippily, wiping his nose with the back of his hand. Verbeck showed all the signs of an addict in withdrawal and would want to get rid of Nik as quickly as possible. Nik could use this to his advantage.

'If you don't mind me asking, what's the um . . . problem?'

'Drugs.'

'And which ones?'

'Coke, for fuck's sake,' Verbeck snapped. 'So I do a bit of charlie now and again. So what? They used to put the stuff in Coca-Cola and no one cared. They should start again . . . might calm people down a bit.' He pressed his hand down firmly against his lap in an attempt to stop the shaking. Nik took out a notepad and wrote something down. He was going to drag the meeting out as long as he could; Verbeck looked unstable and his eyes were springing in all directions, as if he was on the lookout for an imaginary stalker. But periodically they would rest for a moment on an antique office desk. Probably where he kept his drugs.

'Did you make any acquaintances at the clinic?'

'Acquaintances?'

'Yes. Other patients, members of staff, doctors . . . ?' Nik suggested. 'People you saw on a daily basis?'

'Mostly just that bastard, Alois.' Verbeck got angry just saying his name. 'Felt like smacking him the first time I met him. Always looking up at the ceiling to think. Arrogant piece of shit.'

'Anyone else?'

'Of course,' he said, turning his palms towards the ceiling impatiently. 'Class leaders, canteen staff, cleaners. What a stupid question.'

'What about Leopold von Waldbach?'

'Never heard of him.'

'Peter Maier.' Nik made up the name.

'No.'

'Viola Rohe?'

Verbeck's eyes darted to meet Nik's, holding them there for just a second. But it was exactly the second Nik needed.

'Don't know anyone called Viola.'

'Oh. That's strange,' replied Nik. 'Because Viola was in the clinic at the same time as you.'

'There were loads of patients there at the same time as me. D'you think I spoke to all of them?'

'Viola wasn't a patient. She helped out at the Wednesday-night orgies. Not as a prostitute. Giving out drinks.' Verbeck's eyes were brimming with panic. 'Coming back to you now?'

'I never went to those parties.' It was so obvious Verbeck was lying, Nik could have laughed.

'If you say so,' Nik said. 'But you see, I've got video footage of you at The Palace on 22 and 23 October 2016. And guess who was working behind the bar that night?'

'Get out!' Verbeck shot up from the couch and pointed to the door. 'I don't need to listen to this shit.'

Nik calmly put his notepad back in his pocket. 'Actually, you do. Just in a slightly more formal setting.'

'Out! Get out!' Verbeck was waving his arms around frantically.

Smiling contentedly, Nik stood up and walked towards the door, which he then slammed behind him. His plan had worked. They had a new suspect. By the time he had got to the street, Verbeck had rolled down the blinds. So Nik climbed over the garden fence and watched him through the glass patio door from behind a hedge. Verbeck was on his mobile, gesticulating madly. The door was well insulated but Nik could still make out some words.

'And why the hell's he turning up at my house?' cried Verbeck, falling back on to the couch. His voice was shrieking and his body trembled. He went on talking for another minute before throwing his phone down. He left the room and went in what looked like the direction of the bathroom. Nik climbed nimbly back over the fence and got in the car. He called Jon.

'It's looking good,' Nik began. 'I'd barely even finished saying "Viola" when he went off on one and screamed at me to get out.'

'So could he be involved in her disappearance?' asked Jon.

'It's possible. But in his condition, he wouldn't be able to hide a thing. Tilo would have never trusted a junkie like that and he also wouldn't have risked Dr Cüpper's career by using him.' Nik sighed. He still didn't understand it. 'Nah, Verbeck definitely isn't at the top of the food chain. What's his family situation like?'

'His dad's dead. His two older brothers manage most of the family property company. And . . . his mum lives in Marbella. There are rumours that the brothers don't get along. Silvio wasn't allowed into a charity event organised by the family company not long ago.'

'So we can rule out the Verbecks as a supporting party.'

'Sounds like it,' replied Jon. 'So what now?'

'Verbeck called someone as soon as I closed the door and he was instantly fighting with whoever it was. Something else will happen today. Either Verbeck will get visitors, or he'll leave the house to meet up with someone. Until then, I'll wait in the car.'

'Would it be worth breaking in?'

'It'd be difficult,' said Nik. 'The door and windows are pretty much impossible to break. You can get into the garden easily but all the glass in the house is safety glass. Unless he happens to leave the patio door open, I'm not getting in. And I didn't see anything of interest inside the place anyway. No computer, no tablet. No files or records. Not even any books. The only thing that might be of any use is his mobile, but I'm not breaking in just for that. I can get it off him when he's out and about. If he's off his face on coke he wouldn't notice a pink elephant following him down the street.'

'OK, well, while you're waiting, I'll try to find some more on our second suspect.'

'Who is it?'

'A young businessman called Eberhard Lossau. Don't know much about him but I know he's on a business trip in China right now. Gets back in a couple of days. So we can concentrate on the rich junkie for the time being.'

The front door opened and Verbeck came out wearing a winter jacket and a woollen hat. He kept his head down, like a Hollywood star who doesn't want to be recognised.

'Show time,' said Nik, getting out of the car. 'Let's see if my new buddy leads me to the big boys.'

Luckily Verbeck went on foot. Following him through Munich's traffic without him noticing would have been a challenge. It was Wednesday lunch time and the pavements were reasonably quiet. The snow had stopped but it was still cold and people would only leave the house if they really had to. Verbeck was waiting to cross the road when his mobile rang. He took a set of Bluetooth headphones out of his pocket and put them in his ears. He began to talk. His voice was calm now and he wasn't gesticulating or screaming anymore. He was concentrating so hard on the telephone call, it made it easier for Nik to follow him. He would have loved to get closer and listen to what he was talking about but he had to keep a good distance. There weren't enough shops on his side of the street where he could hide if Verbeck suddenly turned around, nor were there enough people to just slip into a group. But he didn't turn around once. Nik followed him for another fifteen minutes before Verbeck stopped at a junction. He looked around, trying to find the right way, then pressed his hand to his ear as if he was listening to directions. He finally nodded and went down a small side street. Nik stayed at the corner and watched as Verbeck walked down the street slowly, looking left and right, trying to find the right number. He finally stopped at a building with a shipping container in front of it and went inside.

Nik waited until Verbeck had disappeared and followed him inside. It was a classic old Munich building made from sandstone, with intricately carved window pediments and a small garden at the front which was separated from the road with a high metal fence. The doors had been left slightly ajar, as if someone was expecting Verbeck to arrive. Nik went in carefully and looked up. The place smelled like screed and the bannister on the wide wooden staircase had been covered with tarpaulin, as had all the landings and staircases. The interior was clearly being refurbished. Nik closed his eyes and focused on any sounds. He couldn't hear footsteps or anything to suggest people were working in the building. He also hadn't seen any vans at the front door. Apparently nobody was working today. The only thing he heard was Verbeck's hushed voice coming from upstairs. Nik couldn't understand a word and waited for other voices to join in the conversation. But none did. Verbeck was still alone. Something strange was going on.

Normally, Nik would have inspected the whole building after getting inside but he knew that if Verbeck spotted him he'd run off. He wished he had his gun and hoped there weren't any surprises waiting for him upstairs. Each stair creaked as he made his way up to the first floor but Verbeck carried on his telephone call regardless. His voice was calm, almost monotonous. It was the complete opposite of how he'd talked back at his house. There was a flat on the first floor with the front door missing. Nik went inside. The floorboards had been taken up and the lights on the ceiling had been covered for protection. Verbeck's voice got louder the further Nik went inside the flat. He pushed a piece of tarpaulin out of the way and walked into a large room with bay windows. Verbeck was standing in front of the window. He'd taken off his headphones and his phone was in his pocket. Instead of being surprised to see Nik, his face was sad and full of remorse.

'I'm sorry,' he said, sinking his head.

Before Nik even had the chance to say something, he heard the clicking of a pistol hammer. A slim woman emerged from a side door, pointing a SIG P226 at Nik. It was an efficient and powerful gun and the distance between him and the woman was minimal. He'd have three bullets to the chest before he could scratch his head.

'Hello, Herr Pohl. Nice to meet you at last.' Her accent had a slightly north German twist. Nik raised his hands and looked harder at the woman. She was wearing a dark grey trouser suit, modern and exquisitely tailored. Her blonde hair was tied back. If it wasn't for her big nose and yellow teeth, she would have been very attractive.

'Do we know each other?' Nik asked.

'I know *you*,' answered the woman calmly. 'You've caused me quite a bit of hassle over the past few days.'

'Because I messed up your connection with the CID?'

'Herr Hübner wasn't our only connection,' she remarked. 'But I'll admit, he *was* one of the best. As was Dr Cüpper, who has had to go underground because of you. And now, without those two, there's been a bit of a hole.'

'Not to mention the clinic closure.'

'Oh, we've got nothing to do with that,' the woman said with a smile.

'But you did have something to do with Roswitha, didn't you?' said Nik. 'You hanged that girl outside my flat and left her to die.' The woman shrugged her shoulders. 'When Roswitha can talk again, she'll tell me who it was and if you had *anything* to do with it, I swear you're finished. And I swear it won't be a nice death.'

She laughed. It was a mixture of surprise and arrogance. She knew without a doubt who would come out of the current situation the winner. 'Why didn't you just leave the case alone? Then nobody would've got hurt. Your colleague would still be alive, and I wouldn't have to shoot you.' She turned to Verbeck. 'You should leave. Wouldn't want you throwing up at the sight of blood.' Verbeck nodded and walked off with his head still hung low.

Nik weighed up his options. The woman was too far away for him to grab her gun. She seemed calm and her hands were steady; she didn't look like someone who would hesitate when it came to the crunch and was clearly experienced in this kind of situation, as if she'd been in the army or worked in security. The hallway was just one step backwards. One jump and he'd be near the staircase and away from the line of fire. But Nik had heard the scrunch of tarpaulin while they were talking, which meant a second person was waiting at the door, probably also holding a SIG in their hand.

A plan began to form in Nik's mind. A very stupid, dangerous and painful plan. But it was his only chance of leaving this place alive. He sighed and waited until Verbeck had reached him on his way to the door. Then he grabbed him by the shoulders and shoved him into the blonde woman. Verbeck fell on top of her, breaking the line of fire. She would need a moment to push him off her. And it was in that exact moment when Nik made his move. He ran to the old-fashioned bay window, covered his head with his arms, closed his eyes and jumped through the glass. If he'd remembered correctly, he'd just miss the container and would land in the snow-covered garden. It hurt like hell when he hit the ground and he'd gathered so much momentum that he rolled, shoulder first, through a cherry laurel bush. He ignored the pain and moved along the ground to the container. He heard a shot. Then a second, louder shot from a bigger gun. So there *had* been a second person behind him. He felt the hissing of bullets pass his head. Pressed down to the ground, he made it over to the fence. The container was high enough so that the woman wouldn't be able to shoot him from the first floor. His trousers were ripped at the right knee and blood was streaming down his left arm, probably from a shard of glass that had lodged itself under his skin. But he didn't have the time to deal with it. He crawled to the pavement, then stood up and limped towards the main street. There was a stabbing pain in his knee but he had to get out of that side street. He took off his jacket and used it to cover his bleeding arm. When he got to the junction, he noticed a sign outside a restaurant advertising a lunch-time buffet. He opened the door, nodded to the staff with a friendly smile, and sat at a small table beside a group of senior citizens who had just got up to go to the buffet. Nik clenched his fists together under the table, trying to hide his pain. Fortunately, everyone in the place was far too engrossed in the buffet to take any notice of him. He sat with his back to the wall, not taking his eyes off the entrance. But neither Verbeck nor the blonde woman appeared. He was safe for the time being.

Chapter 14

Nik made his way by taxi to the U-Bahn, took it to the next station, and then walked for two blocks. He needed to make sure nobody was following him. When he arrived at his flat, Balthasar was waiting at the front door with a first-aid kit in his hand. While Nik got himself a beer from the fridge, Balthasar spread out his equipment in the living room. He cut Nik's sleeve open and looked closely at the wound.

'It'll need eight stitches,' he said, wiping away the blood and disinfecting Nik's arm.

'Let's go then.'

'Without anaesthetic?'

'Wouldn't be the first time.' Nik took off his boots and pulled up his trouser leg. A large shard of glass had got wedged in his leg between his ankle and the middle of his calf. The pathologist nodded, impressed at the size of the wound. Nik took out his phone and called Jon.

'What happened?'

'I got away by the skin of my teeth. But we're getting closer to our answer.' Nik sucked in air through pursed lips and screwed up his eyes as Balthasar positioned the first stitch. 'I met the person in charge of all the dirty work. Sorry, the *woman* in charge.' Nik told Jon every detail. Her height, appearance, accent, hair colour and that unnervingly pale skin. 'When we find the person giving her orders, we've got our culprit. Blondie only tidies up loose ends.'

'I could put the info through the database but if she's a pro I'm not going to find much.'

'No, there's no point. I'll get the information out of Verbeck.'

'It was him behind it all?'

'No, Verbeck doesn't have the balls or the brains to set up that kind of trap.'

'So what d'you want with him then?'

'Blondie's number. That alone is worth a second visit. But this time I won't be as friendly.'

'Don't forget your new girlfriend will be waiting for you,' Jon warned.

'Oh, I know. I'm sure they're watching Verbeck's place as we speak,' said Nik. 'I'll need a diversion.'

'What you thinking?'

'The hire car is still outside Verbeck's front door. Find some petty criminal who's my height and size and give him the spare key. Whoever it is has to take the car and race it away past Verbeck's house. If Blondie's anywhere nearby, she'll follow it and I'll have time to get to Verbeck.'

'And how are you going to get inside? He'll not let you in a second time.'

'With a sledgehammer.'

'What?'

'Like I told you, the windows are so secure breaking in is impossible. The front door had a safety lock that's linked to the frame in six places. Getting in with a crowbar would take me ages so I'll just smash the wooden door apart with a sledgehammer . . . and march on in.'

'The police'll be there in two minutes.'

'I reckon it'll be more like five. There's no station nearby. And that'll be enough time to at least get hold of his phone and beat him up until he hopefully gives me a name.'

'Do you *want* to go to jail or something?'

'I'll put something over my face and take a couple of things away with me so it looks like a robbery. Hopefully, Verbeck will be high, so he can't give the police a clear statement or spew out the real reason I was there.'

'And how d'you plan on getting away?'

'It'll be dark, so a thirty-second lead will be enough time . . . even with a smashed-up knee,' replied Nik. 'Two or three fences later, they'll have lost me. I'll dump any crap I took and disappear into the woods. Five hundred metres and I'm at the U-Bahn.'

'In the dark?' Jon's voice was sceptical. 'So when d'you want to go over there?'

'Tomorrow around five a.m. There'll be no traffic and whoever's watching the house will be tired by then. By the time Verbeck notices I'm doing something to the door, I'll be inside.'

'You know if Blondie pops the driver before he even gets to drive away, the plan is useless. Or if a police car's nearby, they'll be on you before you get inside, or the door might actually be made of iron with a timber covering, or—'

'I know, I know,' interrupted Nik. 'Loads could go wrong. But that's what makes it so thrilling, isn't it!' He felt another shot of pain searing up his arm. 'Are you nearly finished?' he snapped at Balthasar.

'Stop moaning,' replied the pathologist, pulling the needle out of Nik's arm. 'If you want to be of sound body tonight, then this has to be sewn up properly.'

'I'll deal with the diversion,' said Jon on the phone. 'I know a guy who's fast-footed and a good driver. Hopefully, Blondie will buy it. If not, the break-in can't even begin.'

◆　◆　◆

Nik took a taxi to Verbeck's neighbourhood. A couple of painkillers had thankfully sorted out the pain in his knee and arm. It was nineteen minutes to five. The cold night and drizzly snow were perfect for his plan. At five o'clock, Jon's driver would arrive at the car and start the engine. If Blondie was clever, she would have put a tracker on Nik's car so she could follow him easily. Whatever the case, someone would appear. A sports bag hung down heavily over Nik's shoulder. He'd wrapped up the sledgehammer in towels so it didn't bulge too suspiciously. When he got to the junction, he hid himself behind an SUV. Verbeck's house was sixty metres away. He'd have enough time to look around and get into a good position before Jon's diversion kicked off. Nik had expected the street to be quiet and free of people but instead a blue light was flashing through the snow and there was the sporadic rumble of voices.

'Shit.' He crept closer and saw a police car and an ambulance parked right in front of Verbeck's apartment building. He was too far away to see anyone on the street but it would be too risky to move any closer. It wasn't as if Nik lived in the area, and walking around with a sledgehammer in a sports bag might call for a bit of explanation. Nik threw the bag over a fence into the next garden and went back to the junction. He walked one hundred metres north before turning into a street that ran parallel with Verbeck's. With a little help from Google Maps, he'd been able to study the area earlier that day and plan his escape route. But before escaping from the police, he would take the route towards Verbeck's house. He climbed over two fences, crossed a large grassy area with a swimming pool and used an overhanging apple tree to reach the garden behind Verbeck's flat. The lights were on inside. Two male police officers, a female medic and two men in civvies were standing around Silvio Verbeck, who was lying naked on the living-room floor. His eyes were wide open and a trail of vomit was running over his cheek and on to the floor. He had a plastic tube in his left arm and there was a syringe on the floor beside him. Instead of dealing with the body, the medic was filling out a form, so Nik could safely assume Verbeck had been dead a while. He must have overdosed.

Nik scanned the living room and couldn't see a phone lying about. At least not from where he was standing. The police had either already packed it up as evidence or Verbeck had dumped it earlier that day at the block of empty flats.

Nik closed his eyes and clenched his fists. Yet again, whoever he was up against was ahead of him and now they were gone.

The smell of the unventilated basement would have been too much for most people. The place was scattered with mouldy Chinese takeaway leftovers and inhabited by a man who washed and changed his clothes once a week, if he was lucky. Everybody else had already turned around and left the bungalow as quickly as possible but Sara was still there. After experiencing the stench of a rotting, maggot-infested corpse, you could pretty much deal with any smell.

She carefully stepped over the mountain of takeaway boxes and old food, trying at least to keep her cashmere jumper clean. Her shoes were already a write-off after stepping into a sticky puddle of coagulated coffee. She could have made the owner pay for it, but it was already going to be hard enough to get him on her side. And she needed him. He was the only person who stood a chance of finding out who Nik was working for.

Damian Inger was schizophrenic, which made it impossible for him to build good relationships. The threat of violence was enough to set off a panic attack that could last for hours, and that was not what she needed right now. Damian also had agoraphobia and never left the house. His computer was his life. His need for food was satisfied with Chinese takeaways, while his sexual needs were fulfilled by a latex doll, which waited for him patiently on a tattered old couch. And it was on this couch where Damian also satisfied his need to sleep.

'What d'you want?' he asked sternly, flipping his long hair out of his face. He looked at her angrily before letting his eyes wander down to her knee-length skirt.

'An amazing hacker who doesn't give a shit.'

'Not interested,' he replied, sitting himself back down at his computer.

'But you need something to get by, don't you?'

'I've currently got two hundred nicked credit card numbers on my computer. That should be enough money for a while.'

'I didn't mean money,' she said, shaking a little bag filled with white powder.

'I'm done with that stuff.' He waved it away.

'Really? That's a shame,' she said seductively. 'Purest coke out there. Right from the source. Catapults you into dimensions you couldn't imagine.' She pressed her thumb into his unshaven chin and lifted her foot on to the side of his chair. He stared at her calf lustfully, biting his lip. 'And I was so looking forward to partying with you.' She licked his ear slowly and grabbed him between the legs. She laughed. Damian was hers.

◆　◆　◆

Waiting had never been Nik's forte but he knew he would have to put the investigation on hold until Verbeck's post-mortem had been carried out and the CID had finished their report. He'd tried to sleep, but after two hours had woken up from a nightmare bathed in sweat. In the end he'd decided to get up and search Alois's records again for clues. But it was useless. He ordered a pizza and worked all evening, but couldn't find a solid lead anywhere.

He stood up and walked over to the wall where he'd pinned up everything he had on the case. Right at the top were photos of the three women: Viola, Kathrin and Olga. Viola and Olga were still registered as missing, while Kathrin had been murdered. Each photo had a piece of string that led to the words 'Rehab Clinic'; it was the only common factor between them. Underneath that were photos of Alois, Dr Gawinski, Gunnar and Leopold. Again, each of the men was linked to the clinic. Leopold's death had proved Gawinski was willing to go to any lengths for his illegal medical trials, but Nik was pretty certain that these trials had nothing to do with what had happened to the women. But even so, he would bet any money that their stories were linked to somebody else they had all met at the Meadows Beauty Resort.

Nik hung up Verbeck's photo beside the clinic and put a strike through it. Verbeck had met the culprit but was just a follower. Nik looked at the photo of the second suspect, Eberhard Lossau. His black hair was combed over in an obnoxious side parting. He was clean-shaven and looked more like a teenager than a man in his late twenties. His smile was fake, as if he'd really had to force the corners of his mouth to go up. He was pushing his shoulders back and held his chin up in the air but even then, he had an awkward air of instability about him.

Nik closed his eyes and tried to paint a picture of Lossau. He didn't seem to have exceptional political influence and his wealth alone didn't make him guilty. Obviously, some rich people are ruthless egotists who take glorious pleasure in annihilating the competition, but that didn't mean they ran around killing everybody. And Nik could rule out organised crime: Tilo might have been an evil piece of work, but he had been too hard to blackmail since he didn't have any family and money alone wasn't enough for him. He wanted power and authority, and that meant the one pulling the strings in all this must at least have some political power, as well as extensive financial resources to be able to afford someone like Blondie. And of course, he had to be callous enough to have no qualms about getting rid of anyone who posed a threat.

Nik opened his eyes and looked at Eberhard Lossau's photo. It was definitely possible he was ruthless and rich. And he looked unprincipled enough to be able to kill people. But neither Tilo nor Cüpper would have trusted him. Not this little boy. Lossau would barely be able to intimidate an angst-ridden junkie like Verbeck.

Nik was ripped from his thoughts when his phone rang.

'Something's happening,' said Jon.

'With the report or the post-mortem?'

'Both,' Jon replied. 'The post-mortem finished an hour ago. I sent on the details to Balthasar. And since then the report has been uploaded on to the server.'

'Good news first, please,' said Balthasar, who was apparently also on the line.

'The autopsy was carried out diligently. Everything points to a suspected case of poisoning, with poison being found in venous blood, stomach contents, organ samples and hair samples. So the given cause of death – Heroin Overdose – is plausible. All the signs are there. Silvio Verbeck fell unconscious and choked to death on his own vomit. What's interesting though is how much heroin was in his system. It was fatally high. Five milligrams of that stuff would be dangerous for someone who isn't used it but Verbeck had *ten times* that much in his system. That would've finished off the most ardent of junkies.'

'Suicide?'

'Not impossible,' answered Balthasar. 'But Verbeck was a coke addict. Why did he suddenly go and inject heroin?'

'What does the CID report say?'

'Three bags of heroin were found alongside drug-related paraphernalia. High-grade stuff. Barely cut.'

'So there are two possibilities. Suicide or murder.'

'The way you described it, Verbeck was definitely in a mess after your visit,' said Balthasar. 'But it's hard to believe he'd OD because of it.'

'Yeah, but the question is, why was he found with three bags of heroin on him?' added Nik. 'As you said, Jon, five milligrams alone would have been more than enough. That suggests it wasn't suicide.'

'OK, so let's assume it was murder then,' said Jon.

'Did the report mention any evidence suggesting the involvement of other people?' asked Nik.

'None of the neighbours saw anything. There was no mention whatsoever of a blonde woman. And no signs of forced entry.'

'So Verbeck let his murderer in willingly.' Nik stood up and walked around the flat contemplatively. 'And he shot up willingly as well. No signs of a fight?'

'Nothing in the report.'

'I might have an idea,' said Balthasar hesitantly. 'Verbeck had an injury on the side of his head. Apparently from hitting it on the sofa when he fell . . . which is possible. He could have done it when he fell unconscious. But . . .'

'. . . someone could have smacked his head on something to begin with.'

'It wasn't a serious injury but enough to black out or get disoriented.'

'And give someone enough time to inject him with heroin,' added Jon.

'As soon as that stuff was in his system he couldn't do a thing,' Balthasar continued. 'And that gave the murderer enough time to prepare the crime scene and clean up any evidence.'

'How did anyone find out about Verbeck?'

'Coincidence,' said Jon. 'The neighbour's dog had to go out around four. The owner couldn't be bothered going for a walk, so he just let him out in the garden. He saw the light was on in Verbeck's place and when he moved closer he saw him lying on the floor. He called an ambulance immediately but the only thing left for the medic to do was pronounce him dead.'

'And when did he die?'

'By the time the medic arrived, rigor mortis had set in on the eyelids and masseters. Time of death was declared midnight.'

Nik sighed. 'Another witness gone.'

'I'm afraid there's no good news about the phone either. None of your CID colleagues picked it up and I didn't see it in any photos.'

'Email me everything anyway,' said Nik. 'It's unlikely, but I might still think of something.'

'Will do.'

'And now there's just Eberhard Lossau to deal with. Hopefully, he'll tell us something before he also gets popped with no explanation.'

'Lossau got back from his business trip this morning. I'll hack his computer tonight and have a look around. By tomorrow morning I'll have a good idea of who he is. Then we can get going on him.'

The CID and forensics reports turned out to be solid and convincing, and any cover-up on that side seemed unlikely. Which didn't exactly help Nik. He still didn't know who Blondie was or who she worked for. At around two in the morning Nik went for a long walk. Munich was covered with a silky, unblemished blanket of snow. But the walk only distracted him a little. He went home and was making his second coffee of the morning when his phone rang.

'What a night,' said Jon, yawning. 'Lossau's business computer was more secure than the CID's.'

'You hacked the CID?'

'Maybe best you don't know all the details,' replied Jon.

'Was it at least worth the hard work?'

'I'm still downloading stuff but as yet I haven't managed to put together a good profile of Lossau.' Jon cleared his throat. 'He comes from a dynasty of bankers who go all the way back to the Royal Bank of Nuremberg. After the Second World War, the three brothers invested their capital in various companies with varying degrees of success, and that brought about a handsome fortune for the family. Eberhard Lossau is the only son of Willibald and Agathe Lossau. After finishing school and his undergraduate degree in Munich, he studied in various places abroad . . . from Boston to Fontainebleau . . . where he sometimes did well, sometimes not so well. Overall, his studies were a chaotic time, but when he joined the family's own holding company in 2012 things began to quieten down. Today he's responsible for foreign business and is almost always on a plane. Officially at least.'

'And unofficially?'

'According to his file, he's a regular at the clinic. Coke and alcohol. From the family's point of view, it's easier to tell people he spends long periods of time on business trips. Probably the reason he has the international position in the first place.'

'Any connection to our women?'

'He could have met Viola at Munich Uni or known of Kathrin's start-up through work. And it's possible he went to Olga for sex. But as usual, our only link is the clinic.'

'Any cross references? To Tilo, Dr Cüpper or Blondie?'

'Nothing,' said Jon. 'Aside from the CCTV of Verbeck and Lossau together at The Palace, there's no connection to anyone else.'

'I'll have to talk to him face-to-face.'

'Compared with Verbeck, Lossau's wealth is off the scale. His company personnel file says he's got a chauffeur who used to work in security. And they have some of the best lawyers out there, so the CID spiel won't work.'

'I'll sound out the situation first and then think of something.'

'I've sent the holding company address to your flat. Along with directions to his family home outside Munich.'

'Did you find anything else about him?'

'Very little—' Suddenly, Jon's voice was interrupted by a shrill beep.

'What was that?' asked Nik.

'What the hell?' said Jon, confused.

Nik heard Jon hitting the computer keys frantically. 'What is it?' Nik asked.

'They've put a tracker on my computer.'

'A what?'

'A program to get my location.' An alarm went off. It pierced the air like a hammer hitting a plank of steel. 'They've found me!' Jon cried. 'They're at my door!'

'Who?'

'The blonde woman and her friends.'

'Go, for Christ's sake!'

'I know, but I have to start the self-destruct first or they'll find you.' There was the smashing of a window pane.

'Just get out!'

'Just a second . . .' Something hissed loudly like a firework before a loud boom sounded over the phone. Nik could hear the room shaking.

'Jon?'

Something crashed to the floor. Men were shouting.

'Good luck, Nik,' Jon said softly, like a man who'd given in to the inevitable. 'Don't give up.' There was a shot and the line went dead.

Chapter 15

Nik walked back and forth around the flat, staring at his phone and waiting for a call that would relieve his anxiety. He'd tried to call Jon back four times, but the phone was dead. He'd also got hold of Balthasar at work, but he didn't know Jon's emergency hiding spot. Nik didn't have access to the CID server, so he turned on the local TV channels, listened to the radio and kept an eye on the news online. But there was nothing. Just a case of bodily harm in Obersendling and a traffic collision in Milbertshofen. Nik's phone rang, snapping him out of his obsessive search. It was Balthasar.

'Anything?' Nik asked hopefully.

'No,' he replied. 'I was counting on you and your skill at finding clues.'

'I don't have access to the CID server anymore. Tilo's account has been frozen and only Jon had the other access info. So I can't see if there's been a shooting. Blondie's probably beating every last detail out of Jon before she dumps him in the Isar.'

'So what are you going to do now?'

'What d'you mean?'

'You're free,' said Balthasar. 'Whatever it was Jon was blackmailing you with doesn't matter now.'

Balthasar was right. Nik could go back to his flat, wait for his suspension to end and start working his normal hours at the CID again.

The Breitling watch Jon had given him would get him through a couple of months until then.

'Jon sent me the address of another suspect not long before he disappeared.'

'So you're not giving up?'

'It's been a long time since this was just about Jon's search for Viola. And anyway, it was the last thing Leo asked for.'

'Do you need help with it?'

'All the help I can get.'

'Well, where do we begin?'

'With Eberhard Lossau. And if it turns out he's responsible for those women going missing, then I'll deal with him my way.'

Three days had passed and Lossau still hadn't shown any sign of strange behaviour. His chauffeur would wait outside his house for him every morning at half past eight. Today he was wearing a navy suit, a white shirt and a red tie. He had a camel hair coat over his suit and was carrying a briefcase. Lossau was fatter than in the photos Nik had seen. He had less hair and his skin was an unhealthy shade of red. He held his head slightly downwards, resting his double chin on his chest. His eyelids were swollen like a boxer's after a fight and his hair was sloppily combed over to the side. The Mercedes made its way into the morning traffic while Lossau sat in the back reading the paper. His driver went via Oberföhring, took a right at the hospital, past the Isar and over the Maximilians Bridge to a modern office block. It took them half an hour. The driver opened his door and Lossau went into the building and took the lift up to the company offices on the second floor.

Nik parked the hire car in a spot in front of the building and waited. Like every other morning, he scanned the local news, but yet again there was nothing about what had happened to Jon. His mobile was still dead and Balthasar hadn't heard from him either. Nik was raring to follow Lossau into the building and beat everything out of him, but the satisfaction from that wouldn't last long. He had nothing he could use against Lossau: the files from the clinic had been sourced just as illegally as the photos from The Palace; there was no obvious connection between Lossau and Blondie or the other women; and he didn't know Silvio Verbeck well enough to claim any link there. But the fact that he was the only remaining person to have been at The Palace *and* the clinic, meant that he was Nik's last hope of finding out what had happened to those women. And if Lossau knew Verbeck, and Verbeck knew Blondie, that was enough to convince Nik that Lossau was involved somehow. He might even be pulling the strings, and if that was the case, a CID agent on suspension was hardly going to shake him, even with the threat of violence.

If Nik wanted to make any progress, he'd have to monitor Lossau and hope he led him to a new location or to Blondie. Nik closed his eyes and sighed. He felt helpless, and having to sit in the small hire car, watching the office block and hoping for something to happen was frustrating.

At ten o'clock the car door opened and Balthasar got in. He was wearing a thick winter jacket and a woolly hat. He handed Nik a takeaway coffee and a chocolate doughnut.

'Still nothing,' said Balthasar.

'Someone I know at forensics described all the bodies that have come in but none of them fitted Jon's description.' Nik held up his phone. 'I'm also keeping an eye on the police ticker. But there's been nothing there either.' He hit the steering wheel with both hands.

'And what about here? You seen anything?'

'It's been three days and I'm beginning to ask myself if Jon got the right man,' Nik said. 'Lossau leads a boring businessman's life. There's not been anything suspicious. No police, no blonde woman and no one else who seemed in the slightest bit suspect.' He took a sip of coffee.

'I'm gonna get closer at lunch time and if nothing interesting happens by the end of the day, I'll go and visit him at his house.'

Nik saw Balthasar's concern. A break-in was risky and irresponsible, but the pathologist was equally anxious and frustrated, so he stayed quiet. He'd put extra make-up on his eyes in an attempt to hide his lack of sleep. There wasn't a trace of his usual cheerfulness; instead he was serious and pensive. He laid his hand on Nik's shoulder. 'Be careful.' Then he got out of the car.

Nik waited until 11.30 a.m., put on a wig and some glasses and left the car. He took his suit jacket from the back seat and pulled his tie up to his neck to make the perfect knot. Lossau's favourite restaurant was about a hundred metres from the office block. He always went there for lunch and took a window seat that looked out on to the street. Nik had watched him eat there alone for the last few days. He sat down at a table with a view of Lossau's back and dug into a roasted pork knuckle with dumplings. Lossau had good table manners but he threw his food down like it was the only meal he'd see that day and drank more wine than was appropriate for lunch time. He didn't receive any visits from dubious business partners or hold any whispering telephone conversations. While an attractive waitress cleared away dishes from the next table, he made sure he got a good look at her cleavage. You could claim he was guilty of disrespecting the service staff after ignoring the restaurant manager's 'Hello', leaving a tiny tip and going without saying goodbye. But none of that made him a psychotic murderer.

After Lossau was back in his office, Nik went to a public toilet, where he took off his disguise and put on some casual clothes. He then made his way back to the car and observed the building until it got dark. Lossau had left work around 8 p.m. every day that week and had been driven home by his chauffeur. There had been a light on in his penthouse until midnight and then he'd gone to bed. Nik had watched the entrance the whole time but never saw Lossau creeping out or anyone going in.

Today, however, Lossau left the office block half an hour earlier than normal. His driver was, as usual, waiting for him in a large Mercedes, suggesting this had been planned in advance. Nik put his coffee cup in the holder, started the engine and merged in behind the car. As usual, they went back over the Maximilians Bridge and past parliament, but today, instead of going left towards Oberföhring, the Merc stayed on Einsteinstraße before turning south on to the A8 towards Salzburg. Nik gripped the steering wheel with his left hand and picked up his notepad from the passenger seat. Jon had given him the address of the family estate in Inntal. Maybe that's where Lossau was heading. The snow and heavy traffic made it difficult to keep on him, but then, as expected, the car changed from the A8 on to the A93 after the sign for Inntal. When the driver took the exit towards Brannenburg, Nik followed him and then stopped at the side of the road. There weren't many cars on the roads at that time of day and the estate was too remote for another car to also be making the trip. It would have been too obvious to keep following him. Nik waited twenty minutes before putting the address into the satnav and driving off. Despite the ceaseless snowfall, the large drive down to the house was clear. The Lossau's family estate sat regally on top of a hill with views of the nearby villages and the Inntal Valley, and the grounds were surrounded by a wall. Although there was snowy woodland all around the building, it would have been easy for anyone inside to spot an approaching car some distance away. He would have to leave the car on a small woodland track and walk the rest of the way.

The snow was getting heavier. Cursing at the stinging snowflakes, Nik lowered his head and went up the drive. He could barely see two metres ahead but at least that would make it hard for any cameras to get a clear shot of him. At the end of the drive there was a large gate. The metal bars were far enough apart to get a look at the estate but too close together for anyone to squeeze between them. The vegetation around the entrance was tidy, but then got thicker the deeper into the wood Nik went. He followed the wall and it became clear from its height and condition that it was more for decoration than for deterring burglars. At one point, some stones had fallen out so Nik placed his foot inside the gap and heaved himself on top. It was very slippery, but he managed to steady himself and land safely on the other side in a small oak forest. Now protected by the trees, he took a good look at the villa. The two-storey building had at least four hundred square metres of room space, spread over one large main house and two side wings. The windows and doors were new and strengthened to the highest standards but were perfect replicas of the original manor house windows. Lossau's Mercedes was parked at the door but there was no sign of the chauffeur. The drive leading from the gate to the house had been laid with cobbled stones and lined with radiant yellow lamps. The rest of the drive was unlit, meaning Nik could creep over to the side wing at the edge of the wood without being seen. Houses like this always had staff, so with a bit of luck, there would be a separate entrance at the back which would be poorly protected.

The back wall of the house had no windows and was lined with tall hawthorn bushes, making it extremely dark. Nik finally reached a small forecourt, where there was a shelter for the rubbish bins and two parking spaces. And just to the side of that was the back entrance he'd been hoping to find. It was almost impossible in the dark to see if there were motion sensors or cameras. The lock on the door was just a regular Yale. No second dimple lock and no other kind of security device. Things were working out well. Nik took out his mini lock pick and put the clamp in the lock. It was a long, thin instrument that would have looked more at home in a dentist's surgery and was the part he would use later to untwist the lock. Thanks to the internet, he'd been able to buy an electropick – a battery-powered device that looked much like an electric toothbrush, but instead of a brush it had a vibrating mechanism that would work the cylinder much faster than a normal lock pick. In just ten seconds, the pins in the lock had been pushed down and Nik could turn the clamp. The door opened.

Nik hurried inside, and just as he was about to close the door he spotted two figures standing in the hall. One of them was a large man who was pointing a gun at Nik, and beside him was a woman, equally neat and well dressed. Any hint of friendliness from the man was ruined by the scar linking his left eyebrow to his ear. As the second figure moved towards him, Nik recognised her features.

'Disappointing, Herr Pohl,' said the blonde woman. 'Did you really think the doors didn't have any cameras?'

Nik groaned regretfully and raised his hands.

'But please, come on in.' She gestured towards the hallway that led further into the house. 'I'd like to introduce you to someone.'

Nik was frisked by Scarface, then the blonde woman tied his hands behind his back with cable ties. He wasn't going to get away a second time. The man led him along the hall by the arm while the blonde woman walked a couple of steps behind. Nik wasn't going to leave the place alive if he didn't get those ties off but they were pulled tight and made of thick plastic. Tearing them would be impossible. He would need something sharp.

They walked through a large kitchen with two hobs, two ovens and an industrial dishwasher. Blondie pushed open a door that led them into a wide hallway with a polished granite floor covered with a red carpet that ran to the front door. On the walls were portraits of men who looked like Eberhard Lossau. Nik had never understood the fascination with displaying paintings like that, but it said a lot about the family.

A large staircase led from the hallway up to the first floor. The high ceilings and elaborate interior all reminded Nik of the old manor houses in *Gone with the Wind*. It was suffocatingly warm throughout, and Nik contemplated that keeping the house in such good condition and heated in the winter must cost the family a fortune.

He was led into a library full of heavy wooden floor-to-ceiling shelves stacked with books. The room felt sinister. Flames were flickering in the fireplace and a candelabra stood proudly on a desk. Other than that, there was no lighting. In front of the fire stood a small, dainty woman with grey hair tied back in a bun. She was looking at herself in the mirror above the fireplace. She wore a long evening gown that fitted snugly at the top but flowed out elegantly on the bottom half. She was playing with a pearl necklace around her neck, trying to decide if it was the right piece of jewellery for her outfit. Scarface shoved Nik closer to the fire then took a step back, submerging into the darkness, while Blondie went to stand beside the woman.

Nik recognised Eberhard's features on the face reflected in the mirror. The years had dug deep grooves into her face but she was slim and still pretty. She would have been breathtaking in her younger years but there was a pinched expression around her eyes; a look that was filled with bitterness and exposed years of shame and humiliation. Nik scanned the room for something he could use as a weapon. The only things were the logs at the fireplace and the fire poker. But they would be useless with his hands tied behind his back. There was also a large sofa with worn-away leather and a small side table on which stood a crystal carafe filled with water and a crystal glass. The woman put down her pearls.

'Do you have children, Herr Pohl?'

'None that I know of but I could call my ex,' answered Nik.

Scarface hit him on the back of the head. Nik was desperate to retaliate but he also wanted to know why he wasn't already dead and lying in the snow somewhere and as he didn't want to spoil his chances of finding out, the hit would have to be ignored. For the time being.

'But if you did have them, you'd do everything you could to make them happy, wouldn't you?' the woman went on. 'Help them get through life . . . Show them the ways of the world?'

Nik wasn't sure where this conversation was leading, especially as the woman in front of him didn't seem to have an ounce of motherly warmth or affection about her. 'Of course.'

'And if that child didn't turn out how you'd hoped. If it was . . . deformed in some way, would you still love it and protect it?'

'It's not the child's fault.'

'Well, then we understand one another.' The woman opened another jewellery box and took out a tasteful and exquisitely made silver chain adorned with small diamonds.

'What's going on here?' asked Nik. 'There's no way you brought me up here to talk about children.'

'Perhaps you're aware that Eberhard is my son.'

Nik gave an impatient hum to say 'yes', and subsequently received another blow to the back of the head.

'Why are you making so much effort to find out everything you can about Eberhard?'

'Because I believe he's responsible for the disappearance of three women and that he murdered at least one of them.'

The grey-haired woman put the chain up to her neck. 'That's not his fault.'

Nik was surprised. It wasn't the answer he'd been expecting. A denial or an angry retort perhaps, but not a confession.

'So he was involved?'

The woman sighed. 'People used to say the Lossau boys were cursed. The villagers were always polite and said hello, but they would hide their daughters as soon as they saw us coming. And quite rightly so.' She put down the necklace and walked back to the jewellery box. 'Nowadays they call it a hereditary disease. A genetic defect . . . or a mutation. But nobody has found a cure that will prevent the insanity from being passed down.' She looked at Nik in the mirror. 'My father-in-law was a horrible man. Violent, heartless. But he had so much power nobody could do anything to stop him. I knew what the marriage to his son would be like the very first time I met him. Every other woman would have run. But I didn't have a choice, as it had all been arranged years in advance.' She ran her fingers over her cheeks. 'I was lucky, you see, because I wasn't Willibald's type. He'd hit me and kick me . . . and tie me up and rape me when he came home after drinking sessions with his friends. But that was nothing compared to what he'd do to all those girls who were stupid enough to get involved with him. Blinded by his money and power.' She took out yet another necklace. Wild pearls with a dark agate heart at one end. 'It was so easy to cover things up back then. No DNA tests, no security cameras, no computers. But things are different now.' She held up the necklace to her neck. 'When I was pregnant, I prayed to God it would be a girl but he only half answered. I was pregnant with twins. Eberhard and Zita. And while my girl grew into the perfect princess, I recognised the Lossau curse in Eberhard. He was wild and unpredictable and prone to tantrums from a young age. All the typical traits of the male lineage. It wasn't an easy time and got even worse when he discovered his sexuality.'

Nik was looking at the woman in the mirror. Even behind the harshness, he recognised sorrow and regret, the longing that everything could have been different. 'That damned blood,' she said, mostly to herself.

'That's your excuse?' Nik asked. 'That a hereditary disease turns all the Lossau men into psychopaths?'

'Ah, you see. Now we've come back full circle to the beginning of our conversation. What would you do if it was your child?'

'Not allow him to kidnap and kill women.'

'I didn't allow it.' She raised her voice for the first time since Nik arrived. 'I did everything I could to try and stop it. I had Eberhard tested, went to the top psychiatrists. Even got him a bodyguard to try to prevent the worst eventualities. But it did nothing. What was I supposed to do? Lock him up?'

'Yes!' said Nik. 'And because you didn't, people died. You could have saved those women's lives. Viola, Kathrin and Olga. Not to mention Tilo, Leopold and Jon.'

She looked at him in the mirror. 'Was that your partner, this Jon?'

'Yes.' Nik lowered his head.

The woman took her eyes off Nik again and looked at the necklace.

'Was it worth it?' asked Nik quietly. 'Killing all these people for the sake of your son?'

'If you were a father, you'd know the answer to that question.'

'Well, I'm a danger to your son,' said Nik. 'So why am I still here? Why am I not lying dead in the snow somewhere with a bullet in my head?'

'Because I need to know what you know.' She closed the chain at the back of her neck. 'If you were able to trace Eberhard's tracks, then so could someone else and I need to close that gap.'

'And you think I'm gonna start talking now?'

'No.'

'So why tell me your touching life story then?'

'You've proved to be a tough opponent, Herr Pohl,' she said. 'And now with Tilo Hübner's . . . absence we will need an able person at the Munich CID.'

'You might not have noticed, but I've been suspended.'

'That wouldn't be a problem,' she explained. 'You don't think Hübner made it that far up all by himself, do you?'

Nik turned his head to the right and spat on the floor. 'Go to hell!'

He saw the hit coming but didn't try to avoid it. The fist caught him on the cheek and hurled him to the side against the small table. The carafe smashed on the floor and he fell on top of it. Shards punctured his skin painfully. The woman turned to her employee. 'Sara, deal with him, please. And make sure he's gone by the time I get back from the reception.'

Sara nodded and waited for the woman to leave the room. Scarface lifted Nik to his feet and shoved him out of the library. 'We've had a lovely meeting room fitted out in the basement for people like you. Thick walls and loads of things we can use to hurt you.' The blonde woman stood in front of Nik and looked him in the eyes. 'Or, you could tell me everything I want to know and I'll just put a bullet in your head. That's your best option for today.'

'Fuck you!' Nik replied.

'You're gonna die whatever the case,' said the woman while Scarface pulled him along the hall.

◆　◆　◆

It was the perfect torture chamber. A floor laid with tiles that sloped down to a drain. A washbasin and steel bathtub. A collection of tools hung on the wall: hammers of various sizes, tongs, screwdrivers, knives and scalpels. In the middle of the room was an examination chair, like the ones you find in a dentist's surgery. It was lit with a halogen lamp that hung from the ceiling. Scarface pushed Nik on to it, and he noticed, grimly, that it smelled of chlorine. Leaving his hands tied behind his back, Scarface tied down his ankles and chest with leather straps. He didn't pull them as tight as they could go but enough to stop Nik from raising himself off the chair. Before Nik could say anything, Scarface hooked him in the face with his right hand. It was a hard blow and Nik could taste blood in his mouth. But if that was where the torture stopped, then he'd be able to hold out a little while longer. The large man took two steps back and let Sara take the stage.

'Let's start then, shall we?' she said with a smile. 'Do you want to tell me everything about your investigation or should he hit you again?'

'I'll tell you everything. But first just let me ask your friend something.'

She nodded her permission.

'What's it like running around the whole day with such an ugly face?' Nik smiled. 'Do you throw up when you're shaving in the morning? Or did you just get rid of the mirror?' The next punch broke Nik's nose and the one after threw his head to the side. Nik tried hard to stay conscious. Another thud to the stomach left him unable to breathe and he started to wheeze.

'We can go on all night,' said Sara. 'You wouldn't believe what the body can endure before finally giving up.' She pushed Scarface out of the way. 'But don't worry. The caretaker here has some experience in burying bodies. Good old Joseph will make sure you get a nice spot.' She straightened out her suit. 'So, back to your investigation. How did you come across Viola Rohe's case?'

Nik's head was slumped over. Blood was dripping from his nose on to his trousers. He closed his eyes, took a deep breath and mumbled something.

'You have to speak louder,' said Sara.

Nik said something again. Barely audible.

She grabbed his head with both hands and pulled it up. 'Louder, or I'll fetch the hammer and crush each word out of you.'

Nik opened his eyes. 'I just wanted you to come closer.' His right hand shot out from behind his back, ramming a shard of glass into her throat, while his left hand went instantly for her gun halter. Before Scarface had time to get out his gun, Nik had already shot him twice. First in the shoulder and then through his forehead. Sara stumbled backwards, holding her hand up to her throat. Blood gushed between her fingers. Nik untied the leather straps, keeping his eyes fixed on Sara, then he walked past her towards the cupboard as she fell to her knees. Just as he'd expected, the cupboard was brimming with cleaning products. He took out a bottle of bleach.

'That was lucky,' he said. 'Now I can wash away all my traces.'

Sara gasped, trying to push out a reply.

Nik got down in front of her on one knee. 'And then I can deal with Eberhard,' he whispered calmly.

She fell to the floor. Her hands dropped from her throat but the blood kept running. One last breath and she was still.

Nik wiped his prints from the gun, placed it in Sara's hand and used her finger to fire one more shot against the wall. Now her prints were on the trigger. He then took the bleach and washed away his blood from the chair and the floor. Using everything he'd learned during his years in the CID, he organised the crime scene to make it look like there had been a fight between the two employees. It wasn't perfect, of course. The wound on Sara's throat didn't fit the knife he'd placed in Scarface's hand, after wiping it in her blood. But leaving the shard of glass would have made the investigator suspicious. It was entirely plausible that a guy like Scarface would have carried a knife in his pocket. That way, nothing suggested there had been a third person in the room and that was the important thing.

Happy with his work, he took Scarface's gun out of its halter and applied a dressing to his own nose. He didn't want to have to wash away any more traces. He wiped down his trousers and made his way upstairs. He wondered if Eberhard was already sleeping. The house was quiet and Nik didn't see any servants or anyone else from Sara's posse. It was possible the house was empty, but there was also the chance the others were hiding. Looking out of a high window, Nik could see that the snow was heavier now, blanketing the surrounding woods in a deep layer of pure white. It looked idyllic. The only sound interrupting the silence was the low drone of a television. He followed the noise and ended up in a large living room with an old-fashioned interior that matched the rest of the house. Eberhard sat on an armchair with his back to the door. He had a glass of whisky in his left hand and the remote control in his right. Every couple of seconds he would flip through to another channel. Nik went over and stood in front of the chair, pointing the gun at Lossau's forehead.

'Hello, Eberhard.' He smiled with true satisfaction. 'So nice to finally meet you.'

A look of surprise flashed across Lossau's face but then the corners of his mouth started to curl upwards and his eyes became bright. It was as if he'd realised what had happened to his employees, and the thought pleased him.

'I always told my mother—' A punch to the stomach shut him up. The whisky and remote control fell to the floor and he sank to his knees, bent over in pain.

'Now, that felt pretty good,' said Nik, relishing the moment. He went over to the whisky decanter and took a gulp. The strength of the alcohol made him cough. 'Oh, delicious,' he said approvingly. 'I'll need that again in a minute.' He jammed the decanter underneath the arm he was using to hold the gun while using his left hand to pull Eberhard up by his hair. 'Awfully loud in here, don't you think?' Nik said. 'Let's go to the library.' Eberhard squealed like a child as Nik dragged him to the library. He thrashed about and cried, and beat his hands against Nik's arm, but Nik carried on hauling him through the house.

When they got to the library, Nik shoved Eberhard into the middle of the room, where, only a couple of hours earlier, he'd stood speaking to his mother. The broken glass was still on the floor, meaning it was very unlikely there were any employees in the house. Lossau had probably sent them home for the night. The fire had gone out. Nik picked up a piece of wood, held it down in the embers until it was lit, and used it to light the candelabra. He put the whisky down on a bookshelf and turned to Eberhard, who was rubbing his head, trying to straighten out his messy hair.

'So, you know the blonde woman, right?' Nik began. 'She's the one whose throat I just slit down in the basement? Well, you probably know her game as well. Answer my questions, and all this will come to a painless end.'

Eberhard pursed his lips together in anger. 'You've got no idea who you're—'

Nik kicked him in the stomach. Eberhard hunched over with a guttural moan. He tried to catch a breath, but his body convulsed furiously. He rolled around on the floor until Nik pulled him up by his hair again.

'Question one,' Nik began. 'Where is Viola Rohe?' He was looking Eberhard straight in the eyes and could tell the man knew the name. Even so, for a moment it looked as though he was going to deny it, but then he bit his lip and looked down at the ground.

'Dead,' he finally said.

'Did you kill her?' Nik took a step backwards.

'She could have had everything she wanted,' Eberhard continued, his body still contorting. He squeezed his fists together, and in his eyes, Nik saw the monstrous insanity his mother had talked about: a rampant anger that made him forget anything else existed. He was capable of anything in that state. Cover-ups, torture, murder. 'But she treated me like a stupid country bumpkin. Me! The heir to the Lossau House!'

'Maybe you weren't nice to her.'

'I don't have to be nice!' he cried. 'I've got money and power and I belong to the kind of society a common whore like Viola could never dream of.'

'Sounds like true love,' Nik said, disgusted. 'And what? You went along to The Palace one night to prove yourself to her?'

'Yes. And what does she do?' said Eberhard. 'She runs off. Like I had scabies.'

'But thankfully, your employees were waiting outside for her.'

He giggled. 'You should have seen her – the way she lay on the ground in the basement in her own piss. Her eyes stretched wide in fear, begging for her life.' He closed his eyes and inhaled blissfully. 'She would have promised me anything that night. Done absolutely anything for me. All her cool dismissiveness was gone. All her lies about some boyfriend who'd apparently promised to marry her. But it was too late for that.' He shrugged his shoulders. 'What else could I do? A man has his honour after all.'

'And where's her body?'

'Not far from here. A quiet place behind our family chapel with a stunning view of the countryside. Under the branches of a spruce.' He clasped his hands and looked up, as though communicating with some greater power. 'She wasn't religious in any way, so she won't miss a gravestone.'

'And will I find Olga there as well?'

'Worthless whore,' Eberhard said, unaffected. 'I roll up with a pile of notes and she can't get in the car quick enough. Nice to look at but too weak for the big games.'

Nik shook his head at Lossau's unapologetic evil. He'd met a lot of murderers before, and even the hardest hitmen had known they'd committed a crime. But for Eberhard, it seemed legitimate to go around killing people. There wasn't a single sign of remorse and he had no notion of right and wrong. The textbook psychopath. But at least he was feeling chatty.

'And Kathrin was . . .' Nik carried on.

'. . . a scheming little hussy,' said Eberhard. 'We really could have had something, Kathrin and I, but then one night she just upped and left. She was so close to getting away but Sara and her bloodhound tracked her down.'

'So they smacked her on the head and threw her off the climbing rock.'

'Well, that all went a bit tits-up really. It was that bloody walker with his headlamp. He turned up before Sara's people had got to the mess at the foot of the crag. So in the end they decided it was better to wait and do a cover-up, even if it did cost us a lot of time and energy.'

'And that's why Sara put together the climbing gear in a rucksack . . . to make it look like an accident.'

'Yeah, she was a clever girl, Sara.' Eberhard shook his head with fake regret. 'I'll miss her.'

'Well, you won't where I'm about to send you.'

Eberhard chortled. 'Come on, Herr Pohl. You can *see* how rich we are. And you've *felt* how powerful we are. Your friend Hübner was just small fry compared to the other people on our list. And you're just a shitty pig, your colleagues don't believe a word you say. There's not a court in the world that would throw me in jail, no matter what you say.'

'I'm not talking about jail,' said Nik, kicking Eberhard in the kneecap with the heel of his boot. He put all his strength into the kick, all the anger that had been building up until this point, and it felt good when he heard the bone crack. Eberhard rolled madly around the floor, holding his leg and screaming. Nik picked up the whisky decanter and poured the contents over Eberhard's face and clothes before setting the bottle down on the floor. He stood on a chair and started to shake the bookshelf. Books started falling out. He kept on shaking until the screws in the wall came loose and slammed the shelf on top of Eberhard. It was only covering his leg but that was enough for what Nik had planned. Eberhard heaved fiercely trying to get out from underneath while Nik took a candle from the candelabra. He took his time, watching Eberhard's futile attempts to push the shelf off and listening impassively as the man screamed in pain and fear, begging for his life. This must have been how the women had spent their last moments, so it was only fair that Eberhard endured the same thing.

Nik turned to him with the burning candle in his hand. 'This is for Viola, Kathrin and Olga.' And with that, Nik put the flame down to Eberhard's wet clothes.

It must have been an excruciating death. Eberhard had continued to scream even as his flaming clothes engulfed him and only when the books around him ignited did his cries finally subside. By the time the fire service got here, the whole wing would be up in flames meaning Nik didn't have to worry about cleaning up traces in the library. Nik picked up his jacket, which Scarface had taken off him earlier, and went along the hall. It was slowly filling up with smoke. On the way to the door, he went past paintings of Eberhard's father, who'd died eight years earlier. Nik also caught a glimpse of a small photo frame standing on a mantelpiece. Two steps later, it occurred to him who he'd seen in the photo. He turned around and grabbed the frame.

'My God,' he said, looking at the photo.

There was a small chapel one hundred metres west of the house. The fire brigade wouldn't take long to arrive but it was long enough for him to climb over the wall and disappear through the woods. Behind the chapel was a clearing surrounded by birch trees with branches that were bent under the weight of the snow. In the middle of the clearing stood a lonely spruce, just like Eberhard had said. The tree was out of place among all the other deciduous trees, but its bare branches were also battling against the heavy white load. Nik walked over to a shed behind the chapel, where he found a pickaxe and a shovel propped against the wall, as if waiting for the next victim. He took them back to the clearing and started to clear the snow underneath the spruce. He quickly found an area that looked different from the rest, about two metres long and one metre wide: a clear sign that somebody was buried underneath. Nik took the pickaxe and loosened the frozen layer of earth. He then took the shovel and started to dig centimetre by centimetre.

Nik heard the sirens approaching but he kept shovelling until he'd exposed the body. He carefully pulled down the zip on the body bag and knelt beside it. He placed his hand on the woman's cheek, slowly and gently, as if she was still alive.

'He's dead, Viola,' Nik whispered. 'You can be at peace now.'

Nik could see Jon's bandaged shoulder through his white T-shirt and a saline solution was flowing into his veins through a catheter in the crook of his arm. The monitor was off and the evening news was playing on a TV that hung on the wall. In front of Jon was a tray with a dry piece of bread and a slightly suspect slice of red ham. Jon hadn't touched it and wasn't planning to. Beside the tray was a closed laptop. Jon opened his eyes drowsily and turned to Nik.

'Hi, Nik,' he said. His voice was weak. 'Didn't expect to see you here. Thought I'd covered my traces pretty well.'

'Konrad Zuse?' Nik picked up the slice of dry bread. 'You could've given a bit more thought to your pseudonym, Herr Computer Whizz.'

'It was good enough for the hospital.'

'Yep, a fake ID will get you far.' Nik took a bite of bread. 'Our blonde friend didn't expect that one.'

'I enjoyed reading the papers the last couple of days,' said Jon, changing the subject. 'After the graves were found, Agathe Lossau was arrested in front of the Munich aristocracy. And her son Eberhard apparently died tragically in a fire.'

'I saw that. Only heir to the family.' Nik shook his head. 'Terrible. Absolutely terrible.'

'A harrowing chain of events. First buried under a bookshelf and then the books caught fire.'

'Just wasn't Eberhard's day at all.'

'No. And his mother wasn't having a good day either. Might be tricky having to account for all those dead bodies on her estate.' Jon reached for a glass of water and took a sip. 'Jesus, we knew the guy we were looking for was insane, but I never expected sixteen bodies to turn up.'

'Now, don't give Eberhard all the credit,' said Nik. 'Some of those bodies had been lying there for eighty years. It'll be months before it's all processed. But at least the cursed Lossau family disease has finally been put to an end. The last male heir is history.'

'And that was their explanation for everything?' asked Jon. 'Viola had to die because the men in the family were sick?'

'Not entirely.' Nik took out the picture frame from a pocket.

'My God,' said Jon, looking at the photo. It was a young Eberhard and his twin sister on a beach somewhere. The two were unmistakably similar, but even more obvious were the similarities between his twin and the women he killed.

'That's Eberhard's sister, Zita. Here it looks like Lossau was totally in awe of her. And one day she went missing. Just left a letter saying she was never coming back. Her parents hired a private detective and used their contacts at the police but no one ever heard from her again. To this day nobody knows where she is, or if she's even alive.'

'So Eberhard just wanted to replace his sister. As soon as he saw a woman who looked like her, he wanted to have her.'

Nik nodded. 'And if she didn't play along, he would get very angry and kill her.'

Jon closed his eyes. 'So many wasted lives,' he mumbled. 'How d'you know all this? I sat for days searching for stuff on the Lossaus but never found anything on Zita.'

'A fake CID badge can come in handy sometimes,' Nik said. 'After Eberhard was found and Agathe had been arrested, the villagers started gossiping. You wouldn't believe the stories their ex-servants will tell you after three beers at The Crown Tavern.' He took another bite of bread. 'So I brought it all to the attention of some ecstatic journalists, who mumbled something about "headlines for weeks". And while Agathe Lossau's been stewing in custody, the tabloids finally ruined her reputation.' Nik looked at the floor. 'I'm sorry, Jon. I hoped I'd find Viola alive.'

'Yeah, well.' Jon smiled sadly. 'I knew something had happened to her but not knowing what was tearing me apart. At least I can mourn her now.'

The two men sat in silence for a while, each deep in their own thoughts. Two nurses were discussing a patient at the door, a machine beeped and a bed rattled past the room.

'So what are you going to do now?' asked Jon. 'Your suspension still hasn't been lifted.'

'At the moment I'm helping a neighbour move house.' Nik smiled. 'An uncle of Jennifer's, who she never really knew, died and left her a small terraced house not far from Perlacher Forest. Along with enough money to send Justin to some special school.'

'Well . . .' said Jon, 'sometimes good things do happen to good people.'

'I've never seen the two of them this happy. The first load of furniture is already over there and tomorrow we'll start with the boxes.'

'It might be a good idea to get to bed and catch up on some sleep then, eh?' Jon suggested.

'I'd rather wait here till you're feeling better,' said Nik. 'And then I can beat the shit out of you for forcing me to work a case that lost me my job and almost got me killed . . . four times!'

'Oh, come on. I'm more scared of the senior citizen with Parkinson's in room twelve than I am of you,' Jon said dismissively. 'And anyway, our blonde friend already tried and got nowhere.' He pointed to his shoulder.

'Any deeper and the bullet would've hit your heart.'

'Yeah, I'll admit . . . After Lossau's people raided my hideout I was a little bit panicky, but you wouldn't believe how fast you can run when your life depends on it. If it wasn't for the injury, I would have made it to my second hideout but the well-meaning woman who picked me up off the pavement wasn't having any of it and drove me to hospital.'

'Which might well be the reason you're still alive.'

'Very true,' remarked Jon. 'But it was a bit annoying having to explain the gunshot wound to the police.' He sighed. 'I'll tell you that story another time.' He took a deep breath, closed his eyes and turned his head to the side. 'Think I'll take a little nap.' Seconds later, he'd fallen asleep. His breathing was regular and apart from the large bandage on his shoulder he seemed pretty much unscathed. A little bit paler than normal, perhaps, but smiling. It seemed like he'd found some peace.

Nik stood up and raised his hand. 'G'night, buddy.' Then he left the room.

Epilogue

'Looks like spring got here just in time for your birthday.' Nik closed his eyes and lifted his head to the sun. Even this high up, the snow had melted. The first shoots were showing and leaves were starting to appear on the bare branches.

'It was always nice weather on my birthday.' Mira smelled the flowers in Nik's hand. 'Oh, I love daffodils,' she said softly. 'Lovely of you to remember.' Mira stood up from the bench and stretched out her arms, as if trying to soak up every last ray of sun.

'I've even got a second surprise for you.' Nik pulled out the locket from under his shirt and opened it. It was empty.

'What did you do with the cyanide?' asked Mira.

'Got rid of it safely.'

'That's the best present you could ever give me,' she said cheerily. 'And how are you getting by until your suspension is finished?'

'Let's just say Jon . . . got the taste again. After getting out of hospital, he logged into the CID database and looked up unresolved cases similar to Viola's. He offered me the job of private detective. It's better money than the CID, no bosses and lots of freedom.'

'That's gonna lead you back to Rachel's case, you know that?'

'It's possible.'

'That case almost got you killed, Nik.'

'Yeah, well, I've got a team these days,' explained Nik. 'Jon has money and can hack into anything and although I might need a bit of time to get used to Balthasar's strange ways, he's still better company than Danilo.' He smiled at Mira. 'And anyway, I won't get to Rachel's case for a while. I'll need weeks to get through the first massive load of files Jon's already sent me.'

'Well, look after yourself,' Mira said gently.

'I will.'

'Don't let me keep you . . . Your phone hasn't stopped beeping for the last hour. Jon must have stumbled across something.'

Nik stood up from the bench. 'He can wait another minute.' Nik went over to the grave and laid the flowers in front of the light marble stone. He closed his eyes and clasped his hands to say a prayer. Carved in black on the marble, beside an angel, were the words 'Mira Pohl. Beloved Daughter and Sister'.

ACKNOWLEDGMENTS

Thank you to all the people who have helped and supported me for so many years. Andreas, without your feedback it would be impossible for me to publish any book. To Franz and the entire Apub Team, thank you for looking after me so brilliantly. And finally, Dominic, thank you for putting your faith in me.

Any success is a shared one.

ABOUT THE AUTHOR

Photo © Oliver Bendig, 2014

Alexander Hartung was born in 1970 in Mannheim, Germany. He began writing while he was studying for a degree in economics and soon discovered a passion for crime fiction. He topped the Kindle Bestseller List with his Jan Tommen series and now, with *Broken Glass*, he introduces us to Nik Pohl, the Munich detective at the centre of a gripping new investigation series. Alexander lives in his hometown of Mannheim with his wife and son.